THE
CHASM

JACQUI CASTLE

This is a work of fiction. Names, characters, organizations, places, events, and incidents are either products of the author's imagination or are used fictitiously.

Published by Inkshares, Inc., Oakland, California
www.inkshares.com

Edited by Sarah Nivala and Adam Gomolin
Cover design by Tim Barber
Interior design by Kevin G. Summers

ISBN 9781950301331
e-ISBN 9781950301348
LCCN 2021937783

First edition

Printed in the United States of America

PROLOGUE

IN A BED in Nevada, in a bunker nestled in the Black Canyon of the Colorado River, the shell of a young man lay motionless. The form of an eagle, wings extended, was displayed on the gray wall behind him. The eagle's posture was at once protective and hostile. It was accompanied by four words.

Security.
Unity.
Pride.
Strength.

A Compliance Officer named Regina Tellman perched on a hard metal chair near the doorway. The same place she'd sat every day for the preceding sixty days. Her wide feet were kicked up and splayed forty-five degrees on an extra chair she'd dragged over for just that purpose.

In the evening, when her monotonous shift was up, she would swipe out and switch places with another officer. For now, there she sat, playing a card game projected into the air, determined to distract herself as the long hours ticked by.

It was the dullest post Regina had ever had, which was saying something, since she was once charged with monitoring an automated wind power plant. She took each appointment with a smile, though. Anything to serve the Board.

Every few minutes, Regina's hand would shift to the directed energy weapon, known as a pacifier, clipped to her hip. Her fingers would wrap around its handle, the way a child would clutch a favorite stuffed animal. Her thumb hovered above the biometric pad that, with a bit of firm pressure, would activate the weapon in an instant. A thin blue light emanated from the hand-length burnished barrel, indicating that the pacifier was charged and ready if needed. Regina's eyes would dart to the man in the bed, assuring her that her ward was still where he should be. He always was. Then she would release her grip and go back to what she was doing before, as if unaware of what she had just done.

It'd been the same every day. Just her, hanging out with an unconscious prisoner. She didn't know who this boy was, or what he had done to warrant this peculiar treatment outside of a standard American hospital. He looked young, and sometimes she imagined what he could have done to end up here. But she didn't inquire further. If she needed to know, she would have been told.

A representative of the Board had visited twice, and while she would have loved the opportunity to brag to her friends and family about meeting a member of the Board in the flesh, she'd signed away her rights to share this information.

Machines were fixed to numerous ports of entry into the young subject's prone body. Magnetic cuffs at the wrists and ankles restrained him to the bed. They were superfluous—he wasn't going anywhere. She was to call at the slightest movement, any sign he was waking up.

A ventilator puffed his lungs while a feeding tube propelled a gelatinous substance into his stomach. A machine supported his sluggish heart. Rods held his splintered bones in their fixed order, and the muscles and cartilage healed around them. His skin was patched together like a quilt in the places where it had been punctured and torn, and a laser had smoothed the pleats like an iron so only smooth pink scars remained. These would diminish with time.

Sensors dotted his body, stimulating his nerves. His brain, underneath it all, was active, unharmed. Raven-black hair, buzzed short months prior, grew during his slumber, and was now long enough that it began to curl over his olive skin. Deep brown eyes darted around beneath pale lids, until all of a sudden, they shot open.

CHAPTER 1

Patch Collins

HOMESICKNESS DOESN'T SERVE reason. It makes no logical sense to miss a country that abused and deceived and destroyed you; still, I missed America. I missed it deep within my bone marrow. Sometimes I would tell myself it wasn't the place I missed, but the people. That was true as well, but it wasn't all of it. I would dream of the desert, ache for the lakes, and pine for the familiar view from my apartment window where I could see my small garden in bloom in the early spring. For the intense Arizona stillness I used to lament. For the taste of the desert air on my lips. For my rock collection displayed on a shelf in my living room, featuring treasures I'd pocketed on my days out in the field, each one its own unique artifact. For a specific teacup, my grandmother's old favorite, with the ivy pattern around the rim, handed down to me by my mom.

On the slow days, when my brain wouldn't move on, I told myself I was being absurd, but my brain was a tornado, tearing up memories like trees from the ground with little care for the wreckage they would leave in their wake.

I couldn't force the feeling of homesickness to disappear more than I could pluck up the parts of America I loved and bring them here with me. I couldn't ignore everything that had taken place since the day we'd left Tucson and return to the person I once was—the girl who found solace in gardening, delight in hiking, and relief in mantras.

"What am I doing here?" I asked myself. I said the words out loud as I stood in the elevator, staring at the pearly octagonal buttons lined up in five rows of ten until I felt as though I were staring right through them. The lights overhead dimmed. Enough time had passed that the compartment was assumed empty. The shift pulled me out of my daze, but the ache persisted.

I remained in the near blackness, closed my eyes, and combed my memory, working backward from the point the door had closed in front of me. You put your jacket on. Where did you want to go? In the bottom-right corner, next to the inter-building direction dial—*R* for the roof. I pressed it. The compartment whizzed left, and then up, and then right.

I stepped into the snow, leaving a trail of fresh boot prints winding behind me. The ground beneath me buzzed ever so faintly as it harnessed the energy from my footsteps.

Nearly two months had passed since the day I'd escaped America. Two months that somehow flew like a falcon and inched like a snail, all at once. *Time doesn't always follow reason either*, I reminded myself.

The billowy powder barely topped the toes of my boots. Large whirling flakes fell from the sky, salting my maroon jacket and winter hat. I pulled the zipper higher, tightening its warmth against my neck. I tipped my head to receive the snowflakes as they fell, and a few perched on my eyelids, their cool sting grounding me.

Rexx would have loved the snow. I imagined him opening his mouth, letting the flakes settle on his tongue. Then he'd turn and playfully pull me toward him and kiss me. I closed my eyes and imagined him doing just that. Standing next to me, as he was last year—vibrant and full of life, his jet-black curls tumbling in front of his face. I thought of him running through the forest and hopping over downed branches as I stood at the base of a tree and watched, not aware of how much I already loved this person.

I laughed, standing there in the snow by myself. It was an unexpected, fleeting moment of bliss. Then the ache in my chest deepened and I took a few more steps toward the edge.

I missed him, especially when I stood outside. The hollowness followed me like a shadow, one that would loom especially large today. We were supposed to do this together. It wouldn't be long now.

My imagination turned without my permission. Showing me the emaciated version of Rexx I'd reunited with at the forest's edge after Officer Webb had helped us escape from the compound near the northern border. The version I'd watched sacrifice himself for me so I could escape. I fought against it. I didn't want to remember him like that.

Putting my hands behind my head, I ran my fingers through my hair. It had only grown to a length of two inches since I'd arrived. I was thankful for the absence of the rough stubble that for weeks triggered the memories of the cold, unwelcome blades on my scalp.

As I stood alone on the roof, the bustling city full of people on their morning commute buzzed around me. I was a heavy rock in the middle of a swirling ocean.

I walked toward the edge. It would be so easy to just step over, then the guilt, the doubt, the hollowness, the aching, and the nightmares would all end. I took a deep breath, reminding myself why I was still alive and what I still had to do.

The city was graceful in her coat of white, the skyline views spectacular. I'd found myself on the roof most mornings since regaining some of my physical strength, fascinated by what this city had achieved. Several of the large buildings were covered in a living facade—an array of hardy plants cascading down the sides like sheer emerald fabric. A soft yellow glow cloaked the skyline, providing warmth to these plants that cleansed the air in the frigid weather.

We never had snow in Arizona. Even though it wasn't officially winter yet, it had snowed multiple times since I'd arrived in a city known as Vancouver. I'd been here, in this hospital, waiting, for eight weeks. Just waiting for a plan to be figured out. Today was the day it was supposed to happen. Today was the day they would tell me my next move, or rather, if I had a next move.

The sun was rising higher in the sky, and with it, my nerves. My thumb stroked the area on my index finger where my grandmother's ring used to be, feeling the indentation. An image flashed through my mind—the ring and other items shoveled haphazardly into an incinerator truck. They had been deemed unworthy, because, like the ring, they had entered the compound attached to a traitor. I shook the thought out of my head.

In the distance, to the west, I could see the ocean, vast and full of possibility. Large desalination ships, which converted salt water into fresh drinking water for the city, moved just off the coastline, back and forth, back and forth. Sometimes I watched them for hours, letting their repetition soothe me, wondering what it would be like to swim in the waters below their hulls. How could it be the same ocean off the West Coast of America? It might as well have been on the other side of the world. There were no guards or barriers. There was just ocean, open and free. Nothing demonstrated the differences from where I came from and where I stood more than seeing people walk, run, work, and play near that open stretch of pure, unadulterated ocean.

I crossed my arms over my chest. The cold was catching up to me, inching its way down my fingertips and up my toes. Today, I could become someone other than the awkward young woman who lacked the most basic knowledge and social etiquette in this new environment. Someone other than the girl the hospital staff always looked upon with pity as they walked on eggshells and whispered to their colleagues. "That's her, the one from America," I would hear them say, then they would scurry away if I raised my head or glanced in their direction.

My scroll vibrated in my pocket with an alarm. I took one last glance at the view, unsure if I would be coming back here. Escorts would arrive soon to take me to the meeting. That was what I'd been told by the hospital staff earlier as they gave me my first set of nonhospital clothing—a long-sleeved sage-green top and a pair of dark gray slacks. I'd studied myself in the mirror as I'd put them on, imagining how I would be received by the people I would meet today. I was still thinner than I used to be, and my short hair still didn't feel like me, but my injuries had healed and that had to be enough for now.

The hospital staff assured me I could keep the scroll and the coat I'd been wearing to the roof, and then handed me a bag with the meager belongings I'd arrived with. I looked in the bag and fished out the tattered gray compound uniform. I ran my fingers over the thin, papery fabric that had adorned my body only eight weeks prior. Then I handed it back and asked them to destroy it. The map, I kept. As I took it out of the bag and slipped it into my coat pocket, the memory of Webb handing it to me in the rain outside the compound gates flashed behind my eyes.

When I turned away from the edge of the roof, I was startled by two people standing at the elevator door. I hadn't heard them approach.

"Hi!" I said, a bit higher than my usual octave, as I tightened my arms across my chest. "How did you know I was up here?"

"The hospital staff told us you come up here every morning," one of them replied. She was a tall, slender woman with dark brown skin and eyes that seemed to sparkle unnaturally. Her hair was dyed a bright purple and a long, neat braid fell to one side. Next to her was a man with bright red glasses and jet-black hair that swept across his forehead. He had a jagged scar, healed over and smooth, but still vivid, on his left cheek. I hadn't seen anyone else out here wear glasses, and I wondered if they were purely ornamental.

They both wore sleek, dark, fitted overcoats that hung to their knees. Hers a magenta, his a dark indigo. My heart pounded in my chest. There was no more waiting.

The three of us stood on the roof in the snow, cloaked in yellow light.

"I'm Rose. Rose Anders," the woman said with a smile as she stepped closer. "And this is Felix Suen."

I felt the pressure of my arms across my chest loosen. Rose had a small silver tattoo about an inch in length on her temple. It glistened against her dark skin with the light reflected overhead, but I didn't focus on it long enough to make out what it was.

"We've been tasked with remaining with you throughout this entire process. Any questions, and you can ask us." She held out her gloved hand, and I hesitated for a moment. Other than the hospital staff, I hadn't been touched since Rexx and I were scrambling over rocks to reach the Northern Barrier.

An image of his face as I looked back at him for the last time flashed into my brain.

I tried to rein my focus back to the people I was talking to. Just like the doctor said. *Pick something in the present to focus on.* Rose's extended hand. I took it, and suddenly I was back on the rooftop again.

I then turned to Felix and he shook my hand eagerly. "It's wonderful to meet you, Miss Collins," Felix said in a deeper voice than I'd imagined would emerge. He rocked back and forth on his heels a bit and continued to smile. "I've—well, we've—heard a lot about you." He and Rose exchanged a brief glance that I couldn't read before he continued. "And I'll be here to make sure everything runs smoothly. Anything you need at all." He seemed a bit nervous, but I didn't know why that would be.

I took a closer look at the people in front of me. They both seemed to be in their midtwenties, if I had to guess—only a handful of years older than me.

"Um. Should I bring anything else with me?" I asked, knowing full well I had nothing else.

"No. We have everything you need," Rose said, then she took a step back and began to stretch on the rooftop, putting one arm in front of her chest and pulling with the other, and then stretching her arms up to the sky as she continued to talk. "You have been cleared for discharge, and we will not be coming back here. Is there anyone you would like to say goodbye to?"

For some reason, hearing her say it hit me harder than I would have imagined. This place had become comfortable, familiar. A nest in a tree above an unfamiliar forest floor filled with who knew what kind of predators roaming below. I thought about the hospital staff. The only person I would want to say goodbye to was my nurse, Kenneth, but we had said our goodbyes the day before, knowing he wouldn't be working today.

"No. Nobody who I can think of," I replied.

"Great," Rose said. "Then we can go."

Before long, I was following the two of them downstairs, and walking across the road to a vehicle that sat clipped into an oval-shaped parking pad. The car resembled others hovering in the surrounding air, apart from color and décor, which seemed to vary slightly on each. This one was silver with a red-and-white band around the middle—so thin, you could barely make it out. Centered on the band, right near the doors, was a small symbol with a maple leaf.

As we approached, two doors slid outward to reveal a seating area with plush swiveling bucket seats that looked more comfortable than any vehicle seats I'd ever seen.

"Here, watch your step," Rose said kindly as she moved what looked like a briefcase out of my way. Then she gestured for me to climb in, her eyes catching the light and looking somehow greener than they had on the roof.

It was the first vehicle I'd entered since the border patrol vehicle had brought me to the hospital, and the memory of that was anything but crisp. In fact, it was the first time I'd been anywhere other than inside the hospital or on the roof.

Once we were all nestled inside, the engine warmed, and the vehicle began to hover—a feeling I didn't know if I'd ever get used to. From my limited research, it seemed like everything hovered or outright flew here, and the ground was for buildings and foot traffic.

I thought back to when I awoke in the hospital. Apparently, as soon as the border patrol car had arrived, I'd been transported to the hospital and then induced into a heavy sleep for over three days once they saw how emaciated and injured I was. When I awoke, it took several minutes for everything to come into focus. The memories of escaping, of Rexx, of the vehicle that found me lying face-first on the ground in the wilderness. It all came back like boulders crashing down on me, one memory after another.

I felt my face, my buzzed hair, my arms, my neck. A thin, waxy substance coated the scratches on my tender skin, my joints ached as I moved them, my feet were bandaged with something cool and soothing. There was a wrapping over the space between my thumb and forefinger. I peeled it back to see a clean incision where the skin used to be raised, puffy, and jagged from Rexx cutting out my chip. I poked the tender skin, feeling around for a moment—not believing completely that I hadn't been chipped once more.

The room didn't look that different from medical rooms in America. For a brief second, panic rose in me like a snake backed into a corner. Maybe I wasn't out at all. Maybe they'd found me. Maybe they had brought me back. Maybe a Compliance Officer would storm in any moment, pacify me, and take me back to a compound, or maybe I'd made it out but was about to be subject to worse treatment at the hands of a foreign government. Maybe the Board was right. Maybe the people out here wished me nothing but harm.

I contemplated pulling myself out of the bed and making a run for it, bandaged raw feet and all, but then a man walked past the open door to my room and stopped when he saw I was awake. The panic escalated, and I pressed myself into the head of the bed as if I could somehow melt into it if I tried hard enough.

"She's up. She's awake," he said. He walked in with a smile on his face and his head cocked slightly to one side. "Hi there! Great to see you with your eyes open! We were getting worried about you."

"Where am I? We have to help them," I said through a cracked voice as he approached. He stood next to me, calmly pressing something out of view, and the bed angled upward as he handed me a glass of what looked like juice. I took it hesitantly, then poured it down my throat like an Arizona cactus receiving moisture for the first time in months. A combination of flavors I'd never experienced coated my tongue.

"What is it?" I asked.

"'What is it?'" he repeated with a curious look on his face. "It's orange juice. Have you never had it before?"

I shook my head. I never knew something could be so delicious. I hadn't consumed anything other than water and bowls of grain since I'd been captured.

"Thank you," I said.

His clothes were not those of the medical personnel in America. There was no emblem on his uniform. I scanned the room to see that no national emblem decorated anything within view, when ordinarily it would appear on everything from the walls to the medical tools on the tray beside the bed. I hadn't been in Board-run hospitals often, never being permitted to visit my parents at work, but I'd had my tonsils out when I was about ten.

"Where do you think you are?" the man spoke gently as he ran a small tool across my forehead. He had a long, thin face, black skin, and kind eyes framed by lines in the outside corners. He was in his late fifties or early sixties, I guessed, from the gray that speckled his trim beard.

My father had been a nurse in America, and I briefly wondered how many people had awoken to his face, and his kind eyes, after a traumatic event or injury. How no one ever would again, because of me.

"Do you know where you are?" he asked again, varying his original question slightly.

I knew where I was, generally speaking—I was outside the Walls. I was in a place I'd been told my entire life would see me tortured and dismembered quicker than I could say *Board help me*. It was a place I was taught was desolate and foreign and terrifying. In this place, I was now lying inside a facility, mended, and cared for by a man who seemed nothing but kind.

"I, well, I don't know exactly," I said cautiously. "But I know, or at least I think, that I'm not in America anymore."

His eyes widened at this. "So, it is true," he said. "You have come from America?"

"Yes," I said quietly, still not fully believing that I was out or that I was alive. Then panic coursed through me, and the words followed. "You have to help them. Please. Someone has to help them," I said with urgency, pleading to this medical professional who likely held no such power. His eyes were sad, confirming my previous thought, and it was as if that single plea took all of the energy I had. My head fell back to the pillow and things started to blur again.

"First things first," he said reassuringly. "Your number one job is to recover, but there are a couple of officers outside who need to get some statements from you."

"'Officers'?" I said, another burst of the panic returning as I tried to sit up and felt the color drain from my face.

"No, it's okay," he said, watching my reaction intently. He put a hand on my shoulder to gently guide me back down to the pillow behind me. "They are just here to talk. They are here to help. They can wait a little while."

I nodded, and my eyelids felt as if someone had injected them with sand. I let them fall closed, then drift open again, over and over for several more minutes. Another glass of juice was delivered sometime later, and along with it was some kind of peppered cracker that was better than any cracker I'd ever tasted.

The room began to stabilize. The nurse, who I saw from his tag was named Kenneth, handed me something. My hand shook as it tried to grab it, so I used both hands.

It was a glossy black cylinder about three-quarters of the size of the average stylus.

"We'll need you to fill this out when you feel up to it."

I took it, confused.

"Fill it out? How do I fill it out?"

He took the cylinder back and the two sides separated lengthwise, breaking apart seamlessly. He pulled them away from each other. I watched, fascinated. When the sides were about seven inches apart, seemingly still connected by something I wasn't seeing, he stopped. A glimmer resembled a thin piece of glass in the middle, but only just barely. He handed it back to me. It was now as solid as the tablets used in America. It displayed a digital form on its face with a black outline to show its horizontal edges.

"Wow." I ran my fingers along the edge of the now rectangular screen, expecting it to be sharp. It wasn't. I wondered what combination of minerals could produce this material, or if they were minerals at all.

"It's called a scroll," he said. "It's for you. If you register your fingerprint here in the bottom corner," he said, pointing to the lower-right side of the screen, "it will register the device to you, and the form you are to fill out will appear. To close, you press and hold here." He showed me where to press with my index finger. "After you complete the registration process, it will open only for you. I'll give you some privacy."

I nodded as I inspected the device further, holding it this way and that, but hesitated on pressing the fleshy tip of my index finger into the bottom of the screen—wishing I had somehow ended up in an alternate reality where my identity didn't have to start with biometrics and words in a file.

I pressed my fingerprint into the screen. Words appeared for a brief moment, then dissipated.

Welcome to Canada. Please fill out this form.

I eyed the form that materialized.

"Kenneth?" I said, just as he was about to walk out of the room. "Do you have a stylus?" I asked, seeing no on-screen keyboard, and inspecting the ends for a possible hidden compartment.

"No need," Kenneth said, walking back over. "Just position your hands above the screen like this." He put his hand in a position as if he were holding a writing utensil. "Then write."

The form asked for basics: name, date of birth, and health background. I mimicked writing, feeling a bit silly as Kenneth watched from a distance, having taken a few steps away to give me some privacy. To my amazement, letters appeared. To my even greater amazement, they were the letters I'd intended to write. On a better day, I would have peppered Kenneth with questions about this new technology, but I didn't.

I held it back from my face and regarded what I had written.

PATRICIA

Then, in a decisive move for my current state of mind, I decided to delete four letters. I "drew" a line through them, waiting to see what would happen, and they pleasantly faded from view. I replaced them with two others. I never wanted to be known by any name other than the one he used to call me. I typed my last name and admired the line in full.

PATCH COLLINS

CHAPTER 2

Robbie Webb

EARLIER THAT MORNING, Compliance Officer Robbie Webb sat in a chair in the corner of his living room. He held a half-empty glass of grail—a bottom-shelf grain alcohol. A steal at three bottles for one credit. Things didn't come much cheaper than that. Rain pounded against the window and the lumicomm post outside lit up the storm. The effect was hypnotic as he watched the orb of light shine through the thick sideways rain piercing through a deep purple sky.

The minutes ticked by, and when he finally turned his attention to the fluorescent numbers blinking on the screen across from him, they alerted him to how long he'd been staring—it was 2:33 in the morning.

I need to be up in three hours, Webb told himself, but he cast his eyes to the storm once again, and the time frame continued to shrink. He couldn't bring himself to maneuver from the couch to his bedroom down the hall. So, he sat and sipped and swirled the amber liquid around the bottom of his glass and listened to the storm. His lips fell to rest on the rim as he inhaled the acquired scent—*if oak and methanol had procreated,* a fellow Compo had remarked one night. The phrase had stuck with him. A smell repulsive to him years ago was now soothing as it pleasantly burned his sinuses.

It will be worse if I fall asleep, he told himself. The headaches, the joint pain, and the fog were always worse when he fell asleep.

It had been the same dance every day for the past two months. If he fell asleep, if he let himself fall asleep, the nightmares would saunter in like an overfamiliar neighbor, and the questions would arise. So the corner of his chair was where he passed out most nights, screens and lights still blazing, distracting himself in every waking moment from his racing thoughts. They kept him from feeling alone and focusing on his failures.

The girl and the boy had upended his entire world and now he had no idea who he was. Sometimes he felt as if he were losing his grip. He would find himself clutching everyday objects—furniture edges, walls, railings—as if the solidity of them would ground him in reality.

The boy was easy. Webb had helped him through the security gates without issue. No one saw through the downpour of rain. The girl, well, someone had spotted them, and it had forced him into a split-second calculation—one he wouldn't be able to return from.

Using his pacifier, he'd disarmed the fellow guard before he rushed Patricia the rest of the way outside of the gates. When he returned, the other Compo was splayed out, facedown in the mud without a pulse. The lethal setting on the pacifier hadn't been used and Webb didn't know what had gone wrong. Maybe it was the electricity combined with the sopping-wet uniform, though Compliance Officers were never trained not to use their weapons in the rain. Maybe the officer had an undisclosed medical issue. Webb rationalized again and again to shift the blame off himself. The officer shouldn't have been standing there. The pacifier must have malfunctioned. That guy was a jerk anyway.

It never worked.

That was the day he became a murderer of his own volition, and not at the order of someone else. In the end, did it matter who gave the command if he had pulled the trigger? He used to think it did. He used to think that he was serving a higher order, and that his patriotism would be rewarded. He used to believe the Board was all knowing and their decisions always just. Now he wasn't so sure.

He inhaled, driving the menthol sensation deeper. His head buzzing, he brought his hand up and pressed his thumb to his left temple.

He didn't know who he was anymore. Reality used to feel absolute. Even if he wasn't always happy with his lot in life, he didn't question the order of things. So why did he recently feel like if those same solid objects he often clutched for stability suddenly evaporated in his hand, were exposed as nothing more than holograms, he might not even be surprised? Why was he suddenly questioning everything?

Then there was his daughter. He questioned their relationship and wondered how he could fix it all while feeling it dissolve underneath his fingertips. He'd been distant since the incident. When he looked at her, he saw himself. He didn't want her to live believing the word of the Board, and under constant deception, but he couldn't do anything about it. Anything he did would put her in danger. He'd been drinking more, avoiding more, and talking less. She was smart. She had noticed.

He took another sip and then let his tongue lick the lingering taste off his lips.

Another death weighed on his conscience. He replayed the words he'd heard in the room on the day Patricia Collins was caught. He shouldn't have cared what happened to her, but she'd changed him. She had changed everything he knew and believed. She had knocked him unconscious, leaving a lump on his head that ached for days, stolen his car, kidnapped him, and made him look weak in front of his superiors. Despite all that had happened, those weren't the memories that revisited him day after day. One specific memory replayed frequently. The details were as crisp as a freshly starched uniform.

The Board member pulled the hood off Patricia's father, revealing the broken and beaten man whom Webb had dragged into the room himself. "Now, I believe I asked you something, Patricia."

After a fruitless interrogation, the Board member nodded to Webb, and Webb pointed the pacifier at Geoffrey Collins's neck. Moments later, Webb's finger closed around the trigger.

He would never forget the look on the girl's face when he ended her father's life. With the pacifier set to lethal, it sent enough electricity coursing through Geoffrey Collins's body that his heart stopped almost instantly. The primal scream that emerged from the young woman as her father's body crashed to the floor returned to visit him almost every night, and often during the day. He remembered how he'd felt the moment it had emerged for the first time. Like it had traveled to him through deafened eardrums, so that he was no longer just hearing it but feeling it with every fiber of his being as it reached deep inside his body and coated him from the inside out. Like it was now a permanent part of him.

If there was anything in life as real as that scream, he had never encountered it. It was an agony that could not be faked.

Her words and her scream . . . He didn't seem to go more than a few minutes without one of them haunting him.

What made her different from the others he'd encountered? Why had he taken so long to see the deception? He had seen the brutality before, but that had been his first encounter with a Board member, and his first post inside a redemption camp. His regular post was in Portland, Oregon, where he had been patrolling when he'd stumbled upon Patricia and Rexx outside Zone 36. He had a feeling he was asked to change postings just to mess with them, and especially her. He was to remain there so that every single day she had to see the man who had killed her father.

Webb had convinced himself, like so many others, that his work served the country. Being a Compliance Officer wasn't his first choice, but he had accepted the call to action without much complaint.

He'd never heard what happened to them. There was chaos at the compound for weeks, as security protocols were combed through over and over. After assessing the entire situation, the Board placed the other Compo's death on Moreno and Collins, and Webb did not correct them. A few days after the escape, when he'd walked into the morning meeting, his chief made an announcement.

"There has been an attack on home soil," he'd said as he paced back and forth in front of the team. "At the northern border. A team is being deployed to resecure it, and to act as a patrol as we stay on red alert. There are evil forces at hand, and we need to be ready. If those terrorist bastards find their way into our country, well, I hate to think what will happen. If I call your name, you are now on the patrol team. Rodriguez. Finley. Webb. Report to my office for an additional briefing."

What he was saying made no sense. He'd been talking about Patricia and Rexx's escape attempt, however it ended, but the Board was blaming it on outside forces. It was in that moment that everything came to a head for Webb. That was the moment when he decided irrevocably that his government and the people he served were, to put it mildly, full of shit.

Webb worked on the patrol team for one month. Then he was reassigned once again and put back on sidewalk duty in Portland.

Webb took another swig of grail. Then, with the rain still pounding outside, his head dropped against the back of the chair and his eyes closed. As they did, his hand loosened, and the grail spilled down the side of his department-issued slacks.

He dreamed of his daughter—of her innocent face as she sat in her evening ideology class. The other fourteen-year-olds sitting around her were nothing but wavy silhouettes, one like the other, but his daughter, with her thick curly hair and dark black skin, she was not a silhouette. Every feature was crisp and clear. Celeste Webb. Her eyes were full of life and possibility. She stood, and the wavy silhouettes angled up as if they were looking at her. Her eyes widened, her smile brightened and stretched, and she opened her mouth until a distorted, other-worldly voice emerged. "Help me, Daddy. Help us."

Webb bolted awake, spilling the last of the liquid out of the sideways glass, then muttered obscenities under his breath. His eyes darted to the screen across from him. It blinked *4:15*. The screen, and the cameras, were recording his every movement. *Just an old drunk, that's all they will think*, he told himself. They weren't wrong. That was all he was. He moved through his days like a ghost and drowned himself in his vice.

The dream rattled him. He told himself that starting today, things would be different. That when he came home later that evening, he would stay clearheaded, he would think. Think of who the hell he was going to be from this point forward. It was a promise he'd made to himself before. He rose, the glass clutched in one hand, pulled his dirty shirt off over his head with the other, bunched it up, and used it to wipe off the chair. Then he walked to the kitchen sink and poured the rest of the amber liquid down the drain, ignoring the pounding in his head as he watched it swirl away, hearing it drip into the gray water tank below. He put the bottle in the all-in-one recomper, downed two pain relievers, and took a deep breath. Today would be different.

CHAPTER 3

Patch Collins

"IS EVERYTHING ALL right?" Rose asked from the seat next to me in the vehicle, pulling me out of my memory of the hospital. *If I don't get my act together soon, everyone I meet is going to think I'm insane. Focus. Stay in the present.*

"Yes," I said a bit too quickly and defensively. "Yeah, I'm fine." I looked around the interior. It was sort of like the SafePod cars back home. Except, well, these did not stay on the road.

I focused on the details.

An unmanned control panel was housed up front, featuring a display with readings unrecognizable to me. There were two rows of chairs, with the front row swiveled to face the back. A table stretched between the rows. The entire thing seemed designed for conducting business and meetings mid-flight.

Felix kicked off his shoes and reclined in the back chair to my right. He opened a container and held it out to me.

"Would you like one? I made them."

"What are they?" I asked as I stared at the inviting array in front of me.

"They're lemon cookies with a ginger icing," he said as I took one of the perfectly round cookies out, the citrus smell wafting into the air.

"Felix loves to bake, and he's really good at it too," Rose said.

I took the cookie and bit into it. The delicate texture crumbled satisfyingly in my mouth, followed by a burst of a flavor I didn't recognize that was somehow delightfully spicy while refreshing and sweet.

"Wow," I said as I devoured the rest.

"Here, take another one," Felix said as he watched my reaction intently, then he handed me two more. "You've had nothing but hospital food for weeks."

"Thank you," I said as I took the cookies, not mentioning that the hospital food was better than any food I'd ever eaten up until this moment.

I leaned back and enjoyed the respite of the snack. My nerves were shot, and I didn't have the slightest clue how to act to convince foreign leaders to intervene into a hostile country even though it had been the only thing on my mind for weeks. What if they saw me as a silly child as I stood in front of them? What if they laughed in my face? What if they had every reason to?

I'd been trying to learn more since I arrived, but there was so much I didn't know. I'd been gifted the scroll, currently in my pocket. With it I could access the Internet, but using it was so foreign to me compared to the limited Board-run websites used in America, and I often found myself overwhelmed by the onslaught of information. I would have to set it down then lie on my bed, just letting my thoughts sort themselves out. Then, after the feelings of anger, resentment, and helplessness, the guilt would come, stronger than the other emotions. Guilt for not being more grateful for surviving. Guilt for not being stronger, or smarter. Guilt for having left everyone behind.

Focus on the present, I reminded myself. I looked out the window and realized for the first time that we were flying a good twenty yards higher than the rest of the traffic.

There were so many questions on the tip of my tongue. Questions Rose and Felix likely held answers to but that I was having trouble asking. Was I walking into a meeting of people who were prepared to help me today? Was I simply being placated? If I left my questions unasked, hope remained.

"Hey, Rose? Does the prime minister ride in here?" I asked.

"No," replied Rose as she propped herself up on her knees and turned toward me. With this action, plus the stretching on the roof, I was starting to suspect she didn't like to be still. "She has her own personal vehicle. Much nicer than this one. We have a fleet of these for anyone traveling on government business."

I thought of the garage full of vehicles for use by the Natural Resource Department. Maybe we weren't so different after all.

I could feel my fellow passengers giving me room, and perhaps being quieter than they would ordinarily be. I tried my best to appear relaxed, wondering if I would ever feel normal again, or if I would walk around for the rest of my life feeling either hollow or like there was a detonator in my chest that could be triggered at any moment. Maybe there was no in-between for me anymore.

"Don't worry. It's not a long flight," Rose said reassuringly as she leaned forward, resting her elbows on the table. "Only about twenty minutes."

I nodded, then racked my brain for something else to ask her, searching for the art of casual conversation I'd been trained in as a child. Approved casual conversation, I reminded myself. Which rules applied out here? Even in a free society, were there things still best left unsaid?

"So, how long have you, um, worked for the prime minister?"

"Oh? We don't work directly for the prime minister," Rose said. "We've been brought here because of you." Her words obviously took me aback, but she kept going. "I work for the Department of Foreign Affairs, and I did my doctoral studies in American history," Rose said. I didn't know what "doctoral studies" meant but gathered that she likely knew more about my country than I did. But then again, didn't everyone?

"Felix is one of our department's top technology specialists, but he's mostly in it for the travel. His home base is actually here in Vancouver, though. We went to undergraduate school together, and collaborated on a project a few years back, but it's been a while." I looked over at Felix, who was resting with his glasses now perched atop his head. A smile spread slowly across his face.

"How many countries have you been to again, Felix?" Rose asked.

"Thirty-seven," he said matter-of-factly.

Thirty-seven out of how many? I wondered but was too embarrassed to ask, and too ashamed to show them how little I knew.

"Prime Minister Austin requested we be your main points of contact during this process. I think she thought it would help to have familiar faces through all of this unfamiliarity." She gestured as if to indicate everything around us, and everything in existence. I found myself stifling a smile.

"And what exactly is this process?" I asked.

Felix leaned forward as if he were about to say something, but Rose shot him a look that I couldn't read and he leaned back again.

"What?" I asked.

"Nothing," Felix said. "Just wondering if you are going to ask for an intervention."

"Felix!" Rose snapped, then turned back to me. "We'll talk about that more when we arrive," she said with a tone that wasn't harsh but indicated that was all she had been instructed to say. I nodded, familiar with the concept.

I looked back at Felix. He nodded gently, but there seemed to be more behind the gesture. Did he want me to ask for an intervention? And did Rose have a different view?

I looked once again at Rose. She was very pretty and had the self-confidence of someone whose mind didn't wander off every five minutes. Her eyes were as green as an emerald, with the sheen of a freshly polished stone. There was now a pulse of tension in the vehicle, and I searched for something to break it.

"I hope you don't mind me saying, but your eyes—they are so bright. Are they contact lenses?" I asked, hoping I wasn't being too forward, and thinking of the lenses my friend Lydia at the department used to wear, switching them to match her outfit on any given day.

"They are semipermanent implantable contacts. They last up to two years. Some people go with permanent ones, but I don't know what color I'll want in two years," she said with resolve. Rose had taken her coat off for the ride. She was wearing a fitted dark gray top that crossed in the front and back, and a matching pair of slacks.

"Can your clothing change color?" I asked, relaxing a bit and trying to enjoy the closest thing to small talk I'd had in months, though I feared the words coming out of my mouth sounded a bit childish and frivolous.

"It can," she said, and she fiddled with a barely perceptible dial on the bottom of her shirt, and the fabric rippled to a flamingo pink, then back again.

"Huh," I said. She raised an eyebrow in my direction but didn't press me for an explanation.

Her clothing was almost identical to our clothing back home, which had always seemed a bit ahead of its time compared to everything else. I wondered if this was one of the trade routes that was still open. Did our clothing come from outside, its source simply scrubbed "for our protection"? I wondered if these common threads had held us all together even without our knowledge. Maybe in a drawer somewhere, Rose and I had the same shirt or the same pair of pants or the same scarf. I don't know why the thought didn't make me happier. Instead of making me feel closer to the people next to me, it made me feel further apart.

I could see the tattoo on her temple more clearly now. Swirls of silver, thinner than a strand of hair, intertwined into an oval shape.

"Your tattoo," I said. "It's beautiful."

"It's in remembrance of a friend," she said, bringing her hand up to her temple. A sad smile spread across her face. "It's her fingerprint."

"Oh," I said, unable to hide my surprise that tattooing someone's fingerprints on your body was done out here. "That is a lovely tribute."

"Yes, well. It was a friend who was dearly loved," she said. "A friend of both of ours. She was in my doctorate program. Her grandparents were American."

"Really?" I said, realizing after I blurted the word out with eager excitement that it was probably the wrong tone to offer when someone was telling you about a loved one they had lost. Rose didn't appear bothered, but when I looked at Felix, I noticed his eyes were turned down toward the table.

"Felix and I haven't worked together since an assignment we were all on four years ago," Rose said. "She was passionate about America. She talked about it a lot and even wrote her thesis on it. She never forgot the stories her grandparents told her. She hid how sick she was very well."

So a mutual friend of theirs who had more than a passing interest in America had died of an illness. I guess the medical advancements out here hadn't solved everything.

"I'm so sorry. If you don't mind my asking, did the assignment four years ago, did it have something to do with America also?"

"No, just something routine," Rose said, bringing her hand away from her temple in a motion that also seemed to suggest the end of the conversation. Just as before, I knew I should ask more, but something held me back.

I started to sink deeper into the seat, bringing my attention back to the window. We were flying over the Vancouver city center. From this angle, the swirls of walking bridges and buildings resembled a DNA helix. With the living facades coating all available surfaces, everything had a hint of green or yellow, with a speckled backdrop of white where the snow was sticking.

So much of my time had been spent trying to research America's past, I hadn't spent as much time as I would have liked learning about the scientific advances of the rest of the world, but one look around told me they were leaps and bounds ahead. I wished Noah could see it. I was traveling across a country in a flying car. No one who saw the outside could deny it.

As I had the thought, it seemed important. I repeated it in my mind. *No one who saw the outside world could deny it.*

"So, where exactly are we going?" I asked after a few minutes.

"We're headed to a government building just outside Vancouver. It also serves as a United Nations satellite office," replied Rose.

"It's a really cool building," Felix said, leaning forward as he talked. "One of the coolest, at least technologically, in the area. I bet you'll get a kick out of it. When they asked me where I wanted to be stationed between assignments, this building was the main reason Vancouver was at the top of my list."

"You were asked where you wanted to be?" The words came out of my mouth more pointed than I had intended, but neither Felix nor Rose seemed affronted.

"Well," Felix started slowly, as if I were a rabbit in a field and he didn't want to startle me, "since I travel a lot, I requested that this area be my home base. I've been to countless cities, but Vancouver remains my favorite. My apartment is about ten miles that way," he said, pointing off in a direction that was neither where we'd begun nor where we were headed.

I didn't reply. Didn't ask him where else he had traveled or favorite cities of his. Questions that the old me would have been so fascinated to know the answers to. I don't know why I didn't. So I just sat there in awkward silence for a moment with this person who obviously had similar interests to me. I felt like something was holding me back from exploring further. Something in my mind was putting up a wall, warning me to not let anyone in.

"The United Nations was originally in America, as you might know," Rose said.

I didn't know.

"But several years after your leaders pulled out of most global alliances, other leaders took the reins and moved locations. Then the Seclusion happened, obviously. Now, though we have a base location in Germany, most correspondence is conducted via satellite office."

I only understood about half of what she'd just said, but I nodded anyway. I went from being one of the most educated people in the room in America to, well, struggling to understand what people around me were saying. People who were well traveled, had multiple areas of study to select from, and spent their days cruising around in flying cars. I felt like I should just take my plate and go sit at the kids' table.

What I understood, and felt the weight of, was that I was about to walk into a meeting in an important location, likely filled with incredibly important people who I had to convince to do something to help a country they had no motive to help.

"Is everything okay?" Felix asked a few minutes later. It took his words a moment to seep into my consciousness, as if they were delivered on a delay. I'd been staring out the window again.

"Yeah. Sorry. I get distracted a lot, and, um, sometimes my mind fixates on memories, or on questions. I have a hard time reining it back in. I was told at the hospital that what I'm experiencing is common after, well, you know."

I expected to see pity in Felix's eyes when I met them, but there was none. He nodded and leaned back again in his chair and smiled as he handed across another cookie.

I appreciated him for it. Pity was the last thing I wanted, and I'd had enough of it from the hospital staff. Pity never has the intended effect. Though it may be offered to show support, it only makes a person feel more broken.

"We'll be landing soon," Rose said, and she started organizing and gathering a few things she had removed from a briefcase back into their rightful pockets, each one organized to perfection in its own spot.

She then took a mirror out of one of the pockets and went to work on her appearance. I found myself sitting up straighter and smoothing out my hair—what little bit I had. Rose saw me, smiled, and passed me her mirror. I wasn't about to win any beauty awards, but with the fresh clothes I'd been given that morning, I felt I looked decent enough.

"Check it out," Felix said as he pointed through the front window and lowered his glasses back down onto his nose.

We were closing in on a complex outside the city. A large geodesic dome came into focus as we approached, and I leaned forward as far as I could. The towering glass building was forty or more stories, if I had to guess, at its peak. Octagonal panes of glass or a similar material interconnected to form its exterior. The panes seemed to wobble slightly, reflecting green and blue hues as the sun landed on their surface. As we got closer, I could see that the green and blue hues were not simply random, but intentionally and intricately placed. It was a map, or rather, a globe.

"It shows the northern hemisphere in the morning, and the southern hemisphere in the evening," Felix said. "That little spot right there. That's America." His fingers were spread open, pressing against the glass like he couldn't wait to be on the other side. He pointed, and I followed the trajectory of his finger.

I swallowed forcefully as I took in the image before me. A small section stood out from the rest. Its green light was dimmer, like a piece of a puzzle had been removed. Suddenly my hand was in my pocket, and I pulled out the only thing that truly belonged to me—the map from the van. Opened it and looked from the map back to the building. After accounting for the coastline shifts, the shapes were the same.

I felt a hand on my shoulder as I absorbed what I was seeing. It was Rose's. I didn't shake it off; instead I let it rest there, accepting the small amount of comfort as I absorbed the picture before me. I absorbed how small that tiny puzzle piece really was in the grand scheme of things and how small I'd been inside of it. What was most shocking of all was how big and bright the world still was without it there.

CHAPTER 4

Oliver Shelling

THOUGH HE DIDN'T know it, Oliver Shelling was being held at the same compound Patch and Rexx had been held. No one had helped him escape, and his interrogation had been stricter than either of his allies'.

After they searched his home and his large supply of "traitorous paraphernalia" was found and destroyed, they thoroughly searched the rest of the zone, including the burned-down rubble from the community center and the office building where Oliver had spent his days.

Luckily, thanks to someone, everything referring to the Veritas Ring was destroyed in the fire.

After the Board got word of Oliver's collections, they assumed he was a ringleader of some kind, though Oliver had never done much more than be an eccentric artist and a witness to what was taking place around him. In fact, leading the Compos away from Rexx and Patch was the proudest moment of his life, and the only time he felt like he'd stuck his neck out. Board knows he'd failed given other opportunities. He'd always convinced himself he didn't have it in him.

It wasn't until the moment came—when it was him or them—that he knew what to do, and that he couldn't lose more people he loved due to his cowardice. It wasn't even a question. He saw himself creating a diversion in his mind, and before he knew it, he was doing what he'd imagined. He hoped every second of every day since that it wasn't for nothing and that they made it. Not that anyone would tell him either way.

He held on to a sliver of hope that maybe, just maybe, they would somehow come back for him.

The first few weeks were absolute hell. He thought he would be prepared after all the conversations he'd had with the elders, and the visions he'd formed in his imagination and paintings of what these places would be like. He was wrong. There was no military redemption, as he'd been told time and time again since childhood. The elders were right. Only isolation, forced labor, and a new world devoid of color.

After he arrived, he suffered through daily interrogations, and was beaten to unconsciousness more than once. He'd wake up in his cell and every bone in his body ached, and then it would happen again.

When he wasn't being interrogated, they left him alone in a cell no larger than his bathroom at home, and less appealing. A toilet sat in one corner, and there was a large drain in the center of the room. These weren't the incinerator toilets used in urban centers, but instead emptied into pipes whose destination you couldn't see. The mild scent of refuse tinged the air, settling in his nasal cavities. It was the type of smell you hoped to never have to get used to, but then one day you did.

The Board member only took part in his questioning one other time after the day of his arrival. He'd displayed photos of the paintings that had been stacked in the corner of Oliver's living room and of the random items he'd scavenged and hidden away in Zone 36.

He was shown pictures of Noah and Sophia, their dead bodies lying end to end, with nothing but the soles of their lifeless feet touching. Tears streamed down Oliver's cheeks when he saw this, and he muttered under his breath, "This can't be happening. Not to you. Not to you. I'm so sorry. So, so sorry." Even though he felt as though his brain were splintering into a million pieces, he still didn't budge when pressed for more information about what the Veritas Ring was trying to accomplish. "I don't know. I've never known," he said, all the while wondering if Rexx and Patch had gotten word of Noah's and Sophia's deaths.

Oliver vacillated between hoping for the impossible rescue and hoping it would all just end. Maybe one day, in between shooting electricity into his body with the pacifiers or the cuffs, and getting so enraged at his insolence, the Compos would switch to using their fists, something would rupture, and he would just cease breathing. Instead he held his tongue through it all.

After a month, apparently, the interrogations ended, his cell doors opened, and lighted blue arrows led him outside to a blinding sun and a sea of gray faces. Though the beatings had stopped, the meager amounts of food were not enough, and he could feel himself getting weaker and weaker.

He was never a muscular guy, always taller and lankier than most. He was always a little awkward in his own skin, like the body he inhabited belonged to someone else, but he'd never been able to make out the knobs of his elbows so clearly, or the bones above his ankles. The bruises on his brown skin stressed the changes his body was going through, and he felt naked without his long hair or beard. When he touched his own face and head, he didn't recognize what he felt. It was the strangest feeling, to touch your own face and feel as if you were touching someone else. He would pace in his cell sometimes, the rage piling up inside him like a volcano ready to erupt.

He thought about Patch and Rexx every day, wondering if they were carrying out the plan. He thought about how much he hated the Board and how impotent he felt at not being able to do a damn thing to help.

Oliver had been tasked with assembling pacifiers during his time in his cell, an activity whose irony was not lost on him. At first, he couldn't stomach the work without having flashbacks to the jolting pain he'd been repeatedly subjected to. Knowing he was participating in inflicting this pain on someone else. After several beatings for moving too slowly, he did the work without complaint, and the flashbacks were merely replaced with grim reality as a necessary disassociation took hold.

The rituals he muttered to himself became tighter.

Don't lose hope. They might come for you. Be ready.

He said the same words under his breath as he worked, for hours at a time. He assembled pacifier after pacifier, eyeing the biometric pad on the handle as he snapped pieces of the forearm-sized weapon into place. It taunted him, how close he was to having something with which to defend himself, but the weapons wouldn't work until they were programmed to their assigned Compo.

He did his best to drown out the images on the screen that played from dusk to dawn. Images of the atrocities supposedly taking place on the other side of the Walls. Images of terrorists and sickness and death, and of pollution and desolate lands.

The ten minutes of outside time were all that kept him from going off the deep end. Most would huddle together, no energy to exercise or even walk in the meager triangular path that lined the pie-shaped wedge of the yard. A few times a prisoner would drop right there in the yard, never to be revived again, then be dragged off like they were no more than an inconvenient obstruction. What did they do with them once they were out there? Oliver wondered, but he didn't let himself fixate on the question for too long.

He made himself move, even if it meant he wasted away quicker. He didn't take the walking path that circled the yard, but instead he walked through the grass.

After about a month, the grass wore where he stepped. He could hear the Compos whispering as he passed, but he kept going. Something about the sameness, about the ritual, was soothing. It quieted his hectic mind and kept him centered. He liked the path he had formed for himself. It was his and no one else's. He wasn't going to let them change him, not completely, at least.

CHAPTER 5

Patch Collins

"LOOK, LOOK!" FELIX said as more of the United Nations satellite building came into view. *Focus on the present*, I reminded myself. I leaned closer to the window.

The dome stood regally behind a curved wall that stretched to the left of the entry, forming a backdrop to an array of flags on display, hovering in an arc around the building's midsection.

Felix named countries as he pointed out specific flags. "Sweden, Australia, Canada, Saudi Arabia, New Korea, Germany, New Zealand, the Netherlands, Norway." There were additional ones farther down that I couldn't see very well. I looked back to Felix. His eyes were wide and his upper-right canine bit on the corner of his lip. He loved it here, and I couldn't help but soak up some of his wonder as I turned my eyes back to the building that was quickly approaching.

"The exterior was modeled after the original, with just a few upgrades," Rose told me. She slung her briefcase over her shoulder, in a move that suggested she was getting ready to depart and it would just be a moment before we were out of the vehicle.

I took in the bright green foliage, which matched the curvature of the wall. Rose pulled a mini scroll out of one of the
briefcase pockets, and after a moment she showed me a picture.
"The old UN building in New York City."

There was a slight resemblance, if you ignored the whole
brightly-lit-dome thing, but I could see her point about the
exterior. The flags, though these were digital, the landscaping,
and the entryway all were reminiscent of the original.

"Other local and national government offices make up the
rest of the building, so expect some heightened security measures on certain floors," Rose said.

"New York City," I said, still focusing on what she had said
a moment earlier. The name sounded vaguely familiar. I pulled
the map out of my pocket once more and scanned it. "Yes. I
remember. It's now underwater, right?"

"Yes. Yes, it is," Felix said in a somber tone. "But for a
very long time, it was considered one of the greatest cities in
the world. A city full of hope, and possibilities." After that he
started humming loudly, a musical tune emerging from the
back of his throat. Rose smiled his way and shook her head.

"What is that?" I asked.

"'New York, New York,' by Frank Sinatra," he said, as if it
were the most obvious thing. "Oh, here we are," he declared
before I had a chance to respond or ask who Frank Sinatra was.

The car dipped, and I wasn't prepared. I clutched the map
in one hand as my eyes shot back out the window to see the
dome quickly approaching. The vehicle ceased its descent and
was now making a beeline for the building. It looked like we
were going to crash. A familiar knot formed in my throat. I
gripped the sides of my seat and shot a panicked look to Rose,
but she was calmly watching out the window, unfazed by the
rapidly approaching building we would be making impact with
any second now.

"Oh my Board!" I screamed, and bit my lip so hard, I started to taste blood.

At the last second, one of the glass panels disappeared behind another, like an invisible garage door several stories up. It had truly been seamless against the building's facade. We drove right through it. I exhaled as the lights switched on and we navigated down a wide vehicle corridor.

Flying into the side of buildings must be so common of an occurrence here that no one thought to warn me.

I patted my fat lip with the back of my hand and when I removed it, there was a smear of blood on my pallid knuckles. The map was in tatters in my other hand. I must have torn it against the sides of the seat. Though my brain started to wander, to catastrophize, I caught myself. *I can't focus on that now.* I folded the map as carefully as I could and put it back in my pocket.

The vehicle danced gracefully through the corridor until it came to a stop next to two identical vehicles. When I exited, the ground beneath me felt as if it were rippling. As if I'd just stepped out of one of those virtual video games where you clip your arms and legs into the straps so it can complete all the action steps as the avatar on the screen—flips, kicks, and all. Those games always made me feel like I might revisit my lunch, even more so as my teenage years moved further and further away.

We exited, identification was flashed by Rose and Felix, and we were led to a small, wheeled open-air transport vehicle that took us out through a different door and up a series of ramps to another floor. I sure hoped I wasn't expected to navigate this maze by myself anytime soon.

"We're just meeting them right up here," Rose said as we wound one final corner.

Two people stood waiting. The first, a woman with wide eyes, tight lips, and a rigid posture that gave you the impression she was being stretched up toward the ceiling by an invisible string. The second, a man about a head taller than the woman, with sandy-blond hair, walked right in step with her. From his posture and proximity, I assumed he was a security guard or assistant of some kind.

Felix climbed out first and, noticing I was still pale from nausea, offered me his hand. "You get used to it," he whispered as I took it. *Oh, great, something to look forward to*, I thought as I started down the hallway on unsteady legs.

"Patch Collins, welcome!" The woman who had stood out was walking toward us, hand extended. She took quick, short steps and her legs seemed to barely bend, reminding me of a grounded bird as she approached. As she came closer and her face became clearer, I recognized her from my research—the prime minister of Canada.

"I've been looking forward to meeting you. I'm Prime Minister Laurel Austin, and this here is my chief of staff, James Welch."

Her sleek blond hair was pulled up into a sort of bun, but not quite—like knots tumbling into one another. A golden scarf and earrings of the same hue added a touch of flare against the indigo suit and a thread of the same golden color was woven into her braid. Her eyes were captivating and a bit unnerving—a deep amber color I'd never seen in a human eye. Did she also have temporary implants like Rose?

The image of the Board member, with his plastic face and his yellow-tinged eyes, flashed before me. I closed my eyes until the image passed and then looked once again at the prime minister. Her head was cocked slightly to the side as she took me in. Had she noticed my brief hesitation?

It hit me how much hope I was putting into this person I was just meeting. Was it warranted? I wanted nothing more than to trust her. To trust them. For these people to have the answers I'd been looking for. For everything sacrificed to be worth it.

"It's so nice to finally meet you," I replied, extending my hand out to meet the prime minister's. She took it and encased it with both of hers as she studied my face with a sort of melancholy expression.

"I know you've been patient," she finally said as she let go, patting one of my hands with hers before she did so—an action that I couldn't quite read.

She turned and gestured for us to follow her, and began walking with the same stiff, birdlike steps. Their succinct rhythm echoed off the corridor walls. "We know that you have been through a tremendous hardship, and we hope today we can begin to make productive inroads into understanding what happened, and to help you start feeling at home here."

"Start feeling at home here"? I didn't like the sound of that. I flashed a look to Felix, but he was talking quietly to Rose and did not notice. I followed the prime minister, picking up my speed to keep in lockstep with her. The ground below us shimmered the same way it had in the hospital with each step, harnessing the kinetic energy.

We walked down two long corridors, past an array of towering doors that lined the hallway toward a set of double doors at the end. Two guards walked ahead and held them ajar for us. The prime minister waved me through in an *After you* gesture. Rose and James followed. Felix stayed outside and offered a thumbs-up as I passed. When I stepped into the room, I stopped and gasped.

I was standing on the circumference of a vast domed room. Everything was gold. The tables, the chairs, the engravings on the walls, the pillars. All gold. And not just a flat gold, but a reflective gold that made it hard for your eyes to concentrate on any one thing, as if you were standing inside a glamorous light fixture.

On the far end opposite where I stood was an enormous engraving centered on the wall—a circular map was flanked by what looked like two branches.

On each side of the carving were floor-to-ceiling screens, both turned off. If this was one of the satellite offices, I had trouble imagining what the real thing looked like.

In front of the screens, a table ran through the middle of the circular room, with several chairs in a row behind it. About ten feet directly above each chair, an opal ring-shaped device was suspended from the ceiling by a thin rod in the middle, like an upside-down lollipop. I noticed identical devices suspended over chairs in other parts of the room as well.

Ms. Austin motioned to a smaller table in the middle that faced the long one, and pulled out a chair for me. Rose took the chair next to me and the chief of staff, James, sat in a chair against the curved wall.

The prime minister walked toward the large table. I sat down, and as soon as I had lowered myself into the seat, it startled me by morphing to meet the shape of my back and rising until I was at the perfect position to the table in front of me.

I noticed a glimmer in one of the other seats. Suddenly someone was sitting there. I hadn't seen her come in. I looked around, confused, then back at the new arrival with her gray hair and rosy cheeks. She cast a curious, rough smile in my direction and nodded at the prime minister. I smiled back tentatively. Then a chair two seats away from the new woman filled with a man who was staring down, appearing to be attending to something outside our field of vision.

Holographs.

The prime minister walked behind them and took the chair in the center, lowering herself into it without so much as a slight break in her perfect posture.

I suddenly felt small as a grain of rice. My eyes scanned the important-looking figures towering over me like redwoods. I knew they weren't the Board; I knew that, but the table, the folded hands resting in front of them, the group of eyes staring down at me—my fight-or-flight instincts were in full effect and I was trapped.

I closed my eyes for a moment and took a deep breath as my brain started to turn to memories of interrogations. *Not now*, I told myself. *Keep it together.*

"Now that everyone is here, we'll start by introducing ourselves," the prime minister began curtly, and I swallowed the lump farther down my throat. "As you know, I'm Prime Minister Laurel Austin, of Canada." She smiled an overextended smile, then turned her wide eyes to the person next to her.

"It's wonderful to meet you, Patch. I'm Osborn Jacobs, chancellor of Germany."

"I'm Skye Robinson, prime minister of the United Kingdom. It is a pleasure, Ms. Collins, and I am pleased to see you safe and in good health."

After they were done with introductions, the prime minister of the UK, Skye Robinson, nodded at her colleagues and then spoke. "We are three of the fifteen members of the New UN Security Council, reestablished in the year 2045 with a renewed focus on global innovation, peacekeeping, and development. We have reviewed your information and the written statements you submitted upon arrival. We are here today to ask a few questions. From there, we will have you work with a team, including Ms. Anders and Mr. Suen, to update our intelligence files on America. Do you have any opening remarks?"

The room went deafeningly silent, and they all looked at me. A light on the table in front of me lit up. Next to it was an embedded speaker, or perhaps a microphone. I may not know much, but I knew it was my turn to speak.

"Hi. My name is Patch Collins. I'm from America," I said, sitting up straighter in my chair, which again morphed behind to match the new curvature of my spine. I looked from face to face for cues as to whether I should be saying more. I put my hands underneath the table and ran my thumb over the space where my grandmother's ring used to reside on my index finger. *You can do this*, I thought. *They aren't the Board.*

"I'm here to formally request intervention in America and, well, I'm looking forward to speaking with you today."

I wiped my palms on my pants as the words I'd rehearsed over and over in my mind fell out of my head. I was shrinking like a sea sponge left out in the sun. This wasn't the conversation I'd imagined—the one I had rehearsed in my mind hundreds of times by now in a setting conjured up by my imagination based on nothing. I'd hoped for a relaxed meeting with the woman I had seen in the pictures, a conversation between me and the prime minister. I had researched her, and I felt semi-prepared for a conversation between the two of us, at least based on the brief biographies I had read about the woman sitting in front of me. Laurel Austin was fifty-two years old and had been the prime minister for the past six years. She was originally from Vancouver and had two grown children and a dog.

Before becoming prime minister, Austin was a senator in Western Canada. Prior to that she worked for the Canadian Security Intelligence Services, though I didn't quite understand what that meant or what her job entailed, but the description of the agency included a lot of words like *threats, security, abroad,* and *national interests,* so I gathered she knew a lot about the rest of the world.

I didn't know anything about these other two people, and this situation felt different. It felt like me against them.

"Whenever you're ready, Miss Collins," Prime Minister Austin said with a smile, "we would like to hear firsthand how you came to arrive here. Please go over everything that happened from the moment of, let's see, the day that you were questioned by a Compliance Officer at the southern border, to the day approximately two months ago when you were found by one of our medical transport vehicles."

I told them my story. It came pouring out.

I recounted that first day at the Southern Barrier, when I was approached by the Compo. I told them about being called into my boss's office the next morning and seeing *Abuse of Privilege* marked in my file and the other words I had spotted on Mrs. Gerardi's computer screen—*Level-Yellow Alert; Third-Generation Family History.*

I told them about Rexx, and about us finding the van in Zone 72 and the contents within, including the books, the signs, and the map. I told them about us leading my parents to the van, and my father recounting his days as an informant. I told them about how Rexx and I watched the van being torched, about receiving the news of my father's arrest.

I told them how we ran. How we cut open our own skin to remove our dorsal chips and then jumped on a cargo flat out of the Tucson Urban Center.

I spoke for what felt like hours, my voice becoming raw as time wore on. They listened intently, interrupting only to ask a few basic questions or for clarification. Otherwise, they just let me speak. Their eyes and reactions were impossible to read.

I told them about the library in Wildcliff—the chain on the door, the musty smell of ash, and the seventy-five skeletons heaped in piles, with only the occasional strip of fabric left to remind us of their humanity.

They looked at me quizzically as I told them about the cargo flat passing the site of the 2029 bombing in Nevada and the impossible magnificence of that bowl-shaped depression and the layers of striation it revealed.

I told them about Zone 36, and about Oliver and the way that he lived. About the earthquake damage, the rappelling, and the freedom.

The night that Rexx and I shared in the church—well, that I kept to myself.

Then I told them about the elders and the Veritas Ring—the video they showed me of the Board's announcement during the Seclusion, their hope that there were still others like them elsewhere, the stories they told me about the transition, and the plans we made for Rexx and me to reach the northern border.

I told them about the night the Compos searched Zone 36, and the events that followed—Rexx torching the community center, us running again, coming across Officer Webb, and finally, our capture.

I outlined my days in the compound, including the interrogation and escape aided by Officer Webb. I told them about meeting Rexx at the tree line and the jumble of events that led to me being here without him.

When I was finished, I looked up and watched as a conversation happened between them in front of my eyes, too quiet for my ears. Then, when they were done conversing among themselves, they turned to me.

I learned I wasn't the first, but it had been over two decades since another defector was declared. So long, in fact, they had to create a new form for me when they heard of my arrival at the hospital.

In the beginning, there were more like me who'd escaped, or "defected," as they kept calling it. The means were simple—extension ladders, the river, a private plane. The Walls were seen for what they were—simply a man-made obstacle to over-come. The early defectors assimilated rather easily, with a lit-tle help from reliable shelter and food to eat, as they still had knowledge of a time before.

Then the narrative, and with it the collective consciousness of America, shifted, and history was rewritten. The Walls were no longer inanimate objects; they were monuments we were taught to worship. So much so that the possibility of going up against them was too unfathomable for most to entertain. I thought back to the admiration I'd felt for the Walls before I learned the truth, and I shuddered at my ignorance.

There was a strong-arm threat of nuclear weapons every time someone tried to intervene. At first, world leaders didn't take it too seriously, but then, in 2029, America went and bombed itself to make some kind of point. I remembered Noah telling me he thought the Board was behind the bombing in Nevada in 2029. When I'd said as much during my interroga-tion, the Board member hadn't exactly denied it.

The firewalls placed around The Board's state-run systems, prevented outsiders from accessing information about the daily lives of American citizens. Satellites and the early stories of defectors told a partial tale. There were even a few classified missions that sent spies onto American soil, but not for the past twenty-five years, as the Board's dorsal chip technology improved, tagging each American and making it harder for an outsider to pass.

The outside world continued to keep an eye on us and assessed us periodically for danger and threats to the outside. Satellite images, obtained from what they told me were cameras that orbit our planet, showed mostly thriving communities in America. Abandoned swaths of land, yes, but the communities seemed to be doing just fine.

Leaders around the globe felt it was best to back off. To keep an eye on us from a distance. To leave us alone.

And so, life kept going outside the Walls, just as Noah and the others had suggested. They were right. They were right, and they might never know.

"We want to put your mind at ease, Ms. Collins," said Prime Minister Austin when there was a lull in the conversation. "There is an alliance among most other nations. Once the minutiae are taken care of and you remaining here is approved by all the right people, others will embrace you as well. You can live safely here or in a number of other countries if you choose. You have skills that will certainly be appreciated anywhere you wish to settle, and we will provide support in the form of a financial stipend and retraining until you get back on your feet."

I listened, I smiled, I nodded, even though I was confused by her meaning when she said "approved by all the right people." I tried not to appear as overwhelmed as I felt, all the while only thinking of those I had lost in the weeks and months before.

"Thank you. I appreciate that. But what I want is to help those who are still there, and I can't do it alone."

The prime minister smiled, though her lips remained closed. "I don't think you quite understand what you are asking of us, Patch." Her words were succinct and clipped, like her steps. "We sympathize with everything you have gone through, and I understand you have people in the United States you care about. It's my understanding your mother is still there, and plenty of friends as well. Humanitarian efforts are one thing, and even that route we left behind long ago."

No shit, I thought to myself but did not say out loud. I could feel any hope I had of getting to Oliver, or of a massive rescue effort, slipping away.

I felt as if I were at the bottom of a well, screaming, while people sat at the top with their feet dangling over the edge, chatting and having a picnic. I scanned the rest of the faces.

All were avoiding looking at me directly. Anger began to rise inside me. I was right in front of them, telling them that people in America were suffering, asking for their help, and it became clear as the seconds ticked by—they were saying no.

"I don't understand," I replied, my voice rising. "You made me wait two months to be told you aren't going to do anything?"

"Getting people to mobilize," the prime minister said, "it could lead to an all-out war. There's a reason we haven't been able to form a bridge with America. We've pored over it from every angle. You can read about it all if you like, in the digital transcripts. We believe America is sitting on one of the largest, and only, nuclear arsenals remaining in the world."

The prime minister continued. "The rest of the developed world struck a denuclearization accord in the forties. We've tried to handle things diplomatically with America. They have shifted to what we refer to as a command economy, with the government controlling the means of production for all goods and services. Others have had similar economies in the past, but they no longer remain. We still have some mutually beneficial trade agreements in place with America. Which is why communication has remained open with your Board. It's our way of helping Americans just a bit. But any more pushing and your Board threatens nuclear war. We've always come out of any negotiation attempts empty-handed."

I sat there in shock, looking between the six sets of eyes staring down at me. Feeling very small. Then something clicked. I realized, even though I was no longer on American soil, I was taking the threats of the Board as truth again and so were they. I came back to my senses.

"How do you know they are telling the truth?" I blurted out. "It's been sixty years! They brainwashed us. They staged fake videos of 'redeemed patriots,' when, as we came to find out, there was only mass imprisonment. They convinced all of us that our powerful military was out here fighting terror. It was all a lie. What if this is too? What if there is no arsenal?"

As I said the words, another thought came to my mind. "Or what if there is but they haven't been maintaining it properly?"

I seemed to have the renewed attention of everyone now.

"I helped clean up contaminated sites for a living and was one of the few to study the aftereffects of various weapons. Without the right maintenance, the weapons will not work. The nuclear material needs other ingredients to make it function correctly. While the plutonium may last for a century or more, the other components that set off the chain reaction need to be replaced. So, for example, if their weapons used tritium, which is a boost gas, it only has a shelf life of about twelve years. How do you know that after sixty years, they could carry out any of their threats?" I could hear my voice continuing to rise and felt my cheeks turning bright red. But I seemed to be outside of my body, unable to stop my words even if I wanted to. "These aren't trustworthy people we are dealing with."

"I know," Austin said after a moment of silence. She had a far-off look in her eyes, and I stared at her for a moment. It was as if she were off in her own universe or remembering something painful. She then turned her attention suddenly back to the room. "That is something to consider, Miss Collins. For now, however, we need to move on."

Then Austin cast a glance to the woman to her right, Skye Robinson, who nodded. What were they communicating to each other? Skye stood up and walked over to one of the neighboring empty seats, raised her hand, and pressed on one of the oval rings suspended over the chair.

"Now, I don't want you to panic, Patch," Ms. Robinson said. There was something in her voice. Something was wrong. "But we have someone who would like to talk to you."

"Who?" I asked, confused. It seemed I was already talking to plenty of people. A former defector, perhaps? I would love to speak to someone else who had left America, even if it was decades ago. Maybe it was one of the spies they had mentioned, or a defector, but why would they not have joined at the beginning of our meeting and why the warning not to panic?

"Just convince him that you won't cause any trouble, and that it's in everyone's best interest for you to stay here, and we will help you live a normal life. A good life," Robinson said.

"I don't understand who . . ."

But there was no time to clarify. Before I could finish, the empty chair to the left of the main row wasn't empty any longer. I stood quickly out of my chair and took a step back. I nearly fell to the ground but caught myself on the table behind me.

My eyes focused just long enough to recognize the image of the Board member. It was the same man who had tortured me. The same man who had ordered the murder of my father.

No.

I didn't know if I spoke the word, but it filled my body, replacing my blood.

NO.

A split second later he was but a shape I could not focus on. I shook my head and tried to step back farther.

NO.

But there was nowhere to go. The table was still behind me, or was it? The surroundings blurred. My eyes burned.

NO.

I lost the fight between the present and my memories. The image of my father crumpling to the ground filled my head, Webb standing over him, having just pulled the trigger on the pacifier. *My clothes are being cut off, my head is shaved, and jolts of electricity course through my body. I sit, rocking, in a dark, lonely cell. A flashing screen that transcends the walls surrounds me, filling my consciousness and never letting me rest. A never-ending hunger encapsulates me. Emaciated bodies of the barely living huddle together in a compound yard, a sea of gray faces. I claw my way up a rock face to the Northern Barrier. I put my hands over my ears. The Board member's voice through a drone echoes in my head. Rexx leads the Compos away, and then he is lost under a pile of boulders.*

"No. No. Why are you doing this? He can't be here. This isn't real." I still didn't know if I said the words out loud or not.

"Patricia. It's good to see you," he said in a hoarse, bubbly voice that sounded as if it were reaching me through water. Just like that, he took the new name I had chosen for myself and ripped it away. Bile rose in my throat, and I couldn't look directly at him. The blurry room started to spin—gold, everywhere gold. A wave of golden fabric was wrapping itself around me in a tight cocoon.

"Why? Why are you doing this?"

I skirted the edge of the table and gripped a chair. It toppled over. I felt skinny arms behind me, catching my fall. The prime minister's head floated above the gold scarf she wore that blended into the wall behind her. My eyes tried to focus on the other members of the council, looking for an explanation, but they were nothing but blurred items on a shelf.

They'd planned this.

The gold room kept spinning, and the cocoon tightened. I couldn't breathe.

Again, the voice of the Board member.

"Patricia. You don't know what you're doing. It's time to come home." Then suddenly everything went dark, and I was lost.

CHAPTER 6

Patch Collins

WHEN I WAS young and would have a nightmare, my mother used to place her hand on the back of my head. The weight of that hand was grounding. Her slender fingers would encase themselves in my tangled wavy hair as the pad of her thumb traced a line between my temple and my cheekbone, over and over.

Did my mother remember this too? Did she miss feeling my small head underneath her hand or was the memory of her daughter nothing but pain and shame to her now?

After I moved to the dormitories at the age of five, I would sometimes wake up scared in the middle of the night. There were strange sounds everywhere. The air-filtration systems that protected us from the harmful chemicals swirling outside were loud, and they would kick on periodically. The Compos' large boots echoed as they patrolled the corridors and my heart shuddered slightly with each deep step.

When I would look over to find Amara asleep, and no comfort anywhere in sight, I would sometimes imagine my mom's hand once again on my head. Sometimes that was enough, but often it wasn't.

When I came to, everything was sideways, and the weight of a hand was on my head. I could hear voices arguing as my eyes opened. I was lying on the floor in the middle of the vast chambers. The gold-domed ceiling was miles away, no longer spinning. There was no sign of the Board member anywhere, and the long table where the members of the Security Council had materialized was empty.

I spotted the prime minister in a heated exchange with her chief of staff, though I couldn't make out what they were saying. Rose's hand stroked my head.

"What happened?" I asked, shaking Rose's hand away. The prime minister walked over and tried to hand me a glass of water, and I found myself scooting away from her as the memories of what had just taken place came flooding back. I scanned the room again, just to make sure the Board member wasn't there, then I looked back to the prime minister. Her amber eyes avoided mine with expert precision even as I tried to catch their glance. I felt more like something that had spilled in the middle of the room rather than a person.

"Why did you do this? I don't understand. Did you know they were going to do this?" I turned to Rose defensively, and she shook her head.

"No," she said, casting a steeled glance at the prime minister. "It was not my place to know ahead of time."

Rose offered me a hand, but I did not take it. Instead I sat up on my own, then leaned against a table leg. I avoided looking at either of them, trying to collect my thoughts.

"He requested to speak to you," Laurel Austin said after a moment, and there was a hint of something in her voice. I think it was guilt, but I couldn't be sure. "And in the interest of diplomacy," she continued, "we said yes."

"You didn't have to say yes," a voice mumbled from across the room. It was James, the chief of staff. The prime minister ignored his interruption.

"We thought it would be a good opportunity to observe your reaction to seeing him," Austin said, "and his to seeing you." She said the words as if what had just happened was perfectly normal. Who the hell was this person?

"We still think it would benefit the situation if you could bring yourself to have a conversation with him." I whipped my head around. She didn't flinch and she continued to avoid eye contact.

I shifted my glance again to Rose, who just looked down at her knees as she knelt on the ground. I then looked to James, who was still standing against the wall, his face flushed, perhaps from the argument that must have started before I regained consciousness. He was the only one who looked me in the eye. He didn't say anything, but he held my glance for more than a passing second, and then he nodded ever so slightly. Whether he was trying to tell me something or simply offering a small gesture of understanding or validation, I couldn't tell. I swallowed down the bile that was rising in my throat, closed my eyes, and took a deep breath. I then turned back to the prime minister.

"You want me to have a conversation with the man who murdered my father?" I raised myself off the ground and began inching toward the large doors, not letting her out of my sight as I did so. "You want me to make nice with him? To pretend he didn't torture me, and that he isn't part of a group that brainwashes millions and lights people on fire inside of locked buildings?"

Rage began to bubble. I was a teakettle; the steam was rising, and I was holding back a scream. Along with the rage, there was something else—a gnawing realization that I had nowhere to go, that even if I backed out of the door I was about to reach, I was leaving behind the only person who could help me. Like it or not, this person had power and I did not.

I stopped, keeping my gaze directed right into those amber eyes. She stared back with a look on her face I could not place. Pity? Intrigue? Annoyance?

"Yes," she finally said, this time looking straight into my eyes. She rolled her shoulders back and slowly took a few bird-like steps toward me, as if she were approaching a cornered cat.

"Again, Patch," she said carefully, as if making it a point to call me by my preferred name as an act of goodwill, "you are the only defector in over twenty years, and we need to know what the Board is thinking. We need to see the two of you interact. I promise we won't surprise you next time."

We stood there, facing each other. The bubbles still simmered but had lost some of their intensity. Hesitantly, I walked back toward her and sat down in a nearby chair. My head sank into my hands and I took several deep breaths.

This was not how I wanted our first interaction to go. I was angry they'd put me in that situation. I hated that there appeared to be some collaboration among them. I was angry with myself for not having seen it coming. For being so naive. I looked from Laurel Austin to Rose, and then even to her chief of staff, James. How was I supposed to move forward with these people after what had just happened? Did I have a choice?

"What is his name?" I asked, trying to keep my voice as steady as possible.

"What's that?" the prime minister said, seeming to not understand what I was asking her.

"The Board member. I don't know his name," I said rather sharply as I raised my head, once again peering into her captivating eyes. "What is his name?"

She looked at me quizzically for a brief second, and then her eyes widened and darted off into the distance, and she started playing with the golden scarf that cascaded down her right shoulder. All went silent, and it was as if she were recalling something. Then James walked over and whispered something into her ear.

There was something she wasn't telling me.

"Right. His name is Elias Stevens," she finally replied.

I turned his name over in my head—Elias Stevens. It didn't seem real. This person who haunted my nightmares having so human of a name. It was like a shadow rising up from the sidewalk to introduce itself to me. Elias Stevens.

"Even though there are thirty members of the Board," Ms. Austin said, "there is still a hierarchy within members. The Stevens family has been at the top since the Seclusion. Elias has been there since, well, since he took over his father's spot in 2058." She recited the information with the wistfulness and timbre of someone relaying a personal event rather than statistics.

"Let's take a break, Patch. Rose, please show her to somewhere she can wait. Excuse me." At that, Laurel Austin walked past me and out of the room, and as she passed I thought I saw the slightest hint of moisture coating her eyes. I watched the door close behind her, suddenly wanting to know everything about who this woman was.

"I'm sorry," Rose said as we entered a room where I could wait while the Security Council spoke without me. "I had no idea that was the plan." She closed the door behind her and motioned for me to sit on the couch in the corner of the room.

I wasn't sure if I believed her. I felt like a child sent to time-out, but I was so out of my element and my head was still spinning that I didn't exactly want to be part of the Security Council conversation at the moment either.

"You have to understand something about the prime minister," she continued as we both sat down. "She, well, before she became the prime minister, she was a secret agent with CSIS."

"I don't know what any of that means," I said matter-of-factly, the worry about impressing or coming across as naive completely gone at the moment.

"It means, well, it is the Canadian Security Intelligence Service," Rose began gently, "and we don't really know exactly what she did during her time as an agent. A lot of it is classified, but what I do know is that she has a habit of testing people, whether it's deserved or not."

"So, having Elias show up, you think that was a test of some kind?"

"I don't know for sure, but I wouldn't be surprised."

"Well, if so, then I assume I failed spectacularly," I said while feeling suddenly incredibly embarrassed about what had happened.

"Not necessarily. We don't know what she was testing you for. She has a messy past and can sometimes be hard to read, but most people out here love her, and she is a good leader, so I wouldn't write her off so soon. She might have her reasons."

Rose reached out and put her hand on my shoulder before continuing. "But I was telling the truth when I said I didn't know that was coming. I want, well, I want us to be friends."

Friends. The word had lost almost all of its meaning. I didn't know if I had it in me to accept friendship, or to even be a friend in any real way. I felt broken and toxic and empty. I just wanted a moment to myself to process what had happened. A moment without everyone looking at me, and without them seeing how close to breaking I felt underneath it all.

"Can I just have a few minutes?" I asked, hoping she wouldn't take offense.

"Of course. I'll see if I can find out anything," she said as she stood, stretched her arms up over her head, and then walked out the door.

What I wanted more than anything, I thought as the door closed behind Rose, was for my old friends to be the ones who put me back together. I thought of Oliver, and my mother, and even Lydia and Jordan, my old friends at the Natural Resource Department.

I leaned back and tried to assess the situation. My wrist ached. I must have hit it when I fell. I rotated it a few times. It was sore and bruised, but nothing felt broken and it would probably be fine. I'd seen worse.

The room Rose had taken me to was simple. It held a couch, two chairs, and a shelf with snacks and a hot-water heater. Large numbers on the wall blinked *1:35 p.m.* Was that really all? I felt as if I had left the hospital days ago.

I walked over to the shelf and made myself a cup of tea, then returned to the chair. I wrapped my fingers around the cup, absorbing the heat in my hands. The tag from the tea bag hung out the side of it. *Jasmine green, sourced from Japan*, it said in cursive letters.

"Huh," I muttered to myself as I held the warm mug up to my nose, and inhaled the soft, purifying, sweet jasmine aroma, wishing I could disappear inside the steam. I felt the urge to research Japan, but it passed quickly. How freely information was given here. Most information.

I thought about Elias Stevens, conjuring up the image of his face and mentally preparing myself to see him again. I thought about what I had learned so far that day.

Power in America was passed down from generation to generation. It made sense with how little the public knew of the Board. As much sense as anything in America seemed to make, anyway. What did Elias Stevens really believe? I briefly imagined him as a small child, a child just like any other, hungry for his father's attention. A child admiring the Board like the rest of us, with an extra dose of pride in his family's lineage. Pride that he would one day hold the torch. Would one day join the all-knowing entity that is the Board. Be responsible for the cleansing of toxic information. For protecting the citizens of America from the dangers on the outside. Was that how it was sold to him as well? When did they tell him the truth and when did he decide the lies were worth protecting?

My thoughts were interrupted when the door opened. I was relieved to see that it was Felix. He was carrying a bag with a symbol on the outside—a silhouette of a leaf with a plus sign in the middle. He was also carrying a plate whose contents I could not see from this angle.

"May I?" he asked as he nodded toward the cushion on the sofa next to me.

I nodded, and he took a seat, setting the plate between us, which I could now see held a couple fruit-and-nut bars of some kind.

"Did you make these too?" I asked as I reached for one.

"Yes! Well, I made some yesterday, but there were a couple left in the refrigerator in our lab, so I thought you might like some. They are cranberry and almond."

I smiled and took a bite, imagining Felix baking. Did he stay up and bake to relieve stress the way that I used to hide out in my garden? The bars, just like the cookies, were delicious and not too sweet. My stomach rumbled as I bit into the slightly chewy center, revealing just how hungry I'd been.

Felix opened the bag he'd carried in and took out a strip of fabric. "They told me that you fell, hard. This is for your wrist," he said, and brought the crook of his elbow up and swiped the hair out from in front of his eyes.

I extended my arm, and he began gently wrapping the fabric around my wrist, then between my thumb and forefinger, then around my wrist once more. As soon as he was done, he pressed something on the outside of the fabric and a cool sensation coated the area, similar to how my feet felt in the hospital. "This will speed up healing," he said.

"Thank you," I said without asking anything else. On any other day I would have been interested in how exactly it would speed up healing, and in the makeup and components of this medical advancement.

"I don't know exactly what happened in there, Patch. Do you want to tell me?" I shook my head and looked out the window, though I did want to tell him. I wanted to trust someone, and at that moment, out of everyone I had met, he seemed the most genuine and worthy of it. Something stopped me. Felix was nice, but like Rose, and like the prime minister, I didn't know him and he didn't know me.

"Okay," he said as he stood. He waited there for a moment, like there was more on the tip of his tongue. "I'll leave you alone," he finally said, and the door shut a moment later.

I kept my gaze out the window, watching the vehicles hovering around and the people walking below. Even in the daylight, the city seemed to have a soft sunset-yellow sheen to it, almost as if it were being viewed through an amber dome.

The building we were in was in the middle of other large, towering ones. The living facades growing on the faces of the structures were all uniform, as if it were part of the building code for each structure to match its neighbor.

I leaned closer to the window and looked down directly at the people. Some words from the prime minister earlier in the day came into my mind—*start feeling at home here.*

What would it feel like to be one of those people? To erase my memories and blend into this new environment? I could get a new job, a new group of friends, and a new purpose in life. Maybe I could work on the desalination project or learn about how they manage soil health out here.

For a split second it sounded enticing. Maybe it would be the reasonable thing to do. Maybe they even had the ability to wipe away memories in this world. Perhaps they could erase all memories of America from my brain and I could just be someone else. What would that feel like?

I took a sip and set the cup down, wondering how I would make it through the next several hours.

I took the scroll out of my pocket, and while I waited, my curiosity got the best of me. I thought about the image of New York I'd been shown earlier that day. I held my hand above the screen and "wrote" out a search term.

Photos America. Before the Seclusion.

There were results. Most of them were labeled with the words *Public Domain* and dated before 2030. I scrolled through them, feeling as if I were looking at pictures of a place as foreign to me as where I now sat, and feeling somehow illicit for viewing something I'd been taught my whole life was unviewable. I didn't recognize the photos I was looking at as America. There were photos of busy city streets, of musical performances, of gatherings large and small.

I searched again.

Photos America. After the Seclusion.

There were not many results. There were what were called satellite images, which showed a view from above and computer-rendered images of urban centers. Then there was a search result that stood out.

America Surveillance Project. Discontinued 2065.

These must be from one of those classified missions that the Security Council mentioned, the ones terminated when dorsal chips became mandatory, before I was born. Who was on these missions? What countries had they come from? I still didn't fully believe that there had been others walking among Americans after the Seclusion, gathering information, and I'd never heard about it. Then again, there were plenty of things I'd never heard of. Did the Board know? They must have, since the council had mentioned the dorsal chips. Was this the primary reason they were invented? I glanced down to the scar, now a smooth line, on my hand where Rexx had cut my chip out.

I clicked on the text and watched several images appear. There were labeled close-ups of the various tiered housings in different urban centers, and the insides of schoolrooms and dormitories. There were labeled photographs of Board members, of the Compliance Department, and photos of abandoned swaths of land. There were photographs of many of the closed-off zones, and I searched them for any that I recognized, but they had either changed so much since the photographs were taken, or they were all of zones I had never visited.

Rose and Felix came in, startling me, and I closed the scroll and put it back in my pocket.

"Are you ready?" Rose asked. It was time to talk to Elias Stevens.

Soon we were again walking down the hall, but not back toward the large double doors as we had before.

"There is a conference room upstairs we will use to patch you through. A less overwhelming environment," Rose said after we'd entered an elevator, speaking to me as if I might crumble right there on the floor. I hadn't exactly proven otherwise.

"It's okay. I think I'm ready," I said, trying to convince myself as much as them.

"Just remember, he is not here," Felix said.

I tried to reassure myself even though I was still skeptical. *They want to watch this conversation. Even though it hasn't gone as planned so far, this means they haven't ruled out helping. It's a good thing.*

I stepped off the elevator to see Prime Minister Austin and her chief of staff waiting. James had his arms crossed and was standing farther from the prime minister than he had been when I met him. Was he disapproving of her actions today? She led us to what she told me was a secure room where Elias Stevens and I could talk freely.

"Thank you for agreeing to do this, Patch. I know that it's not easy," she said through pursed lips once the door was closed and only she and I were inside. I tried to smile, and to pretend I didn't have a peculiar feeling about the woman standing opposite me, whose golden eyes seemed to dodge my gaze. *I need her to like me*, I reminded myself. *I need her to want to help me.*

"I know it won't be easy," she said curtly, repeating herself. "The members of the council had a brief conversation with Mr. Stevens and two other Board members about the situation we find ourselves in. While we did not disclose to him all of what we discussed, he remained adamant about you not being truthful, and that the situation in his country is not what you describe."

"I'm sure he did," I said, any guise of hiding my frustration quickly disappearing. Then panic started to rise as a detail I had neglected was suddenly all I could think about. How could I have been so stupid? Why had I told them everything?

"Officer Webb," I said. "You didn't, well, you didn't tell them he helped us, did you? Or that he was the one responsible for that other officer's death? Please tell me you didn't."

I searched her as she cocked her head to one side, making me wait for an answer. The lump in my throat grew as the seconds ticked past.

"No. No, we didn't." I exhaled in relief. "The Board seems to believe you and Mr. Moreno were responsible for the death of the Compliance Officer at the rehabilitation center." The way she kept her head cocked as she spoke the words made me wonder if she also thought we were responsible, and that my story was rather convenient.

"Mr. Stevens reiterated that their military is one of the strongest in the world, and he was sure to remind us of the nuclear arsenal once again. I also want to let you know, Patch, that for years the common consensus has been that the Board has been training underground, knowing that we have the ability to monitor them via satellite."

Hope. Just a tiny sliver, but it was there. She was starting to question things. But after the surge of hope, there was another emotion: anger.

"So you have no actual evidence of military activity or an active nuclear arsenal?" I said, unable to hide the harshness of my voice.

The prime minister took a step back, obviously not used to people talking to her this way. She let out a quick and airy sigh as she regained her composure. I knew I should tone it down, but there was something about her that kept rubbing me the wrong way, and I couldn't put my finger on it. There was something else she wasn't telling me, and I thought about what Rose had said about Austin's tendency to test people.

"What is our goal here?" I said, looking around the room. It had a sterile smell to it, and at first glance, it was remarkably similar to the conference rooms at the Natural Resource Department back home. There was one notable exception—the floors, ceilings, walls, and even the doors were all flexible screens. The floor, which looked like a green tile, was merely an image of such a design. It was the same with the walls. Three were set to a muted ivory color, and the fourth displayed an array of picture frames set to look like they were hung in a row, rather than encased in one giant image.

There was a round table in the middle of the room that looked like it would fit about ten people. My brain paused, imagining Rexx walking in, holding a coffee in one hand and jumping with unnatural morning energy into a chair. A familiar ache filled my chest.

There were halos suspended above the chairs, similar to the ones in the chamber that morning. I wondered what the room was generally used for in a government building such as this, and what sort of meetings took place between its walls. Had the Board member patched into this room before? Did American leaders take part in these discussions regularly? Would I ever know all the answers?

I steeled myself and stood up straighter. "If I'm going to do this, I feel like I need to know why. Like, is there specific information I should be trying to get out of him?"

"As we discussed, the goal is simply to watch how this conversation plays out. How the Board responds. We have analysts watching in. It's almost time. We will be outside this door," the prime minister said. She put her hands on my shoulders and gave them a squeeze. I think she meant it to feel maternal and comforting, but it was just awkward.

After she turned and left, I stood in the room alone.

My arms prickled as I walked to the right side of the table, past several empty chairs. I walked the circumference of the table, unsure where to sit and not wanting to accidentally sit where Elias Stevens would materialize. So, instead of sitting, I just stopped and stood, waiting for a signal as to what I should be doing.

After about two minutes, the form of the Board member materialized across the table. It was instantaneous. One moment, the space across the table was empty, and the next, the man I now knew to be Elias Stevens was standing there, looking as real as me.

It's only a hologram, I told myself. He looked as if, were I to reach out and touch him, my fingers would graze the impossibly crisp fabric of his black suit. I imagined myself doing just that, then his fingers curling around my arm and slamming me against the wall, a Compo then storming in to subdue me. I took a step backward, my brain not accepting he couldn't harm me. I promised myself I wouldn't cower, and I wouldn't let my memory run away with me. *Stay in the present. Embrace the anger you felt a moment ago. Pick something to focus on.* The chair behind him cut through his knees at the seat, because he was not yet sitting. I picked the chair. The chair was real. The chair was here. The image of the man rising out of the center of it was not.

His hands were clasped in front of him. His eyes met mine, and we stayed locked like that for a moment, analyzing each other. Was the technology on his end as crisp? Did I look as real to him as he did to me? Was it driving him crazy that I was out of his reach?

A chill ran up my spine, but I didn't flinch, not wanting him to see my fear. He'd seen enough of that and I wouldn't let him have it twice.

His lips parted, and I swallowed down the panic. There were so many things I wanted to know. Things I didn't have the answers to, even out here.

I wanted to know if Oliver was still alive. If he was suffering additional torture because of us. I wanted to know if the others in Zone 36 had been arrested. I wanted to know what was happening with my mother. Had they punished her for my crimes, and how was she spending her days without me, and without my father?

I wanted to know if they had made the connection between my escape and Officer Robbie Webb. I knew asking any of these questions would put all of their lives in more danger, so I just stared.

Elias was the first to speak.

"Your hair is different. I liked it better long." He smirked as much as one can when their skin is tighter than a tourniquet. I didn't reply to his obvious attempt to goad me. My hair would still be long were it not for him.

"Let me ask you this. Is it everything you hoped it would be?"

I was caught off guard by his question. I thought he would start with a threat, and that our conversation would be like the one we'd had in the compound.

Was it everything I'd hoped for? I'd hoped that once outside, people would hear my story and swoop in to help. It was a naive thought, I now realized. I'd also hoped I would prove the Board wrong, and in that case, my hopes had come true.

I'd hoped I wouldn't cross the Walls to find the terror we were shown each day growing up. What was waiting was direct proof that life had continued outside the Walls. That our leaders, the one in front of me and the twenty-nine others, had lied.

I kept my eyes on his. "Well, I know we were right, and that you are all lying. Though, to be honest, I still haven't figured out exactly why. Is it just power?" I paused, but he didn't answer, just stared analytically.

Suddenly the fear dissipated, and the words began to flow. They were the words I'd been wanting to say for months—a version of the words I had practiced saying to the Security Council but which were left unsaid after I had frozen up. The words, I realized in that moment, I had really been saving for him.

"Because from out here," I went on, "no one respects you. You've created an illusion of power, but really, there is no power. I mean, you might have everyone in there fooled, I guess, but out here you're the mess someone shoves to the back of their closet when cleaning up. It's still there, but it's out of the way, at least. They've moved on without you in mind."

His pale face reddened, creating splotches on his forehead where it looked as if his skin might rip as easily as fabric stretched past its breaking point. His brow furrowed, and even under his heavy suit, I could tell his muscles tensed. His yellow eyes narrowed, boring into mine.

"There are reasons you cannot possibly understand, Patricia. The Board works for the greater good. It has always been that way. You don't see the whole picture. You're messing with something very delicate, something beyond your understanding. Something it is simply not possible for someone like you to understand," he said curtly.

"Now you're just repeating yourself. I've heard that before. It's not going to work." My voice rose, and I leaned forward on the table. "You're not brave, Elias." He flinched at the mention of his name, as if knowing his identity took away some of his power. I relished it. "You're just too damn stubborn to admit your mistakes, and you know, also the mistakes of your father and grandfather, and, well, possibly someone even before them. Don't you see your misdirected pride has caused you to be left behind by the rest of the world?"

"We aren't being left behind, my dear. We are upholding the very values the rest of the world has forgotten. Values like strength, security, and unity. Values that, when ignored, make nations weak and broken. One day they will realize their mistakes."

"I guess you and I have different views on what strength means," I said. "I may not know much, but I know without their help, like their resources and trade agreements, you wouldn't be able to keep going. The world has moved on without you, Elias."

He shuffled slightly on his feet, causing the image of his body to be dissected slightly by the conference table.

"You don't understand, Patricia. Why don't you just come on home, and we can get this sorted out? Get you reunited with your little friend. We can protect you."

What did he just say? What "little friend" could he be referring to?

"Oliver? Is he okay? Tell me." I pictured Oliver still in one of the compounds, wasting away. His eyes, more full of life than those of anyone I'd ever met, turning empty and gray.

"That's right—you don't know," he said as that smug smirk spread across his plastic face, creating deep, crescent creases in the corners of his mouth. My heart quickened and time slowed to a syrupy drizzle as I waited for what he might say next. He watched me, not answering right away, knowing the suspense was threatening to overtake me. I hated how clearly he saw through me.

I searched his eyes for a clue. He left me hanging a moment longer before he answered.

"Mr. Moreno. He's alive. Just barely, mind you."

I felt as if someone had just squeezed my chest in a vise. My legs liquefied beneath me and I clutched the back of the neighboring chair. The dizziness I'd felt in the council chambers returned.

I pressed my heels into the ground as my mind started to wander. "Stay in the present," I hissed at myself with a stinging ferocity and self-hatred. Elias Stevens raised an eyebrow, analyzing my reaction.

"Wait. What do you mean? Do you mean he's alive?" I spit out through dry lips. I picked something to focus on until the room stopped spinning: the back of the chair in front of me. I had to remember who I was talking to. It was a blatant attempt to get in my head. *This is what they do. This is who they are.*

"No. You're lying. How can he be alive?"

There's no way Rexx could have survived. The boulders that came down on him were massive. He would have been crushed instantly. At least, that was what I thought. When he turned and sacrificed himself so I could escape, he knew he was giving his life. I never once considered he might have lived through that.

What if he had? What if he'd been waiting for me to help him these past two months? What have I done?

"You're looking a little pale. Why don't you have a seat in that chair you're clutching?" he sneered. I didn't want to give him the satisfaction, but passing out again would probably leave him with more. I sat.

I put my head in my hands and tried to think of where to go from here. What if it was all a big trick? What if it was true? I looked to the door, but no one came in. My pain was just a show to those watching through the glass.

"He survived?" I said, not prepared for the actual answer. With just a few words, he'd taken my power and my rage. He had taken it all. I was in a different country and yet still completely at his mercy. I hated myself for it.

"Yes, he's alive. We've been treating him. His injuries are extensive. But yes, he is alive, and he will survive."

The holographic Board member sat down in the seat across the table. The effect was uncanny, and I instinctively leaned back in my chair and gripped the edge of the tabletop.

"Why should I believe you? All you've ever done is lie to us. There's no reason to believe you. He's dead. Either prove it or this conversation is over, Mr. Stevens."

I stood and walked toward the door, willing my liquefied legs to carry me the whole way. I was finished with this mind game, from both the Board member and the Security Council, and I didn't care if anyone was angry with me for leaving. I would leave. I would come up with a new plan on my own. To hell with all of them.

"Patricia. Please," he said, an octave higher than usual. "I will prove it to you." There was something in his voice—a hint of fear. A sign that somehow, in the dynamic the two of us had now, he was nervous about what I might do.

What exactly was he afraid of? Did he know the Security Council had all but taken offers to intervene off the table? How quickly power could change hands. I knew not to trust it. We were playing tug-of-war, and we were both holding on to frayed rope ends with raw fingertips.

The form of Elias Stevens evaporated, and I was again in the room by myself, looking around for a clue as to what I should be doing. Did "I will prove it to you" mean *I'll be right back*, or *I'll prove it to you another day*? How long was I supposed to sit there?

I again cast a glance to the closed door, but no one came. If they were still watching, they must think he was coming back.

My heart drummed inside my chest, and I stroked the scar on my hand and took several deep breaths, reminding myself that people, possibly more than I could ever know, were watching this interaction. Reminding myself of Rose's words, and that this could be a test.

There's no way Rexx is alive, I repeated to myself as I waited. *Elias is trying to break you down. He doesn't know what you've been saying about him, about the Board, and he doesn't have any control. You're out of his reach and he's trying to break you.*

For the first time since I'd left, instead of wondering what the leaders outside would do to help, I wondered what conversations had taken place among the Board members in America over the past two months. How many times had my name come up? For the average citizen, had anything changed?

After five of the longest minutes of my life, Elias Stevens rematerialized. His hands were folded in his lap, and he stared at me.

"I've created a patch to one of our hospitals. Regina, now please," he said, speaking to someone out of view. Next to the Board member, underneath another swirling silver ring, a bed hovered in the air—about 20 percent of its actual size.

A body was draped underneath thin off-white blankets. I stepped closer. Hot tears filled my eyes, and my throat caught. The thin drape over the body rose and fell ever so slightly.

Lying on the hospital bed, unconscious but breathing, was Rexx.

"No."

Relief, guilt, longing, and all manner of emotions clawed toward the surface. The urge to go to him, to touch him, to tell him I was with him, consumed me, but it was only an image. He wasn't there, and why should I believe it was really him at all? It could have been a recording taken the day they dug him out as the last gasps of life faded from his body. Or it could have been completely manufactured based on Rexx's likeness or from footage from one of the compounds. I'd seen them do it before with those *Portrait of a Redeemed Patriot* shows I'd watched since childhood. They were nothing but manufactured theatrics, like avatars created from a citizen's likeness in a video game.

"How do I know this is live?" I meant to say the words with ferocity, but they came out as a squeak. The Board member scoffed.

"You'll just have to trust me." I stared at Rexx, and then I stood, walked around the table, and reached my hand out toward him. It slipped right through, and I choked at the emptiness.

"You see, Patricia, we are merciful."

"What do you want? Why didn't you leave him to die? Why do this?" I said as the anger and resentment started to build once again. I already knew the answer to my own question before the words left my mouth. There was a reason he was ready to meet with me today.

Though I didn't know what the prime minister had said to him, he had to know that my escape, the first one in decades, would change things when it came to their relationship with the outside world. Rexx was his bargaining chip.

Suddenly the weakness I'd felt minutes before was replaced with an all-consuming rage. I charged at the hologram of Elias Stevens, my fingers outstretched, searching for his throat. I slipped straight through his pixelated body and tripped on the chair. My already injured wrist shot pain up my arm as it slammed on the floor.

I glanced at the door, and still, it remained closed. For that moment, I hated everyone and everything.

Elias stood over me, amused and unfazed. I wished he were there in the flesh. I wished I could wrap my hands around his neck and feel his life cease beneath my thumbs as that infuriating smirk faded away. I wanted to see how tough he really was without his weapons or his precious Compos.

Instead I looked up at him from the floor and asked him a question. "What do you want?"

"I want you to stop telling lies about us, Patricia. I want you to come on home. We can help you forget all the toxic ideas you've been exposed to out there. Help you see why the Board's way is the only way. Why American values are the future. The righteous way. Why this is the way it was always supposed to be."

As Elias spoke, a glazed, depraved look came over his face. *He's delusional*, I thought.

"Power is not meant to be distributed, Patricia," he said. "My father taught me that. Having power in the hands of those with limited knowledge would be nothing but chaos. Citizens are not equipped to see the big picture. Humans are not creatures of objectivity. We only see what is in front of our own faces. The Board though, well, the Board is all knowing. It is our job to look at the big picture so that you don't have to."

I watched him gaze off into the distance as he waxed poetic about this version of America he saw.

"It is the reason that I have taken on my father's mantle, and why I believe with every fiber of my being that there is no room for compromise. Not with insubordinates such as yourself, and not with outsiders. They will see one day where their paths have led them, and they will come groveling back to America for guidance. They aren't your friends, Patricia. You don't feel safe out there, and lying to yourself isn't going to change that."

When he was finished, Elias looked directly into my eyes as I lay on the floor below him. "It must be so confusing for you. So scary. We want to help you see the light. We want to teach you why following the Board, why finding your place in society, is the only righteous way to live. I truly believe, like my father and my grandfather before me, that we are the greatest, safest, most united nation on this Earth. Come back and I will show you, and I promise redemption for you and your friend."

"Redemption is a lie," I said meekly. "You aren't going to get away with this. They know, Elias. They know there is no longer an active military. They know there are no redeemed patriots. They know about you burning people alive in libraries. They know the truth behind the redemption camps. They know that your nuclear arsenal is not what it used to be. They know, and now they have seen you threaten me. They won't let this stand. I won't let this stand."

The image of Rexx disappeared, and Elias continued to look down at me. Then, of all things, he chuckled. I stared at his face. There was something he wanted to say, and he seemed to be struggling with whether to say it. In the end, his ego won.

"Don't you understand, Patricia?" His yellow eyes seemed to deepen, and his smirk widened. The words the prime minister had uttered earlier came flooding back into my consciousness.

Once the minutiae are taken care of and you remaining here is approved by all the right people.

I knew. On some level, I knew.

He folded his hands in front of him and leaned forward. "They aren't deciding whether to intervene in America. That's not what this conversation is about. They are deciding whether to send you back to me for repatriation, and my guess is, they're starting to think you're not worth the trouble."

CHAPTER 7

Rexx Moreno

REXX WAS WOOZY, and he stared at the sterile ceiling above him. Bright, elongated fluorescent lights shined down and he closed his eyes once more at the unwelcome onslaught of stimulation. He didn't know where he was or how long he'd been there.

He opened his eyes again and moved his head slowly from side to side, wondering if this was real, or if he was caught somewhere between life and death. It was too blurry to focus. He squeezed his eyes tight until the nausea passed. He tried to swallow, but something was in his airway and he gagged.

Panic bubbled to the surface as the air refused to come. His mind fought against the obstruction in his throat. There was movement to his right. He thrashed in the bed and his ankles and wrists burned. He tried to sit up, but he couldn't move. Something restrained him at the arms and legs and across the waist. Someone, a blurry figure with a mask covering the lower half of its face, appeared above him. His heart raced so quickly, he thought his chest might explode. A hand lowered toward his mouth.

The figure gave the obstruction a firm yank until it dislodged. Rexx gasped, and the air burned his raw throat. His lungs screamed in agony and gratitude as they filled. The figure who had taken out the obstruction looked around as Rexx painfully gasped beneath. He was drowning, he was sure of it. Somehow he was drowning in fresh air. Everything in his body told him to sit up, that he shouldn't be lying down, but he couldn't move. The figure seemed unfazed and soon walked away and out of view.

"He's awake. Yes. Yes, sir," spoke a female voice from the corner of the room. The drowning feeling started to subside as Rexx's lungs accepted the oxygen. Rexx tilted his head in the direction of the voice. It was a Compo speaking into her wrist.

"Just now. No, someone just unhooked his ventilator, but the doctor has not come in yet. What do you want me to tell him? Right. Okay. Yes, sir."

Rexx's muscles tensed and he grabbed at the sheet underneath him. His fingers were barely strong enough to grip the fabric.

As he watched her, the memories of what had happened the last time he'd been conscious came tumbling back nearly as quickly as the rocks that had crushed him. It had all happened so fast. He'd fallen, then felt a large boulder land on the back of his thigh, crushing the bones beneath. Searing pain like nothing he'd felt before coursed upward, worse than the jolt of a pacifier or jumping from a moving cargo flat. Another boulder had then landed on his back. That was the last thing he remembered. After that was nothing but blackness.

Patch, he mouthed, but even that hurt. Tears came to his eyes. He never meant to survive. Questions flooded his brain. Had she made it out? Had it all been for nothing? Had she been killed? Where was she now?

He tried to move his limbs within their restraints, to test them, to see if they were still communicating with his brain. He could feel the cuffs digging into his ankles, and his spine protested the movements—a good sign that he could feel the pain, at least. He did the same with his arms, and his wrists burned at the tension against the thick metal. *I'm not paralyzed,* he thought to himself. Then another question followed—*Where am I?*

"No. No. Yes, sir. Been at this post for just over two months," the voice continued. "Since he arrived, yes. It's the first time he has opened his eyes. Yes."

Two months? I've been here for two months, Rexx thought in a panic. Good Board. Two damn months? So much could have happened in that time. If Patch had made it to the other side, what did she find there? Did his plan fail? Did they catch her anyway? Where is Oliver? Is he still in a compound? Did she already send help? Is the country being invaded at this very moment? Was it possible he wasn't even in America anymore?

No, he was still in America. There was a Compliance Officer next to him, and he tilted his head far enough to search for something on the wall behind him. Yes, there it was—the national emblem, stretching from floor to ceiling. Rexx closed his eyes once more. *Think,* he told himself.

Rexx wanted to run, wanted to find her, wanted to get answers, but he was at the mercy of the metal cuffs. If he had been there, unconscious for two months, then his injuries must be extensive, he rationalized. *I likely wouldn't even make it to the door,* he thought, *even if I weren't restrained. Why did they save me? Why didn't they leave me to die?* He had no answers.

The Compo continued with her conversation. "Sure. Yes, sir. I will. It's such an honor to talk to you directly. Later today? Yes, sir. Thank the Board."

The voice went silent and Rexx listened for as long as he could for something else to happen, until the energy he'd spent by simply being awake was too much. As he drifted in and out of consciousness, the guilt that began to fill every inch of him was overpowering.

He couldn't protect them, either of them. The image of Amara's lifeless, emaciated body burned Rexx like a hot iron. When he shoved the memory aside, another came. He was teasing Patch, convincing her to go into the van, all while knowing deep inside where it could lead. How immature he had been. He wished the rocks had killed him.

There was nothing left in that moment—no changing the past, and no promise of a future. There was nothing but overwhelming, insurmountable guilt. He stopped fighting, closed his eyes, and let the images wash over him until they tossed him into a sea of regret and shame.

The tears streamed down his face, but he ceased to care about the Compo in the corner. Let her come for him, punish him. Nothing anyone could think could be lower than what he thought of himself.

The Board member walked into Rexx's room hours later. It was the same man who had interrogated him upon his arrival at the compound months before. The man sat next to Rexx's right-hand side, inches from his face, and the bed sagged as he lowered himself onto it. Rexx stiffened in response.

"Mr. Moreno. I am glad to see you awake. How was your nap?"

"I don't understand why you kept me alive," Rexx finally said, unable to hide the pain in his throat. He tried to scoot over, to give just another inch or two of space between them. "You should have just let me die out there."

"I think you know why you are alive, Mr. Moreno. Don't play stupid. You are how we get to her. I'm not going to pretend otherwise by talking in circles. I think we are past that, don't you? So why don't you tell me? Tell me what the goal was here. I need to know what plans your friend has."

"If she continues to think I'm dead, then you will probably never hear from her again," Rexx said, and part of him believed it though he didn't want to. Part of him thought, maybe even hoped, that with her father's death, and now with his, Patch may have just moved on and abandoned the goals set forth by the elders.

None of it seemed to matter anymore. He just wanted her safe. "You should just leave it alone," Rexx said to the Board member. "Just let her move on. It will be better for everyone. Kill me if you have to."

"Well, sorry to disappoint you, son, but she knows you are alive. Truth be told, she didn't look too happy about it either."

"You've spoken to her? How? Is she okay?"

"We've communicated, yes. She is putting everyone in a great deal of danger, Rexx, herself included. We need to stop this. Stop this before more people are killed."

"People won't be killed unless you kill them," Rexx said steadily, then turned his head away, wondering exactly what it was the Board member was thinking.

Patch had defied everything the Board stood for. Was he wishing that he had killed her when he'd had the chance?

"Someone needs to pay for what the two of you have done," the Board member said. "You have made others question our security. You've sacrificed our standing in the world. A standing that has remained steady for decades. If you think upending that will make anyone safer, then your naivety is showing, dear boy. Now, you don't want to go back to the compound, do you? Did you know that the life expectancy there is, oh, about five years? So I'm asking you again. Sometimes a man needs to be broken down to the core before he has a real chance at redemption."

"Redemption is a lie," Rexx spurted out through a dry throat.

"Far less common than the average man believes, but not a lie, no. Not if the Board deems someone might have a better use. People are put where they are needed."

He stared at the tubes decorating Rexx's body. Rexx took a deep, shuddering breath, and the pressure caused a sharp ache in his lungs on the right side.

He forced the air into his lungs once more, filling them past the point of comfort. Then he turned his head back and bore his brown eyes into the Board member's icy yellow ones.

"I will leave you to rest. Guards, unshackle Mr. Moreno so he can build up his strength. Just the legs for now. Light leg lifts only," he said. "I trust you won't push your limits."

At that he stood.

"Wait!" Rexx said before the Board member vanished from view. He turned to look back at him.

"Yes, Mr. Moreno?"

"What is your name?"

The Board member laughed under his breath, then disappeared out the door.

CHAPTER 8

Robbie Webb

WHEN WEBB WAS sixteen, he sat in his classroom surrounded by other sixteen-year-olds. They were the same children he'd been sitting in a room with since he was five. His instructor, Mr. Richards, stood at the front of the class, supervising their virtual lessons. Like his classmates, his instructor had been a constant since Robbie was five.

Mr. Richards leaned over, hands splayed out on the desk in front of him as he read names, and coordinated postings, off a digital roster. The day that was simultaneously dreaded and excitedly anticipated by all had arrived. The day that would determine what the students would do with the rest of their lives.

Webb sat with a leaden stomach and feet tapping as Mr. Richards made his way down the alphabet, shooting congratulating glances to friends who received their top choices, and *It will be all right* glances to those who received their second or third choice. As Mr. Richards neared the end of the alphabet, Webb repeated three words over and over to himself under his breath: *Please say* engineer, *please say* engineer, *please say* engineer. Eventually Mr. Richards reached the *W*s.

"Robbie Webb," he said loudly, shooting a glance in Webb's direction. Webb thought Mr. Richards looked hesitant to continue, and he steeled himself for whatever was to come next, but not before whispering one more time under his breath: *Please say* engineer.

"Compliance Officer, posting Portland, Oregon," Mr. Richards announced. Webb's leaden gut tightened.

"But that wasn't even on my list," Webb blurted out. Audible gasps surrounded him, and his neighbor kicked him under the table.

"You will contain yourself, Robbie," Mr. Richards snapped back, his brown eyes narrowing as he glared in Webb's direction. It was customary for a student to press the call button on their desk, turning on the light in front of them, then wait until being called upon before speaking.

Mr. Richards seemed to weigh the options of disciplinary action. In the end, he simply sighed.

"I'm sorry, sir," Webb continued. His hands trembled slightly.

"Go on, Webb. What is it?"

"It just seems that everyone else got one of their first three choices. I mean, isn't that why we give three? I just don't understand how this happened." Mr. Richards shifted in his step and his lips tightened.

Mr. Richards pressed a few times on the device he was reading from as Webb watched, the seconds seeming to drone by. His leaden stomach became weightier with each breath. He resisted the urge to drum his fingers on the tabletop. It had to be a mistake. It would be remedied. He couldn't be a Compliance Officer. He just couldn't. He appreciated everything they did and all, but they scared him and the thought of someone feeling that way about him made him queasy.

"It looks like you showed tremendous aptitude for work with the Compliance Department," Mr. Richards said. "It's stamped PRIORITY. That's all it says here, Robbie. It's out of my hands." He avoided Webb's despondent eyes as he moved on to announcing the last student on the list—Marty Zimmerman, Transportation Department.

A week later, fully clad in a department-issued training uniform, sixteen-year-old Webb had found himself standing in front of the exact same Compliance Department he was now about to walk into as a grown man.

Webb swung open the doors to the Compliance Department in Portland, Oregon, wondering how different his life would have turned out if he had become an engineer. Different, but maybe not great, he rationalized. All the engineers he'd talked to over the years spoke of the monotony involved. They rarely worked on designs and instead their time was spent on execution and installation.

At least you get to work outside, he remembered his friends saying to him when he was young. *At least I get to work outside,* he would repeat to himself when things got low. When he was pinning a suspicious-looking teenager to the ground, his pacifier inches from their neck—*At least I get to work outside.* When he was searching an apartment with a scared toddler watching from the hallway—*At least I get to work outside.* When he was loading suspicious paraphernalia into an incinerator truck, closing the door, and flipping the switch—*At least I get to work outside.*

Recently the mantra that had helped him for years was about as effective as fixing a burst pipe with a handkerchief.

After completing all security checks, Webb headed into the locker room with just enough time to clean up before his shift.

He hoped his coworkers couldn't detect the hint of grain alcohol still on his skin, and he ignored the sticky feeling under his clothes from where he'd spilled the glass that morning. Though he'd put on a fresh shirt, he knew it was still detectable. Webb liked to think maybe his excessive drinking wasn't noticeable to the outside world. Everyone had their vices, he rationalized, and it was true. Antianxiety meds and other mood-altering pharmaceuticals were part of the morning routine for most, and he'd managed to avoid taking those except for when they used to be issued at the dormitory during exam weeks.

IT'S HUMAN NATURE TO FEEL OVERWHELMED, one of the billboards downtown said next to a photo of a bottle of mood stabilizers. REMEMBER, THE DEVIL LIES IN THE DETAILS. LEAVE THE DEVIL TO US.

He breathed a sigh of relief to see the three-chambered locker room was empty. The damp, minty smell indicated the cluster of showers in the far chamber had been used recently. He would need to hurry, or he'd receive an earful from his shift commander and possibly a mark in his file.

Webb showered quickly, washing away the stench of alcohol on his skin. He swiped his chip in front of a locker, then pulled out a fresh uniform, which he quickly changed into. He loaded his gear, clicking his scanner into its holster, and his pacifier on the opposite side. He double-checked everything was clipped in tight, an action as habitual as breathing. He opened his locker and pulled out a small bottle of painkillers from the top shelf, and with shaky hands he opened the lid. Though he'd taken some that morning, he could feel the hint of a headache returning behind his eyes.

"Headache," he mumbled to the camera overhead as he shook two small blue pills into his palm. He poured them into his mouth and swallowed without water before shuffling out of the locker room and into the briefing room, where, as he knew they would be, his nine shift mates were already lined up like dominoes.

Webb slipped into an opening between Jason Stokes and Evan Graham. He could feel their eyes turn toward him, though their rigid bodies did not move. Webb planted his feet and stood straight, as if slipping in would fool his commander. If Commander Lewis wanted to know exactly what time Webb had arrived, he would simply check his logs. The information was not private. His ID recorded every move.

Surveillance wouldn't miss his late-night drinking session, or the morning heaving in the bathroom. It was all recorded, available if needed to use against him for any reason. There were no secrets from his superiors—well, almost no secrets.

Webb thought back to the day of Patch and Rexx's arrest. Here were two people who had knocked him unconscious shortly before, careening down the highway in the Compliance Department vehicle they'd stolen out from under him, presumably using his own fingerprints.

Webb figured out who they were the minute his brain started to straighten itself out, when the outside world and the interior of the back seat finally ceased wobbling. He'd watched as they came to an abrupt stop, tumbled out of the vehicle, and tried to outrun their inevitable fate. He'd seen the young woman toss her belongings into the brush as she ran.

He'd pulled himself out of the back seat, grabbed the item out of the brush, and thrown it in his car. Then he took off after them, wobbling as he went from the aftermath of the concussion. He rounded a corner just in time to watch Patch collapse face-first from the sting of another officer's pacifier.

He'd held his tongue when he was ordered to pack his things and accompany the unconscious prisoners via a Compliance Department plane to the redemption camp in northern Montana, where they were to be detained. He'd held his tongue when accepting the temporary reassignment to the camp—an ordeal that involved several hours of extended virtual training. After all, citizens were educated to do their job and nothing more, and Compliance Officers were no different. There had never been a need for Webb, as an urban-center patrol officer, to be trained on the redemption camps.

He'd looked around that first day, expecting to see rows of soldiers practicing military drills, or rooms full of people taking courses together, working on bettering their patriotism skills. He didn't find any of that. Instead he saw prisoners weak and starving.

For the first time, he saw with his own eyes the fate he was sending people to every time he'd labeled a traitor. He would never be able to unsee it. One to two a month for over twenty years, he quickly calculated. It never felt like a lot, but it added up. He had sent at least two hundred and fifty people to this fate.

A week or so after being at his new posting, he left his ID and gear in a compliance vehicle by the side of a road and trudged through the Montana woods until he found a quiet space.

Webb took the backpack he'd grabbed out of the brush the day Collins and Moreno were arrested and carried it to a nearby tree, hanging it on a low branch. It was a slate-gray backpack, with the national emblem staring up at him, and the words NATURAL RESOURCE DEPARTMENT above it. He slowly unzipped it to reveal the contents.

He sighed a huff of relief. There was a bit of water damage, but otherwise everything was intact. He pulled out the item in the front—a laminated map of some kind. He slowly opened it, careful not to tear the aged seams. He looked at the image propped on his knees as he squatted near a tree. He focused on the map, and as he did so, Patricia's words from the ride played in his mind.

None of it's true, you know. . . .

Webb looked around to make sure he was alone. He was in the middle of nowhere. There was no one around for miles, probably. No cameras, either, yet he always had the feeling he was being followed.

He turned his attention back to the map. It wasn't a map of America as he knew it. The entire country had shifted its shape, and land had disappeared from both coasts. He examined the edges for any sign of a date. There. In the lower right-hand corner. He found it.

©*2028*

If the date was correct, this map had been manufactured two years before the Seclusion, in 2030. To hide something like this, well, Webb didn't want to think about the depth of the lies that would go into that.

He looked at the thin strips at the top and bottom of the page, hinting at land beyond the borders. His hand made its way to his temple, then to his eyes. He wanted a glass of grail.

None of it's true, you know, her voice repeated like a bad song.

Most of the cities on the map did not exist, and there were strange shapes drawn in odd places.

∞

One was drawn in Oregon, in a zone near the area where Webb had initially stumbled upon Patch and Rexx—or rather, where they'd stumbled upon him.

What were they doing there? Did it have something to do with this map she carried? Had they visited other places marked on this map before law enforcement caught up to them? He found himself touching each of the symbols in turn, letting the pad of his index finger linger for a moment.

He could almost taste the amber liquid on his lips, the craving was so strong. He shook his head, folded the map back up, and set it down for the time being.

He grabbed the bag once again and pried it open, revealing the rest of the contents, and let out an audible gasp when he saw what was at the bottom. He quickly looked over both shoulders to once again make sure that he was alone.

It was an old book. It was the kind of book he had thrown into countless incinerator trucks, watching the amber flames lick the pages into nonexistence. He closed his eyes for a moment. Every urge in his body, maybe not an urge, really, but rather everything he had ever been taught told him to destroy this and make it go away.

The devil lies in the details. Leave the devil to us.

Without thinking, his hand found its way to the torch clipped on his belt. He kept it there, like a child clutching a favorite toy for comfort.

He brought his eyes down to the dark binding. The corners frayed, so the inner layers were exposed. Dampness had traveled its way up the pages, and now a musty smell made its way from the book to his nostrils.

A feeling of melancholy washed over him, but he couldn't pinpoint why. He held it in his hand, afraid if he were to open it, it would fall apart, as if his hand itself were the flame.

He squinted to see the title, disappearing against the water-damaged binding so that it was barely visible—*Les Misérables*. The title meant nothing to him, but it still evoked an overwhelming sadness.

He lifted the bottom of the shirt to his uniform and instinctively wrapped it around the pages, trying to will the damage out. Of himself, or the book, he didn't know.

CHAPTER 9

Oliver Shelling

OLIVER COULD FEEL two Compliance Officers stationed near the fence watching him as he walked in his usual way around the yard. His head was angled down the entire time, never leaving his own feet, which were covered in their soaked-through flimsy compound boots.

Though he could feel their eyes and hear their muttered voices, he did his best to drown them out and never looked up. He just kept walking and walking—right, left, right, left, right, left. Then, after several minutes, about seven to be precise, or half the length of outside time, he'd stop, turn around where he stood, and start walking the other direction. Left, right, left, right.

He didn't walk in a straight line, or around the diameter of the wall, either. There was focus, and the placement of his feet was critical.

"What the hell is the matter with this guy?" Oliver heard one of the Compos say to the other as they passed on their patrol of the fence.

"I dunno, man. I heard he isn't right in the head," replied the other. "Maybe he was injured on intake. That happens sometimes to these damn gadflies. They rough them up a bit too much, then they just don't work right anymore. Every day for the last few months it's been the same. He just walks." Oliver tried to ignore them, but with his head angled down, his eyes flitted to their location along the fence. *Just keep walking,* he said to himself.

"You should go talk to him. Ask him what the hell he's doing," one of the Compos continued.

"Eh. He's not bothering anybody. If you care so much, you do it. Be my guest."

"He's bothering me," the shorter Compo replied firmly. "Fuck this guy for making my life harder," he hissed as he began to walk over to Oliver. "I've got enough shit to deal with."

He leaned down and looked up at Oliver's face and Oliver imagined what he saw—deep bags under his eyes, magnified by his bushy eyebrows, which grew very close together. His light brown skin was thin and dehydrated. Oliver knew this was a relatively average look for the prisoners, and he'd heard guards remark in passing that the prisoner's faces, in varying levels of sickness and decay, couldn't be looked at for more than a passing second.

The rest of the prisoners stood near the same door they had been let out of, huddled together on the concrete slab, looking like a pack of ghosts more than humans, with graying faces that almost matched their jumpsuits.

Oliver kept his large, round eyes pointed down, and he could almost feel the rage beginning to boil in the Compo's belly.

"Hey, you, Shelling!" the Compo finally said, as if he were shouting from across the yard and not standing right next to him, blocking his path and looking at the top of Oliver's downturned head. "Why you out here every day like this, man?" Oliver heard him, but he didn't look up; instead he kept mumbling something under his breath. *Left, right, left, right.*

"What are you saying, man? I can't understaaaand you. Say it so I can hear you." When Oliver didn't lift his head, the Compliance Officer did what Compliance Officers always did when an inmate wouldn't comply—he took out his pacifier and aimed it at Oliver's neck. He then used the elbow of his other arm to give Shelling a sharp jab to the ribs.

"You a damned idiot, Shelling? Huh? They mess you up when they dragged your sorry ass in here or are you always this stupid?" The officer smirked with a sense of pride as Oliver doubled over in pain, clutching his midsection and pulling in a deep breath.

Still, Oliver didn't answer. He tried to straighten himself up, feeling the barrel of the pacifier against the back of his neck as he did so. The Compo pulled the trigger.

* * *

Oliver started seizing in front of him and collapsed to the ground into a patch of dead grass worn thin from where he'd been walking.

Though Oliver was lying unconscious, the Compo delivered an extra kick for good measure. Then he cast a satisfied nod to his coworker, who approached shaking his head, not with disapproval, but accompanied by a laugh and a smile.

Oliver lay in a heap on the dead grass, his arms splayed out unnaturally to either side. It was obvious he wasn't going to regain consciousness anytime soon. The Compo stepped over Oliver and clipped his pacifier back in and then brushed his hands together and looked around.

"He's damaging the damn grass out here with his nonsense. Look at this." He pointed at a strip of dead grass—a path, the width of approximately a pair of boots sitting side by side—and shook his head.

"Well, this is a damned first. What a damned idiot. Let's get him back to his cell," the Compo declared to the other officer as he grabbed one of Oliver's arms. "Come on. Let's get him out of here. And we'll program the pad outside his door for a couple days of solitary while we're at it. See if that shows him to reply when an officer is talking to him."

The other prisoners watched as Oliver's limp body was dragged across the yard and back into the building. A few had stepped closer with mild interest, but they quickly shuffled back when the Compos' eyes trained on them.

"What the hell are you all looking at? Go back inside. Playtime's over early today."

CHAPTER 10

Patch Collins

PRIME MINISTER AUSTIN opened the door, and her golden eyes searched me. I found myself turning away from them, and away from her. "Is it true?" I asked, my eyes still focused on the space where Elias Stevens had been. "Are you considering sending me back to America?"

My skin prickled, and I stood and crossed my arms over my chest as I waited for an answer, unable to dislodge the image of Rexx unconscious in a hospital bed from my brain.

"It's been on the table," she said, and a sinking feeling spread through my chest. "We still have functioning trade agreements with America. They are stripped down to the bones, but they are still there. Supporting repatriation when possible is one of the terms, though we haven't had to consider it for over twenty years. A lot can change in that amount of time, and the current Security Council is overwhelmingly against it." She stopped, waiting for me to meet her eyes, before continuing. "Myself included, Patch."

"So, before twenty years ago, how many of us did you send back?" I asked, thinking about the defectors mentioned during our original meeting. I couldn't recall everything they had said, but I remembered they'd said there hadn't been one for twenty years, until me, and that others happened early after the Seclusion, which was now sixty years ago. There was a large gap unaccounted for.

The prime minister was quiet for a moment, and I wondered if she was going to grant me an answer. She looked briefly to the window beside us, before turning back to me and saying in a swift, staccato voice, "All of them since 2042, when our new agreements were put into place."

Forty-eight years. So, minus the past twenty years, in which no one escaped, that meant that everyone who'd made it out of America over a twenty-eight-year period had been sent back. Why had they made it seem like I could stay out here, like I could work out here? This entire time, they had simply been sizing me up, wondering if they should chuck me back over like a baseball that had ended up on the wrong side of the fence.

"I suppose I should start packing my bags, then," I said, looking to the window, wondering who exactly was watching this interaction. I suddenly felt incredibly exposed, and the foundation of frustration was starting to not be enough to hold me up any longer.

"I don't think we will be sending you back," the prime minister said. She shuffled on her feet a bit, and I noticed that the stiffness I had seen in her before was starting to soften. "Not yet, at least. You are the first defector in twenty years, and there is new leadership out here."

I breathed a sigh of relief.

"No. I think for now, while the Security Council continues to deliberate, we will have you fill in the team we have assembled on more of the details of your journey. Do you think you can do that for us?"

"Of course," I said, still shaken and feeling buried by the aftermath of what I had just learned on top of learning that Rexx was still alive.

"Rose, please show Miss Collins to the lab."

"Come on," she said, and Rose's hand was suddenly on my shoulder, leading me in the opposite direction. I walked with her, my head still reeling. *Stay in the present*, I reminded myself, but the words felt meaningless as the vision of Rexx lying prone in a hospital bed imprinted itself on my brain.

Rose and I made our way down to the lab. As we walked, she explained that our first assignment would be for me to identify my travel route from Tucson to the Northern Barrier. I tried to listen. I felt like I was being placated, and I had to prove that I was needed here, and I wasn't going to be able to do that if I couldn't focus on something for more than a few seconds at a time.

We took an elevator down to a part of the building I hadn't visited yet—the basement. When the elevator doors opened, Felix was waiting, and the three of us stood on the precipice of a large oval room. The sight of it snapped me to attention.

The entire facade had a silvery-blue tint to it. There were no windows, but framed displays around the room projected the open-air views from outside. An abstract work of art, featuring many interconnecting ovals and orbs, covered the ceiling.

A few groups of people chatted here and there, many circling countertop-height tables where they were gathered with cups of coffee. Doors to private rooms ringed the perimeter.

As we walked into the room, people turned and whispered to one another. A couple of them pointed. I felt a little bit like one of the native animals on display at an American zoo.

"This floor is reserved for special projects," Rose said as we walked, her purple braid bouncing against her shoulder. "I've actually only set foot in here two other times before this morning." She led me through a door into a room where a table with four chairs sat in the middle. I noticed this room, like the conference room where I had spoken to the Board member upstairs, featured walls, doors, and tabletops that doubled as digital screens.

Rose and Felix sat down at the table in the middle and invited me to join them. Felix kicked his feet up on the remaining empty chair beside him. Rose grabbed each of her feet one by one and pulled them under her until she was sitting cross-legged on the chair in a position that didn't look entirely comfortable to me but seemed natural for her.

"I'm just going to dive right in," Felix said as he pressed a few buttons on the tabletop. The entire table was filled with an aerial image of land. "Because of America's firewall, most of what we know about your country comes from satellite photos, the word of the Board, and accounts of foreign operatives and defectors from the past. Any attempt to infiltrate the firewall would be considered an act of cyber warfare. So, for now, we are simply updating our records by taking down any information you have for us, Patch, and checking it against what we already know."

"'Firewall'?" I asked. "I'm sorry. I've heard the word tossed around, but I still don't have a clear grasp of what it is."

"Sorry," Felix interjected as he turned to face me. "In America, you were able to use a limited Internet, yes? Only Board-approved sites, run by the Board itself, correct?"

"Yes, that's right," I replied.

"Well, the firewall is the way that America keeps what we provide our citizens, an open and free Internet, from being used by its own citizens, and keeps outside countries mostly uninformed about what American citizens are currently seeing on their devices," Felix said. He didn't say the words patronizingly; rather, they were laced with the excitement of someone who thoroughly enjoyed teaching someone something new. He reminded me a little of Noah in that way, though decades younger.

"But it has also kept us fairly in the dark regarding many of the activities taking place within America right now, especially close-up issues like the government's treatment of its citizens and modern-day American life," Felix continued. "With most foreign countries, we can see what their citizens are thinking or saying, and what the citizens of those countries are communicating to others outside of it. This information can then be used to impact our foreign policy. America's firewall prevents that easy accessibility." He pointed to the tabletop and zoomed in on an image.

Then he smiled largely and leaned toward me. "So, when it comes to the behavior of the modern Board, you, Patch Collins, are our most-valued asset."

As he said the words, I could feel the blush come to my cheeks. I had not felt like anything resembling an asset since any of this started. An annoyance, yes. An asset, no.

I looked back at Felix, then to Rose, and they both looked at me with eager eyes and genuine smiles. The vulnerability started to build, and so I searched for something to change the subject, something that would bring a reprieve from all the eyes on me.

"And you're also a technology expert?" I asked Felix, wondering what that entailed.

Felix smiled proudly, as if he'd been waiting for someone to bring it up. "Yes, I am. I also design weapons and surveillance technology, but those will not be needed for what we're working on here." Then he changed the subject rather abruptly so that I wondered if there was something he wasn't telling me. "Let's talk about what we're going to start with here today." The screen he had pulled up changed shape and was now occupying half of the table, while the other half filled with a different image.

"So, as I mentioned when we were coming down here, we're starting today with something simple," Rose said. "By tracking your route from Tucson."

She made hand motions above the table, and the image shifted. A long, snaking gray shape covered most of the screen, and I realized after a moment that it was the Southern Barrier.

A concrete mission, a first step. I was eager to get started.

CHAPTER 11

Robbie Webb

"LISTEN UP," COMMANDER Lewis said after walking authoritatively through the door in the far corner. "I've received notice from the Board that all Compliance Officers are to be on alert. Expect a briefing delivered to your face shields this morning."

Webb's spine stiffened like that of a cat being tossed to the ground. He knew his briefing would include everything *he* needed to know, but not everything that was to be known. He told himself not to panic. It was likely something he'd dealt with before, such as an extra-large stash of contraband or multiple occurrences of disparagement of the Board occurring in proximity. Still, a sense of foreboding cloaked him like a second skin.

He searched the commander's face for hints. Did Lewis know the whole story? He was starting to think maybe the Board didn't even know the whole story. He thought about Celeste and considered sending her a message to stay inside the dorms today, but then quickly rationalized that thought away. It was probably nothing.

"Eyes and ears turned on, people. Someone so much as looks at you wrong, and you are to perform a thorough search and scan and pacify at will. Understood?"

A chorus of "Sir, yes, sir" filled the room as Webb studied the commander's face. It was the face of a man he'd once looked up to. It was the face of someone he sometimes even aimed to be like on those occasional days when he shoved his childhood dreams down far enough and let his achievements as a Compliance Officer temporarily fill him with pride. Some days he received an exuberant pat on the back from his commander for a job well done and thought, *Maybe if I try hard enough, I can be a commander myself.*

Now when he looked at Lewis, he felt only a blurry resentment.

"Permission to ask a question, sir?" Evan said from Webb's left.

"Permission granted, Officer," Lewis replied.

"Is this level jump nationwide, or contained to our territory, sir?" Evan's voice was laced with the determination of someone eager to prove himself in a time of crisis. All the officers knew he was gunning for the commander job once Lewis aged out of it. It wouldn't be long now, as Lewis, at fifty-eight, was nearing the forced retirement age of sixty.

"Nationwide, Officer," Lewis replied. "The entire force is to be on alert."

Webb started to feel nauseous; he had to keep the pain reliever he'd swallowed down, or it would do him no favors. Something big was going on. A nationwide alert would not result from simply a contraband stash or even a clandestine conversation involving multiple parties. Perhaps it was an outside threat or unapproved communication across urban lines. How was he going to find out?

"You're dismissed, officers. Contact me through visacoms if you have any questions." At that, Lewis turned abruptly and walked into his office in the corner.

Webb didn't leave the line behind the others, but his shift mates were already sitting at their own individual cubicles, their faces hidden within their face shields, when he arrived in the briefing room. Webb took a seat in an empty cubicle, behind Evan, who was leaning back in his chair, right foot propped on his left knee, animatedly nodding as he listened. *There's someone who's always known he wanted to be a Compo*, Webb would often think when he looked at Evan.

Webb took his helmet from the specially molded port where it was currently plugged in and put it on his head. His nausea was finally subsiding, and it didn't push him over the edge to slide on the face shield.

He held his right hand up to the chip reader installed by his temple. A light chirping noise indicated he was recognized, and inside his face shield the screen turned on and the words *Welcome, Officer Webb* scrolled. He opened his eyes wide for the iris scan. When it was done, he blinked twice in succession, and the briefing began.

Your assignment today is to patrol Zone 38.

A map appeared with a highlighted area several miles south of Portland. He'd patrolled the zone multiple times in the past.

The area is unoccupied. Pay special attention to the cargo flat lines, thoroughly searching the vicinity. Report any signs of recent activity or unauthorized citizen sightings immediately. Any persons encountered are to be apprehended and brought in for questioning. Our drones will be circling the area. If you encounter any aerial objects not marked by the national emblem, aim your face shield at them for at least ten seconds to capture footage and then send an alert to the Compliance Department. Blink three times if these orders are understood, and four to repeat this order.

Webb blinked three times. The scrolling text vanished, and the face shield returned to its normal presentation of a menu of options in the upper right-hand corner, with the rest clear for an optimal visual field.

The day proceeded rather normally, with Webb patrolling the outskirts of the Portland Urban Center, both in vehicle and on foot.

Webb's commander checked in more often than usual, looking for updates on what he had seen or not seen, though the info was available if he just checked Webb's records. Every chip he scanned and search he performed was recorded. Lewis could even view the reel of the footage captured by his helmet. Something was definitely up. He could sometimes go an entire week without any personalized check-ins.

He didn't run into a single citizen or spot an unmarked drone all day. What exactly was he supposed to be looking for?

When Webb's patrol was finished, he began driving back to the station, but a thought clung to his brain like a burr clinging to clothing. Then, as if his muscles acted alone, he turned his vehicle so he was no longer returning to the station but instead driving slightly northwest toward Zone 36—a fenced-off quarantined zone. It was a zone he had never entered, but the same one whose perimeter he'd been searching when he was knocked unconscious by Patricia Collins.

He couldn't stop thinking about the map he'd found in the girl's backpack and about the symbols. This zone just happened to be very close to one of the symbols he'd seen drawn on the map. It couldn't be a coincidence, could it?

You're putting yourself at risk, he told himself. *This is dangerous. The department can monitor your every move.* He knew he should stop, but the burr clung, not so easy to brush off. He kept driving, closer and closer to Zone 36, his adrenaline climbing with each mile, telling him to keep going—no, begging him to keep going.

As he drove, he sent a voice-translated text message to Celeste's ID.

I know I don't say it enough, but I love you.

As he got closer to Zone 36, the first thing he noticed was that the fence he had once spotted surrounding the zone was no longer there. He drove closer still. Then the view of the zone came into focus. Something was wrong.

A black, burnt landscape lay before him. Everything in the entire region had been scorched. The buildings and trees were no longer there. This wasn't the rogue path of a wildfire ignited by chance—this had been a controlled, calculated burn and demolition all the way down to the soil. It was a burn meant to leave nothing.

Webb had participated in calculated burns before, but never anything of this magnitude. Zone 36 was no small zone. It was approximately eleven square miles. Everything, as far as Webb could see from his current vantage point, had been completely decimated. A tangle of metal equipment of some kind was barely visible in the distance.

Webb quickly put his car in reverse and got out of there, driving back to the station wondering what the hell he'd just seen and how long it would be before his lapse in judgment caught up to him.

Back at the station, Robbie practically ripped off his equipment, leaving as quickly as he could. He started home, but then changed his mind, transitioning to a jog and heading the two blocks to the girls' dormitories. He was craving a drink, but he shoved the feeling down and thought of his daughter.

The woman at the front desk snapped her head up as he skidded through the automatic doors almost more quickly than they could slide open to accommodate his broad frame.

The woman's hands fanned out and clutched the desk in alarm. Webb was off duty, but still had his uniform on and he realized he'd startled her. They were two blocks from the local Compliance Department and this place was all but filled with the children of officers. Still, he felt embarrassed. He took a step back, then flashed an unconvincing smile and asked if she would let Celeste know her father was here.

The woman pressed a few buttons on the display in front of her. "Her lessons are just finishing up. I'm going to need to see some form of ID, Officer."

Robbie extended his wrist so she could inspect his ID. It always felt odd, and a tad disorienting, for him to be on the opposite end of such a scenario. She then scanned his dorsal chip.

"Have a seat, Mr. Webb," she said after a moment, apparently satisfied.

Robbie leaned his head back and tried to analyze the mix of adrenaline and dread he was feeling. He felt like he had just done something catastrophically stupid and misguided. There were trackers in the Compo vehicles. It was only a matter of time.

As he sat there, he wondered if maybe part of him wanted to get caught, to be punished the way he knew he deserved. He could only hope it didn't happen in front of his daughter. He needed to see her, even if it was only to say goodbye.

Celeste walked into the waiting room.

Her black hair was pulled tight against her head with a puffed bun in the back. She was wearing an ivy-green top and leggings that complimented her black skin. When she smiled, her brown eyes sparkled.

In two more years, Celeste would be an adult and placed on assignment. *She will be okay*, Webb reassured himself as he looked at her, trying to see the capable young woman she was on the verge of becoming and not the child she once was.

An unpleasant image flashed in Webb's mind of the dream he'd had days before—the wavy silhouette of his daughter asking for help. Would her final memories of him be of the distracted and distant thing he had become since the incident at the compound, or was there room for an apology as well as a goodbye?

"Dad, what are you doing here? Is everything all right? Is someone hurt?" She stepped back and looked him up and down as if searching for something wrong.

"No, nothing like that. I just had a long day, and I wanted to see you. That's all. How about I take us out to dinner?" He tried to give her a reassuring smile, but she was smart. Smarter than he had ever been at that age. She saw through him and he knew it. Maybe she would also start to see through the Board, even if he wasn't there. He didn't know if the thought made him feel better or worse.

"Sure. Let me just go grab my jacket."

They ate dinner at one of their favorite restaurants. Webb tried multiple times to open his mouth and say the words that he wanted to say to his daughter.

I'm sorry. I shouldn't have pushed you away. Something happened, and it shook me. I'm not the person you think I am. I've done terrible things. Remember when you were seven, and you used to tell me I was your superhero? Remember me that way. Things are changing. Don't trust the Board. Just promise me, you won't trust the Board.

Instead they ate their dinner, talked about safe topics, watched the screens littered throughout the restaurant, and spoke of nothing of importance.

Webb hugged his daughter longer than usual when he said goodbye that night, inhaling the lemongrass scent of her hair and trying to keep the tears from falling onto the top of her head as she nestled into his neck. She was going to be tall, and he may never get to see it.

"Are you sure you're all right?" Celeste asked as she pulled away. "You've been acting strange all night."

"Yeah, yeah, it was just a long day, that's all."

"Okay, I'll see you next week?" she asked as she turned to go.

"Sure, pumpkin," he said, utilizing a nickname he hadn't used for nearly five years. "I'll see you next week."

When Webb got home, he began walking toward the cabinet in the kitchen, ready to reach for that half-empty bottle of grain alcohol only to find it wasn't there. Right, he'd dumped it down the sink the night before. For a moment he thought of putting in another order. The Board-run shopping website could likely have it delivered by drone within the hour.

He took a deep breath and stopped himself, despite the pressure behind his eyes and the lingering pounding that had returned to his head in the middle of dinner. He brought the heels of his hands directly over his eyeballs and pressed. Sometimes this relieved the pressure. Sometimes it helped.

When he brought his hands back down, and when the little white orbs stopped spinning in his field of vision, Webb walked back to the kitchen and filled up a cup of water and chugged it down. He filled up another and tapped a few pills out of a plastic container and swallowed them too.

He changed into clean clothes and spent a minute cleaning up his apartment—putting away the glasses left out and scooping dirty towels and underwear off the floor. He even pressed a button on the wall a few times that emitted a room-freshening spray he usually hated, but he realized it smelled a heck of a lot better than the mix of alcohol, vomit, and left-out dishes that currently filled the air.

Looking around at his straightened-up apartment, he felt some anxiety lift and his shoulders dropped slightly. He grabbed a protein bar out of a bowl on the counter and sat in his favorite chair. He swiped his chip against a device mounted on the table next to him, and the screen taking up most of the far wall flipped on. Webb selected the mandatory viewing for the day—the daily episode of *America One: Helping Our Nation Succeed*—and leaned back.

Aelia Ramey bounced in front of the camera with, it seemed to Webb, an extra dose of her usual vigor.

"Welcome to today's episode of *Helping Our Nation Succeed*! Today we have a very special game-style episode!"

Webb grunted. These "game episodes" were organized like games, but often involved "homework-like" assignments when a participant answered a question wrong. So really, they were national exams. The sense of foreboding he'd felt earlier returned.

"Today the Board sent me a very specific theme for our game." Canned gasps erupted from the screen. Webb knew the Board always had a hand in the programming to a point, but Aelia almost never mentioned the Board dictating a specific episode. It was a thinly veiled call for citizens to pay closer attention than usual. Webb eyed the screen with suspicion. This was the only time recently that he'd watched unencumbered by the amber haze of alcohol.

"So, everyone grab their individual controllers. Each citizen over the age of five will be able to submit a response!" Her chipper spin on things didn't fool Webb. Everyone was legally required to submit a response, was what this meant. He had a weird feeling there was a reason he had talked himself into being sober today, and he committed to paying very close attention.

"Our theme today is civic duty!" The words *civic duty* lit up the stage behind her in a playful font. "Winners who receive one hundred percent will be given five extra miscellaneous credits this month! Take someone you love out to dinner, or to a movie! Or visit one of the Board's holiday displays in your urban center. The entrance fee is only two credits, and they will be live all of November and December and are worth a visit!"

Webb thought back to last year's Portland holiday display, which consisted of the national emblem lit up hundreds of times within a few city blocks, and tunnels filled with advertisements and mantras to walk through.

The term *5 credits* appeared in an equally obnoxious font inside of a little prize box next to *civic duty*. Maybe if he won, and somehow wasn't caught for his excursion today, Webb could use the five extra credits to buy something for his daughter to make up for being such a pathetic father.

Aelia wasted no time getting on with the game. "Question one," she chirped. "When you see someone breaking one of our laws, you can report their behavior using the following methods. A: an anonymous see-something-say-something kiosk. B: by filing a report at your local compliance office. C: by filing a non-anonymous complaint directly through your idecation device. Or D: all of the above."

Webb wasted no time moving his cursor to select D, though he felt that being a Compliance Officer gave him a bit of an unfair advantage with that one. He also knew the Compliance Department monitored the see-something-say-something booths closely, and that no report made in those was ever anonymous.

The word *CORRECT* scrolled across the screen.

"Below you will see a running tally of the results so far today," Aelia said after a few more seconds. Webb glanced to the bottom of the screen, where a number was quickly scrolling up from zero until it reached 72 percent.

"For those of you who got the answer right, congratulations!" Aelia said as she clapped her hands. "Within twenty-four hours, everyone over the age of ten who submitted an incorrect answer is required to submit the correct answer as well as an explanation for why you were wrong. For younger children, virtual instructors will receive an automatic alert as to which topics need to be refreshed. We need to be on the same page, after all! It's how we stay safe in the greatest country on Earth." Webb imagined his daughter in the dormitory answering the same questions and wondered whether she would get any wrong.

He almost hoped she would. Maybe something over the years hadn't stuck. Maybe she had already watched her episode earlier in the day in the common room. She hadn't mentioned it at dinner, but it wasn't really the type of thing you mentioned.

"All right! Next question! Recent history is an area we encourage our citizens to become widely versed in, because it is not toxic and dangerous like ancient history, which the Board remains fluent in so you don't have to be. So, when discussing history, when is the earliest you are permitted to discuss provided you avoid other illegal topics? A: 2055; B: 2016; C: 2030; or D: 2085?"

Again, Webb had an unfair advantage, being one of those who enforced these rules. He knew that as long as people were not discussing traitorous topics such as books, banned media, or outside culture, or disgracing the Board's decisions, they could discuss events that took place after the year of the Seclusion, in 2030. Webb selected C, and the word *CORRECT* once again scrolled across the screen.

Webb watched the number tally until it reached 84 percent.

"Excellent, excellent!" Aelia said. "Look at what model patriots you are! Seeing these answers gives me so much hope for the future of our country. Give yourselves a pat on the back!"

Aelia had appeared on his television screen every night for as long as he could remember. Though she never really seemed to age and was obviously chosen because she had a sort of charm that resonated with a large group of people. Webb actually felt himself smile, then he felt angry with himself for being so easily manipulated. He knew that because this message could be watched anytime today, Aelia had recorded this before the results had come in, and therefore had no idea what the rate of correct responses would be. Webb could only assume that because the answer to this question was drilled into every citizen with such vigor, the Board and the *America One* Studios could confidently predict a high success rate.

"Question three!" Aelia piped up again. "As most of you should know, there were many escape attempts in the early years after the Seclusion, by traitors who did not heed the warning of the Board about the dangers of the outside world, and most likely paid the ultimate price for it. Escape attempts today are nonexistent. How long has every single citizen remained safe inside our borders?" For this she turned directly to the camera and her expression looked stern.

The hair on the back of Webb's neck stood up. *This can't be a coincidence. This question is the reason for this quiz today. This is the way they let every single person know that regardless of what some have heard, no one has tried to escape.* "A," Aelia continued, "One year. B: five years; C: twenty years; or D: forty years."

Webb paused on this one. He wasn't 100-percent sure of the answer, and he suspected he wasn't supposed to be. They wanted everyone to reflect. So, the question was: What answer would prove their point the most? This was more information than they would usually give to citizens, so what was the reason? Webb's joystick navigated and clicked—forty years.

CORRECT scrolled across the screen. Webb let out a deep breath. The last thing he wanted to spend time working on was an explanation about why he got this answer wrong.

Aelia kept her gaze on the audience as Webb watched the numbers tally up, stopping at a mere 36 percent. Aelia hung her head and shook it dramatically, indicating her disappointment, and Webb knew instantly that whether the correct rate had been 36 or 90, it didn't matter. It wouldn't be one hundred, and that was the reason they were doing this now.

"It saddens me to see that some of you did not automatically think that the Board had been succeeding as long as absolutely possible. After all, every decision they make is to protect you. Forty years they have succeeded in making sure even the traitors among us are kept safe and given a chance at redemption instead of letting them over the Walls and into the arms of terrorists who would do unspeakable things. Things that, because of the Board, all of you have had to witness only through your screens and not in real life. So, for those of you receiving an 'INCORRECT' on your screen, I would like you to submit an answer as to why you doubted, and what you are going to do to show your patriotism in the days that come. The eyes of the law are watching you and we know that you believe in the Board."

Aelia then perked up and smiled. "For those of you outstanding patriots who answered all three questions correctly, you should be very proud of yourselves! Five credits have been added to your account! Spend wisely! This has been today's episode of *America One: Helping Our Nation Succeed*. Tune in tomorrow as we discuss job placement and what you can do to always make sure you are giving your best."

Webb clicked off the screen and sank back in his seat. Pride was the furthest thing from what he was feeling.

CHAPTER 12

Rexx Moreno

THE TELEVISION ON the far wall across from Rexx's bed turned on. A familiar tune began to play and Rexx found his eyes dart to the screen—*America One: Portrait of a Redeemed Patriot.*

Aelia appeared on the screen. She'd had a haircut sometime recently. Her hair, usually a straight dove white bob, was styled in a pixie cut with streaks of gold and one side a great deal shorter than the other. She flicked her hair back and walked toward center stage.

"Today we would like to introduce you to Oliver," she said in a chipper voice. Rexx's stomach dropped, and he felt what little color he had drain from his face.

"No," he muttered under his breath. *There's more than one Oliver, you idiot,* he said to himself, and for a split second he held on to the hope it wasn't him. Then Oliver Shelling appeared on the screen.

He was sitting behind a desk. His hair was clean and combed back into a ponytail. He had a professional-looking uniform on and was leaning back in an office chair behind a computer. He appeared younger than he had been when Rexx met him.

This must have been from his days working in the upper echelons of the Natural Resource Department. He'd been in a Tier 2 office space prior to his assignment at Zone 36. Oliver's honey bronze skin was rosy around the cheeks and he looked healthy and young as he smiled and conversed with an employee sitting across the desk. There was no sound accompanying the video clip.

"Oliver Shelling was one of our Tier Two employees at the Natural Resource Department, but he thought it was all right to compromise national security by diving into topics outside of his privilege." Aelia's tone turned down, and she cast a serious look at the camera, like one a mother would give you if you had disappointed her. "Because of his Tier and aptitude, Oliver was given the opportunity for reform, but he took his responsibilities for granted and eventually ended up in custody and sent for military redemption."

The next image caused Rexx to involuntary clench his stomach muscles. He tried to bring his aching hand up over his mouth, but it was still restrained. Sound now accompanied the footage.

The reel showed Oliver on the night of his arrest, after he'd run away to divert attention from Rexx and Patch and give them a chance to escape. One officer pinned Oliver to the ground underneath a shield while another shot him with a pacifier. Oliver screamed. It was the same scream Rexx and Patch had heard on that dark night right before they had gone back into the tunnels.

Tears filled Rexx's eyes. Oliver twitched on the ground, not going to cause anyone harm, but the Compo hit him hard across the face with the back of his pacifier anyway. The footage cut away, and the focus of the camera returned to Aelia.

"Mr. Oliver Shelling endangered his life and the lives of others, including our beloved Compliance Officers, who put their lives on the line every day, because of his selfish actions. Now, we would have been well within our rights to leave Mr. Shelling to rot somewhere, but we don't do that here in America. We are a virtuous and forgiving country."

An unseen crowd erupted in canned applause.

"Mr. Shelling was given the chance to redeem himself, and now he will have the privilege of serving our great nation in the capacity we believe he was always meant for."

An image of Oliver standing at attention in front of the national emblem in full military gear filled the screen. He was smiling. Rexx was awash with confusion. It made no sense.

Oliver would not have put up with this, and Rexx knew firsthand the promise of becoming a "redeemed patriot" was bullshit. The Board member had all but admitted it. Something was going on.

Rexx focused on Oliver's face on the screen, and then he noticed something. The face was young and did not resemble Oliver now. The eyes, the same ones he'd first felt were erratic when he met him but that he had grown to love for their sincerity, were all wrong. His face did not reflect the lines and the creases and the scars of everything he had been through to this day.

The image on the screen was not Oliver.

Instead the face on the soldier resembled the young man with sleek hair laughing behind his office desk. Rexx chuckled a self-deprecating laugh under his breath at how stupid he had been.

It was an avatar, plain and simple, like the faces of the players superimposed on video game characters.

Then he let his mind wander to Oliver and wonder, *Where is he really?*

For the first time since he'd awoken, Rexx tried to move something other than his arms. He thought of Patch, and of her face, of her hair, and of her laugh. He kept the image of her in his mind, and with all the strength he had, he lifted his right leg. It fell back down with its full weight. He waited a moment, then forced himself to do it again. Then he tried the other leg, raising it about two inches from the hard mattress. He waited five minutes to regain his strength, then he did it again.

CHAPTER 13

Oliver Shelling

OLIVER SAT IN his cell during his days in solitary, trying not to go over the edge. A timer on the face of his door told him he had three days left. He paced back and forth and stretched from side to side, doing everything he could to avoid remaining stagnant. He forced himself to eat the bowl of mixed grains they brought three times a day.

He was having a hard time imagining a world in which it would be different—a world in which he wouldn't simply waste away in this cell and become nothing more than a pile of bones thrown into the ground.

He knew he had to hold on, to keep it together, and to grasp that slim sliver of hope that maybe someone would come for him, but it was fading fast. Though he reminded himself that the weather was too cold, it was as if he could feel the grass regrowing outside in the path that he had carved, his hard work disappearing underneath the leaves.

His well of hope was so empty, its contents wouldn't fill a spoon.

Patch had asked one day, when they were out in the garden, about his family, friends, and lovers, but he'd changed the subject. It was too painful to talk about then, but now, feeling that his days were numbered, he let the memories come just for a moment.

He dug his head back against the concrete wall of his cell, closed his eyes against the horrific images that played on a loop opposite him, and thought of someone he missed very much.

America had a strict one-birth policy and sterilization after a first birth was mandatory, but Oliver was born with a twin—a sister. Her name was Yasmine and she lived to be ten years old.

They had the same smile, people would say. They also had the same sparkling brown eyes, the same beautiful brown skin, and the same hair with a mind of its own, but the smile was what people would notice first.

When they were walking around in public, people would stop and stare. Siblings were a rarity, and it was almost as if people did not know whether to look upon them with suspicion or with admiration. Friends of their parents liked to come over just to watch them play, and when Oliver and Yasmine got frustrated, their foreheads wrinkled in the same way, making everyone around them laugh.

When Oliver and Yasmine moved to the dormitories at five years old, they were lucky enough to be across the street from each other. They were put into the same virtual training course and saw each other every day. When occasions arose that they could be together—walking to and from the dormitories or in the dining halls for meals—they would be. They were different from the other kids, and it was obvious to everyone. They giggled more, and they loved more.

When they were ten years old, Oliver received a message on his idecation device. Yasmine had become sick during her lessons, and she didn't make it. His parents pressed for more answers, but they didn't come. When they wouldn't leave it alone, they were taken by the Board. Oliver never saw them again. Within the span of one week, everyone he loved was gone, and he didn't even know why.

After that, Oliver was often on the receiving end of discipline from the instructor for disrupting the class. He spent many full days in a solitary room they reserved for children who were being disruptive, with *disruptive* having quite a vast umbrella assigned to it—not sitting still, wiggling too much, laughing at inappropriate times.

He'd always been taught that his instincts were wrong. As far back as he could remember, Oliver wanted to make things to sort through these feelings. When he was at the dorms, he would collect found objects, make things with them, and display them by his bed. One day his dorm leader dramatically scooped them into a trash can and shamed him in front of all of his bunkmates.

He was told his instincts were dangerous and selfish. He needed to ignore them and set them aside in pursuit of becoming a contributing member of this great society. So he hid them, stuffed them away. When he was assigned to the Natural Resource Department, his aptitude tests showed his intelligence to be unrivaled by his graduating class.

When Oliver was sixteen, he'd dared to open his heart again and fall in love with a boy in his training sessions. He laughed at Oliver's jokes and smiled knowingly and lovingly when he stuttered or tripped over his words. He would put his hand firmly between Oliver's shoulder blades when he'd start to get worked up in a way they both knew was dangerous. A week before Oliver's eighteenth birthday, he lost him too.

Their training instructor declared he'd been relocated. No more information. No more details.

The memories came and went as Oliver sat in solitary. Soon he was conjuring the faces of the two who had brought him back to life—Patch Collins and Rexx Moreno.

Oliver opened his eyes. He bit his lip, pressing his canine down until he felt the skin break. He lifted his thumb and brought it up to wipe the blood away, but then he had another thought. He turned to the wall, wiping down the cool concrete like paint. He did it again and again and again, until his face was swollen and his fingers ached.

Several hours later he collapsed on the ground and admired his work. To anyone else it would just look like blood on a wall, but to him, it was a waterfall cascading down to a river.

After three days, his door finally opened, and those blissful arrows lit the way out to the yard.

CHAPTER 14

Patch Collins

WE SPENT THE next few days hard at work. I was given a room in the same building, and we started each morning early, usually with Felix meeting me at the elevators with some kind of portable breakfast dish he had whipped up that morning.

Rose and I fell into a rhythm, working through satellite images laid out in a grid, and I did my best to mark things that I recognized as we charted our route from Tucson to the northern border.

Felix worked with a goofy smile on his face and earbuds in his ears. I looked over multiple times to see him mouthing the lyrics to a song no one could hear but him. Sometimes he would simply make excited declarations like "Awesome" or "That's what I thought," though he rarely explained to the rest of the team what was going on in his head. Then his energy would pick up, his head would go down, and he would approach whatever he was working on with a renewed ferocity. I couldn't help but smile whenever he did this.

Every once in a while, Felix would take a piece of technology out of a nearby case, hook it up to the central display in the table, leave it for a moment, and then unhook it.

"What are you doing?" I asked after a few times, when curiosity got the best of me, having to talk loud enough for him to take out his earbuds.

"I want to make sure we have this information saved somewhere portable," he said. "Just in case."

I began to feel more comfortable and even had a little fun as I got to know Rose and Felix. The two of them were absolutely captivated when I talked about the redeemed patriots, and how we thought the footage and stories we watched of young men and women telling their tales of redemption, the national emblem swaying behind them, were real all those years.

They thought it fascinating—and horrifying—the media we were forced to consume daily. They listened respectfully, documenting everything I said as I outlined what the inside of my cell looked like, or what a day at the compound consisted of, or what it felt like to be shot with a pacifier.

Rose would jump up without warning every so often and start to stretch in the middle of the room, and it took me awhile to realize she was still listening, but that she could not sit still for long without needing to move and bend and twist.

She had a stellar memory, and she and Felix worked well together. Rose, with her reference-rich brain when it came to history and geography, and Felix, who seemed to always be solving several puzzles at a time and had a true, enthusiastic passion for technology and innovation.

I learned that they really had been hoping for an assignment like this for years, that it felt like honoring their friend's memory. Their curiosity and concern surrounding America ran deep, and they assured me they weren't the only ones.

Eventually we neared the end of mapping my journey.

"Do you think you would recognize the compound you stayed in?" Rosed asked one afternoon.

"Yes, I think so."

"Here, pull your chair over next to mine, and we'll look together."

Rose used her finger to drag the map around until she found an area in the northwest near the border.

"This is where you were found." She pointed to an area directly over the Northern Barrier. "Which means you must have escaped from this complex over here."

She moved the image around once more until she was zoomed in on a complex. I could see the telltale pie shape of the compound yards divided into wedges, the central tower and the double fences surrounding the entire enclosure.

My stomach lurched at the memories it elicited, but the image itself was quite something. When taking it in, it almost resembled the sun. Compos here and there resembled scout ants, out looking for scraps before alerting the colony. It reminded me of the scene Rexx and I had seen when we passed by the site of the bombing. She zoomed in more.

"The prisoners must be inside, if this is live," I said. "There's no sign of them in the yards and they only go out once a day. In the afternoons. Well, that's when our section went out, anyway."

I found my eyes darting around the image. I didn't know why I was searching for him, but I was. I was searching for Officer Webb. All the officers looked the same from this aerial view.

I tried to remember his gait. I tried to recall if there was anything about his body language that might give me a hint and help me separate him from the rest of the figures, but I came up blank. I kept at it, hoping for some kind of sign, until my eyes scanned over one of the yard sections and my chest tightened.

"Stop! Zoom in here!" I yelled, pointing to a region in one of the yards. Rose zoomed in.

No, it can't be. Can it?

"What is that?" Felix asked, standing up from his side of the table and leaning in toward the image.

My heart rate sped up, and a gasp escaped my lips. There, in one of the sections, taking up the spread of almost the entire pie wedge, was a shape, dark brown against the rest of the faded winter lawn. A shape quite familiar to me.

An infinity symbol.

I stood up and my hand hovered in front of the symbol reflected on the dirt, having been worn into the compound grass. It was the symbol used by the Veritas Ring. I couldn't help but picture the work that went into him sending this message, and the danger he must have put himself in. Had those who had seen him realized what he had been doing? Had they punished him for it? It wasn't until I felt a wet drop on my lips that I realized my cheeks were streaked with tears I couldn't stop from coming. His name emerged as a rusty squeak.

"Oliver."

CHAPTER 15

Patch Collins

FELIX AND ROSE had stepped out of the room to contact the prime minister. I stared at the image of the infinity symbol, with its imperfect curves but perfectly perceptible shape on the compound yard. I imagined the work that had gone into making it, and I thought of Oliver, alone in a cell, waiting for me. There was nothing to keep him company but his own consciousness and memories, which, I knew from experience, made terrible company.

As I stood there alone, waiting for the others to return, I was sinking in overwhelming guilt for every laugh and moment of enjoyment I'd had over the past few days. I felt trapped in my own skin, as if it were tightening itself around me. I wanted to claw myself out of it, peel it off, and run as fast as I could, continuing until I reached the Barrier and then Oliver. I knew it wasn't logical, but the impulse was there. Suddenly everything I was doing felt wrong. Updating the files on America? Waiting until the Security Council members changed their minds? How would any of this help him?

I heard the door to the lab slide open behind me and felt a slight shift in the air, but I didn't turn around. I kept my eyes on the symbol. "We have to help him. We have to get him out," I said, speaking to the prime minister, though I knew she wasn't alone.

There was no reply, but I felt someone walk up behind me, and then there was a hand on my shoulder. "We can't. Not yet," Rose said, and she squeezed slightly. "Any act of aggression will be noticed and chance putting everything at risk."

Three other people walked up and stood beside me—the prime minister, Felix, and James, and together we took in the image.

"I can't just ignore this. How am I supposed to ignore this?" I said, my eyes still on the symbol.

"Try to look at it this way," Felix said. "He is still alive. Now you know that he is still alive."

I swallowed hard, and something seemed to stick in my throat, and I could feel the memories of the compound threaten to pull me in. *Stay in the present*, I reminded myself.

"Can you excuse us for a moment?" a voice said, and I turned ever so slightly to confirm that it was the prime minister's. I noticed her eyes. They weren't looking at me, but rather were captivated by the image in front of us, and it was as if her pupils were tracing the shape over and over. Her mouth was turned down, and though I don't think she realized she was doing it, she bit the edge of her lip ever so slightly. There was a strange energy between us, as if an invisible tether tied us together, not pulling us closer, just there for a reason I couldn't name yet.

"Of course," said the fourth voice in the room. It was James, standing on her opposite side, and he nodded before he, Felix, and Rose left the room, with Rose giving my shoulder one final squeeze before her fingers slid from their perch.

The room emptied, but the tether remained, and I felt as if, were I to move to the right, she would as well. It was almost as if this woman standing next to me held her own gravitational pull.

We stood there for a moment, and then, as the silence of the room and the gravity of this woman became too powerful, I spoke first, opening my mouth before I even knew how to articulate what it was I wanted to say.

"I don't think you understand. He's alive now, but you don't understand how much my body changed, how much I changed after just two months in that place. I could barely walk. Getting to the Barrier took absolutely everything out of me. He's not going to make it, and I can't even imagine what they will do to Rexx over that time . . ." My voice started to crack.

Laurel Austin shifted slightly on her feet, and I found myself shifting too as I waited for her words.

"I'm going to tell you something about my past," she said, and her eyes stayed on the image. She crossed her arms over her chest before continuing. "It's classified, and it's something that not even my closest advisors know, but after everything you have been through, I think you deserve to know."

I thought about what Rose had told me regarding the prime minister's past and braced myself for whatever was going to come out of her mouth.

"I used to work as a secret agent for CSIS, which is our secret service agency. That part of my record is public, but the specific locations of my postings are not."

As the next words came out of her mouth, I wasn't as surprised as I thought I would be.

"I spent a year in America, undercover. It was before your chip technology, and long before I became prime minister. I was stationed at the Chicago Urban Center, and I was one of the last agents to walk on American soil. I was young, still in my early twenties, and to this day it remains one of the most difficult things I have ever done."

I turned away from the image, and so did she, and we stared at each other. She was a few inches taller than me. Her eyes were still golden, but they, like some of her other features, had softened slightly. They didn't seem as rigid and harsh as they once had.

"What did they do to you?" I asked as I crossed my own arms over my chest just as protectively, mirroring her, as if I weren't in control of it, the tether moving my limbs for me.

"I don't want you to worry about that; it was nothing compared to what you have been through," she said. "But I want you to know that I have seen it up close. I have seen what your Compliance Officers and your Board are capable of when someone steps out of line. I saw the devastation to the land outside of your urban centers, and that was over twenty-five years ago."

"What were you doing there?" It was the only thing I could think to ask.

"I was undercover as a Tier Four worker in the Transportation Department. We were trying to pinpoint the location of the new Board headquarters, which we believed to be close to where the nuclear weapons are stockpiled."

"Did you ever find it?" I asked hopefully.

"We had some guesses based on what we could find out, but no, we don't know specifically where it is. While most of your leaders used to operate out of Washington, D.C., before the Seclusion, the rising oceans forced a change, and the new headquarters location was never made public."

"I . . . Well, I don't know what to say," I replied, still in shock. "But if you've seen it up close, then how can you still refuse to help?"

"Because it wouldn't help, Patch. An all-out war would not help, and that's what it would be if we intervened fully. No, the best course of action is to have you continue to work with Ms. Anders and Mr. Suen to update our intelligence. After that, we can revisit the negotiation table with the Board, using our trade agreements as leverage to hopefully implement higher humanitarian standards."

Images flashed through my head—Rexx lying in a bed out of my reach; Oliver leaning against a cell wall; the prisoners in the yard of the compound. None of this would help them. Any help would be too late. I'd failed everyone.

I felt myself being pulled into my memories again, and then suddenly there were arms around me, holding me tightly, and I didn't fight them off. I let her arms hold me, let her gravity overpower the memories. I buried my face into her shoulder.

"So what am I supposed to do now?" I asked. She grabbed my shoulders forcefully and held me up so that she was looking straight into my eyes.

"Patch, I, well, I barely survived one year in there and you survived twenty-two, but you are out now. You survived. Take a deep breath, enjoy yourself, and let us worry about things for a while. Go out, have a drink, and see what this outside world has to offer."

CHAPTER 16

Patch Collins

THE PRIME MINISTER instructed Felix and Rose to take the afternoon off and show me around for the rest of the day.

"Why don't you show her the technology lab while I close out our work from today?" Rose said to Felix with a sly grin on her face. "I'll meet you in there."

I followed Felix, hesitant, my brain still reeling from the compound image and the conversation that had followed, yet I was intrigued and, to be honest, I did just want to think about something else for a while.

We took the elevators up to almost the top floor, then Felix pressed one of the directional buttons and the elevator moved sideways, skirting the circumference of the building I knew to be a semicircle. I pictured the globe-like architecture, wondering where we would end up.

The elevator came to a stop and Felix pressed his thumb to a pad on the wall and the doors opened. We stepped out of the elevator into a room entirely encased in glass. Above us were lights, projecting the blues and greens that made up the globe on the outside of the building while also bathing the room so it felt like we were underwater creatures. I held my arms out in front of me and let the lights dance on my skin.

"Where are we? What is this?" I asked as I looked around. Shelves containing various items lined the edge of the circular room, but their existence was almost entirely drowned out by the eye-capturing items before me.

There were several gigantic glass domes, each the size of my old living room, and about the same height as me, and their placements formed a ring around where we had emerged from the elevator. I counted them, and there were eight.

I walked up to the closest one, and felt the breath catch in my throat as my hand seemed to be drawn to it of its own accord. It held plants I had never seen in my entire life. It held trees and soil and vines. I put my hand against the dome, and it gave slightly, like the exterior was made of silicone or something similar. It was the strangest feeling, and I suddenly wanted to be inside one—to dive my hands into the soil.

"These," Felix said, like an announcer on a game show, "are ecosystems."

I turned to him, seeing a sparkle in his eyes as he drank in my reaction.

"Only eight of them, of course. Scientists use these for study. Come on, I have one you will want to see." He spoke fast and held out his hand. I took it. I almost pulled away as his fingers wrapped themselves around the edge of my hand, but I didn't.

He led me around one of the giant domes to another on the other side, and my heart ached with the familiarity. It was a desert. My desert. Not really, but for all intents and purposes.

The letters lit up on the dome read DESERT SCRUB.

I spotted spider milkweed and straggler daisies, exserted Indian paintbrush, and a couple of small saguaro cacti—not fully grown of course. I squatted down, dropping Felix's hand,

and spread my hands out across the wobbly bulbous exterior and looked at the layers of soil. The pH level was displayed on the bottom of the dome—7.6. There was a digital thermometer reading imprinted above it—37 degrees. It must have been in Celsius and not Fahrenheit, a difference that still threw me a bit.

"What is this? This material encasing them?" I asked. Felix pushed his hand into the side of the dome firmly, then pulled it out again. The dome rippled back into shape.

"That? We call it Glastic. It's like glass, but probably not as you're familiar with it. A few decades ago, scientists started playing with the heating and cooling process of glass and discovered that if you heat a powdered iron composite to a very specific temperature using electricity, and then cool it rapidly, what was traditionally known as glass can hold on to varying levels of elasticity. We're still building and learning what we can do with it, but it's a really exciting field."

I pressed my hand up against the dome again and pushed slightly, letting the material ripple under my fingers.

"I want to see all of them," I said, turning to Felix excitedly.

"Of course," he said, obviously thrilled. So around the room we went, Felix introducing me to different ecosystems and telling me where they occurred in the world. Some were remnants of our past, from a time before temperatures shifted and destruction reigned—like the domes labeled CORAL REEF and ARCTIC TUNDRA. Others showed the future hopes of damaged ecosystems restored.

"People in America," I said to Felix as we walked, "they have no idea that half of this exists. We . . . we had no idea. We weren't allowed to learn about it. Anything outside of our borders."

Standing in front of these domes, I felt like the realization was fresh. Like it bore repeating. "If there is a future. A future for me other than this one," I said as Felix and I stood there in front of the temperate grassland, "this is what I want to do. I want to show them everything they have missed and help America become part of the solution."

"I could see you being really good at that," Felix said. I smiled, letting that imaginary future settle on my shoulders for just a moment.

"Do you want to see some of the other technology we've been developing?"

"I'd love to," I said, and I really meant it. We walked over to the edge of the room, and the shelves I had spotted upon our arrival were filled from top to bottom with gadgets I didn't recognize. Some gadgets were encased in what looked like glass, with warning signs on them and biometric security locks flanking their covers.

"That one right there," Felix said, gesturing to a particularly treacherous-looking item on the wall. "That one isn't active, but one of those bad boys gave me this during testing." He raised his red glasses and ran his finger down the scar on his cheek.

"Yikes," I said, and he smiled and lowered his glasses back down to the bridge of his nose. "I know there are plenty of surgical options these days, but it helps remind me that sometimes the perfect solution can't be rushed, and that innovation takes time."

I couldn't help but wonder if he was talking about more than the technology we were admiring. He picked up a small object about the size of a thumbnail; it resembled a boxy beetle. There were several others like it nearby and I noticed that they didn't require a locked case.

"Here, hold this," he said, and placed it in my outstretched hand.

"Is it safe?" I said as the little gadget started moving. Things resembling legs protruded out on both sides, and it scurried across my palm. Felix smiled again.

"Yes. That one isn't a weapon. Just surveillance."

He opened a scroll from his pocket. "You can program an entire fleet of these to communicate with one another, then control them with just the push of a few buttons," he said. He studied my reaction, and it reminded me of the way Amara used to watch me watching a movie she loved, just to make sure I liked it too.

"This little baby is one of our newest inventions." Wings suddenly extended out from the tiny thing, and it started hovering out of my palm. It moved so quickly, it was difficult to see, and before long, it had all but disappeared into the surrounding air. I closed my eyes to listen. There was no noise.

Felix pressed another button, and I saw a blur in front of the wall, then caught sight of the gadget as it landed on one of the vertical surfaces of the bookshelf. Before long, it shifted from its original bright white to the subdued yellow of the surface behind it, disappearing against its new background.

Felix beamed with pride and excitement. He was truly in his element. He radiated joy and passion and he passed it to me like he was letting me in on a secret.

"Did you invent this?" I asked him.

"It was a team effort, but I was part of it, yes."

He pressed some more buttons, then held out his hand. The gadget landed on his open palm.

"How fast do they travel?"

"About one hundred miles per hour at top speed, but look here: it has a tiny camera on the top, and one underneath, for a different view. Its legs cling to fabric, watch."

He held it against his sleeve, and it wrapped its "feet" to cling, sort of like a Venus flytrap. He started to laugh. I laughed too, and then I watched Felix. His eyes behind the red frames of his glasses were bright, and focused. Suddenly his passion hit me at full force. It was the look in Rexx's eyes when he saw the van in the forest. It was the look in Oliver's when he clipped the harness around my waist and looked out over the edge of a cliff to the waterfall below. It was that sense of wonder and excitement that I used to feel when finding a new insect, or a new stone, or setting up the portable lab in a new closed-off location full of possibility. That integral part of me that used to define who I was.

"So what would these be used for?" I asked, my words catching slightly in my throat.

"They can be used for all sorts of things, mostly tracking and surveillance in areas where airspace is monitored and larger drones cannot be deployed. They can capture footage and save it, or send it to an outside source via satellite. They are almost imperceptible to the human eye when in motion, and their camouflage technology makes them hard to see when stationary unless you know what you're looking for." He pinched the item between his thumb and forefinger and held it up in front of his face, turning it back and forth as he admired it. "They really are the perfect tool for seeing what is not meant to be seen."

As he spoke, I wondered if he was showing me this for a reason.

"What do you call it?"

"We haven't come up with a title, but I've been calling it the beetle for now."

"Of course," I said, watching as he put the beetle back down on one of the shelves. I heard the elevator doors open and turned to see Rose joining us.

"Almost finished?" she asked as she walked toward us. "I was thinking maybe we could take Patch out to dinner."

My heart raced in my chest as that feeling of excitement, of wonder, remained at the surface like sea-foam that wouldn't retreat. It was a feeling I didn't want to end, though behind it was the guilt of feeling that way. Of hating myself for the enjoyment. I shoved it aside for now.

"Absolutely," I said.

"Great," said Felix. "I know a place that will blow your mind."

Soon we were in a vehicle headed toward the coast. As Rose and Felix chatted happily beside me, I watched out the window as the sunset began. The prime minister's words played on a loop in my head.

You survived. Take a deep breath, enjoy yourself, and let us worry about things for a while.

The vehicle set us down in front of a restaurant with a wraparound dock. We stepped out into the cold evening air, and the smells of salt and seaweed greeted my nostrils and made my eyes water slightly. My instinct was to breathe deeper, and so I did, letting the salty air coat my tongue and fill my head.

Twinkle lights lit up the area around the restaurant, covering the dock and the beach below. As we walked toward the front door, I noticed there were people swimming in the ocean.

"Wait here," Rose said. "I'll go get us a table."

I walked toward the edge of the dock and watched the swimmers. They were free and happy, diving in and out of the water and laughing with friends.

"Wait, how are they swimming?" I asked. "It's freezing outside." I turned to Felix as I wrapped the coat I was wearing tightly around my body. He was leaning against the railing of the dock, his eyes cast over the water. His red glasses fell down the bridge of his nose slightly.

"Do you see those markers out there in the ocean?"

I looked out to where he pointed, and saw some large round objects floating in the distance. I nodded.

"About twenty years ago," he continued, "we did this giant plastic-collection project to clean up the ocean, and we used part of what we collected to build a barrier. It's about a mile wide and a mile long, and everything within that area is heated as the tide comes in. So, you're looking at the only area on the Canadian coast where you can swim all year long."

Felix was smiling as he watched the swimmers in the sunset. A heavy feeling came over me, and I turned around, away from him.

"So, you and Rose," I said tentatively. "Is there something there?"

"Oh." Felix laughed, but I didn't understand what was so funny. "No, Rose and I love each other, but she only dates women."

I nodded. Why was I asking?

I distracted myself by looking out at the ocean again. People covered the dock and the beach below, walking here and there. A few children played at the water's edge, chasing the small tide as it came in and went out. I knew why I was asking but didn't want to admit it. For the first time since Rexx, I found someone else attractive. I looked around for something else to distract myself with.

A family with a baby in a stroller and a young child, about five or six years old, walked up to the dock railing beside us. The young child held the father's hand and gripped the side of the stroller with her other tiny hand.

Every once in a while, a member of the quartet would peek into the stroller to check on the baby. As I watched the gesture, a dull ache shot through my chest, and I turned my head away for a brief moment. The baby started to cry. "Let's just go around them," Felix whispered. "We can go closer to the beach." We were starting to bypass them when I heard the father say something.

The words felt like sharp tools drilling into my skull.

"Get the pacifier."

CHAPTER 17

Patch Collins

I DROPPED TO the ground, hard on my knees, the moisture from the light layer of snow on the dock sinking into the fabric of my pants as I covered my head. The logical part of my brain told me I couldn't possibly have heard what I thought I heard, but I ignored it, squeezed my eyes shut as hard as I could, and waited for the fallout to come.

When it didn't come, I opened my eyes slightly and looked at the father who had spoken the words. He was staring at me with wide, alarmed eyes, and in his hand was a small plastic item of some kind. He turned briefly and put the object inside the crying baby's mouth and in an instant the baby was quiet.

In confusion, I looked to Felix, and it was as if clarity suddenly hit his face. He dropped down to his knees too, and with a gesture waved everyone else away.

"It's okay," he said as he put a hand on my shoulder. "It's not a weapon here. It's, well, it's something a baby sucks on and it helps calm them down when they can't nurse or have a bottle."

I sank farther down onto my knees, suddenly feeling incredibly stupid.

"I'm sorry. I, um . . . Well, the only way we use that word in America is—"

"I know," Felix said, and he extended his hand to me and pulled me up off the ground. "It's okay. Come on. I bet our table is almost ready."

I ignored the pain in my knees as we walked toward the restaurant, and I tried to shake off what had just happened. Rose was waving us over from a table on the patio overlooking the ocean.

The sun was now almost completely gone, but the sky held on to a soft yellow glow due to the nearby streetlights and the lights illuminating the swimming area below us. A trio of dimly lit candles sat in the middle of the table and soon a basket of bread containing several kinds that I had never seen before was delivered to us.

"Oh, these are so good. You have to try this one—it's my favorite," Rose said as she reached for a slice of bread that looked like it contained dried fruit of some kind.

I grabbed a slice out of the basket, ripped off a corner, and put it in my mouth. It was soft, light, a texture I had never experienced with bread before, and it burst with a sweet flavor that coated the inside of my mouth.

"This is incredible," I said as I ripped off another piece.

"You should try it with some of the fresh garlic butter," Felix said. "Here." And he pushed a small dish in my direction. I spread some of it on what was remaining of the slice of bread and took another bite. The silky flavors were incomparable to anything I'd ever experienced.

"Why don't the two of you just order for me?" I said with a laugh as I savored the remaining bites of the bread. The rest of the meal did not disappoint. I was presented with a fresh salad featuring radishes, pumpkin seeds, and a basil dressing that burst with flavor on my tongue. A creamy entrée featuring an array of seafood from just off the coast followed, and by the time we were finished I almost felt at peace.

Afterward, Rose leaned over and whispered something in Felix's ear, and a smile spread across his face as he listened.

"What?" I said. "What is it? Is there something on my face?"

"No, we just thought . . . Well, would you like to go swimming?"

"Swimming? Down there? But I didn't bring anything with me."

"That's okay. There is a shop right next door," Rose said.

"I don't have any credits," I said.

"Out here we call that money, but don't worry. I'll cover for you. I don't want you to miss your chance to swim in the ocean."

Swim in the ocean. I thought about the Compliance Officers patrolling the waterline in America. I thought about the prime minister telling me to live a little. I didn't want to miss my chance either.

Soon the three of us were standing on the beach in the cold, crisp air. All around us people laughed and played or sprawled out on the beach under heat lamps. A few smiled at us, welcoming *Come join us* smiles. Music was playing from somewhere nearby, loud enough for everyone in the vicinity to hear.

I stepped one foot into the lapping water, and it was warm like bathwater. I waded deeper and deeper into the water, letting it cover my calves, my knees, my thighs, and soon all the way up to my abdomen.

I nearly forgot I had company with me. It was like I couldn't stop taking steps until the water covered my shoulders, its warmth lapping around my neck. The waves were not overpowering. They were gentle and rhythmic. Though I had improved slightly during my time in Zone 36, I still did not consider myself a strong swimmer, but this water felt safe and, in that moment, I felt content. The feeling swelled within me as water encased me like a cocoon.

I turned slightly to see Rose and Felix watching me from closer to the shore. I dipped down into the water and let it coat my hair, allowing the thoughts that had been held at bay come swirling into my head as I tried to sort through the emotions I felt. Then thoughts I wasn't expecting came crashing in faster than I could control them—thoughts of what my life could have been. I let my head completely submerge under the water.

I imagined growing up in Canada. I imagined having a brother or a sister and taking walks as a family, like the family I'd just seen on the dock.

I surfaced for air and took a deep breath, then went back down again.

I imagined dinners with my parents, and easy conversation as we said anything and everything that came to mind, without cameras and cheat sheets and lessons on acceptable communication.

I took another deep breath, and then went back under.

I imagined being a teenager, talking freely with my friends, laughing and playing without surveillance, like those on the beach beside me. I imagined us staying up late, reading books and listening to music.

I came up and breathed in more air, then descended again.

I imagined Oliver, being exactly who he was and being not hated for it but loved. Imagined his art and his music and his joy spreading to those around him, and how successful he would have been had he grown up here instead of there.

The happiness started to give way to rage as I surfaced once again and took a deep breath.

I imagined taking a shower, a bath, or just sleeping, without the constant knowledge that someone was watching me.

I imagined my father, Noah, Sophia, and Amara still alive, still thriving, just living life as ordinary happy people who were allowed to have their own thoughts and beliefs as long as they didn't hurt anyone else.

When I emerged from the water, the happiness was gone. All that remained was anger—anger at who we could have been had the world not abandoned us.

I walked out of the water and straight over to Rose and Felix, who were both stretched out on two towels on the beach. Their eyes became wide as they saw me approach and noticed the expression on my face.

"How could they just abandon us?" I was yelling, unable to control the volume of my voice. Rose and Felix jumped up, and I grabbed one of their towels and wrapped it around my dripping body.

"How can you just watch what is happening and not do anything? Any of you?" I could feel the rage filling my face as I angrily dried off my hair with the bottom of the towel. "How could you see what I saw this morning and then just decide to distract me like I am a damn toddler? People are dying in there and you all just go on with your lives." I gestured around at all the people swimming and laughing and eating on the patio above us.

"Patch, it's not that simple—" Rose started to say.

"Stop! I am so tired of hearing that. From you, from the Board, from the prime minister. Just stop. There are decisions being made and ignoring us was a decision. You could have helped more than you did. You could have fought harder for us. You could have, but you didn't. You let it get this far."

Rose and Felix both stared at me, their mouths slightly agape. I knew that it wasn't these two people opposite me who I was angry with, but in a way it was. It was everyone who decided that we weren't worth an interruption in their perfect lifestyle. Everyone who decided that they could just shut the door on the mess in the closet and pretend it wasn't there.

"I just want a straight answer," I finally said, firmly. "I gave up my entire life. My own father is dead because of me. All because I thought I could help. I mean, I know intervening in America is dangerous, but if everything I read about the America of the past was true, how could the world have just forgotten us? There must be more to it. I'm so sick of being lied to. I just want the truth."

Rose looked around us. A few people glanced our way, but she held up her hands to indicate that everything was fine and it hit me how loudly I had been yelling.

"Are you sure?" Felix asked, and his words sent a fresh ripple of anger through my body.

"Yes! I wish everyone would stop treating me like I'm a damn child."

Rose nodded, then she dropped down to her knees and straightened out the towel that was still on the ground. She gestured for me to sit.

"Please," she said. "Sit down and we'll talk. It's not pretty."

I sat, but continued to clutch the towel as if it were the only thing holding me together. After a brief moment, Rose spoke again.

"You became the example," she said, lowering her head. I let the words sink in, trying to extract more meaning from them than they held for me.

"What do you mean?" I finally asked.

Rose fiddled with the sand next to the towel. "Nationalism and totalitarianism were sweeping the globe," she said, "threatening to grab hold of humanity as people's worst behaviors became normalized. It was an incredibly scary and divisive time." She raised her head and looked directly into my eyes. "Extremist leaders were popping up everywhere, feeding on the fear, taking the actions of a changing America as a green light for chaos. Until the Seclusion."

As she said these words, I was reminded of what the Board used to say about viruses spreading. Suddenly my surroundings felt anything but safe. The urge to vomit rose in my throat.

"You became what we could point to. You became the face of extremism, of separatism. The model to show others what would happen if we didn't stop it. We could point to you and say, 'This is where your misguided pride and hate will lead you'—a country once considered the greatest on Earth, willing to seal itself off from the rest of the world rather than admit its mistakes and move forward."

Rose didn't take her eyes off me as I absorbed her words.

"So what are you saying? Are you saying you never intended to help us?" I asked.

"No. We—I mean they—did at first. That is, until the world watched as you fell. It broke everyone's hearts, but then something else happened. Order began to restore itself in many of the other developed regions of the world once you were silenced. You were considered a necessary sacrifice."

CHAPTER 18

Patch Collins

THAT NIGHT BROUGHT one of the most vivid dreams I'd ever had in my life. I was back in Zone 36, in Oliver's front yard. I was digging in the garden with Oliver and could see Rexx through the window cooking dinner. Music filled the dream, and the smell of lavender surrounded Oliver and me as we talked about our day. We worked side by side, and planted seeds in neat little parallel rows. He dug the holes, and I followed, placing a seed in each indent made with his fingers.

His fence, painted a rainbow of colors, was visible in the distance. An amber sun was shining high in the sky, and we made plans to go swimming in the river after dinner. A few moments later Rexx walked outside with samples of what he was cooking up in the kitchen, to feed us as we worked.

"I'll need more mint as a garnish. Do you mind getting some? Dinner will be ready in ten," Rexx said as he leaned down and kissed my cheek, then ran the fingers of his free hand through my hair as he pulled away. My heart swelled.

In my dream, I knew I'd found the life I wanted. In my dream there were no thoughts of leaving. We would stay in

Zone 36 forever. We would not venture into the community center where we were destined to meet Noah, Sophia, and the others. We would not give the Board any reason to find us. We would keep a low profile, swim in the river, hike, and cook. We would visit with Oliver in the evenings and hear secondhand stories of his work.

Then we were back in the church. Oliver was teaching Rexx to play the piano as I hung in the back and fiddled with Oliver's art supplies. I'd painted something—a waterfall, with a rust-colored hue. It was pretty good.

Then Oliver was gone and Rexx and I were on the floor of the church, in each other's arms. "I love you, Patch Collins," Rexx whispered in my ear. I let my head fall into the nook in his shoulder and felt his breath on my forehead. We would stay like this forever, and no one could touch us.

I reached up to run my fingers through his hair, and as I did, the silky black curls disappeared, replaced by stubble. His vibrant face morphed into sunken eyes and prominent cheekbones jutting out unnaturally. I searched him. Where my hand had just been on his bare chest, he now wore a compound-issued uniform. I felt the top of my head, and my hair was now gone too, replaced by stubble.

"Rexx," I pleaded, but he grew thinner, his eyes sinking with each second. His body decomposing underneath the papery gray uniform.

"Rexx! Don't leave!" I yelled at him as the last remnants of his body disintegrated into the floor of the church. I pawed at the ash as it fell out of an empty compound-issued jumper.

With ash-covered hands I pushed myself off the ground and tried to run away, but the doors of the church closed and the room shrank in on me. Flames became visible outside the barricaded doors. I searched for another way out, the sweat pouring from my body like rain.

Rexx's body was now back and stacked on top of several other skeletons in the corner. I tried to reach it, but I couldn't. Flames licked the ornate walls and the vaulted ceilings, and beams fell in front of me, blocking my path. The walls closed in, closer and closer.

Then the building disappeared, and I was inside one of the incinerator vans. Elias Stevens stared through the small window, smirking, and his hand moved to press the button.

I awoke, drenched in sweat and breathing heavily. I felt the bedding underneath, reassuring myself it was not the cold floor of the compound cell. I wiped my face with a pillowcase.

"Light," I said, and a dim blue light illuminated the room. *I am safe. I'm in a guest room in a government building outside of Vancouver.* I repeated the words until they sank in and everything started to settle.

I am safe.

I am safe.

I am safe.

I found my scroll on the side table and opened it to check the time—3:57 a.m.

My hand stretched across the emptiness next to me on the bed. "You're alive," I whispered, reminding myself. "You're alive."

This isn't over yet, I thought.

After an hour of attempting to go back to sleep, I gave up and hoisted myself out of bed. I made some tea and waited for clarity to come. I paced the room, sat in the office chair, sat on the edge of the bed—determined to come up with a plan. The edges of plans teased me like fish swimming under the surface of a lake, visible in bits and pieces through murky waters. They were there, but I couldn't see them clearly and I couldn't catch them.

A knock on my door around eight disrupted my anxious pacing.

"Good morning," I said when I saw it was Rose. A bit of the tension from the night before still hung in the air between us. "What's going on?"

"I've been thinking about our conversation last night, and there's somewhere else I want to take you."

A short ride later, we came to a stop in front of a large building. Behind a bow of thin columns, a light patina coated the exterior of a stone facade, like copper exposed too long to the elements. Above the arched entryway, there was a sign.

THE AMERICAN HISTORY MUSEUM: IN MEMORIAM OF THE USA

"'In memoriam'?" I asked. "We didn't die. We're still there," I said too pointedly.

Rose didn't say anything, and my throat burned as I stared at the building that was somehow intimidating and yet beckoned me inside its walls.

"That image, there on the sign, what is that of?" I asked, admiring the somehow familiar silhouette of what looked like a woman wearing some sort of crown. Her color matched the hue of the rest of the building.

"That," Rose said as we walked, "is the Statue of Liberty. There's going to be a lot to absorb in here," she added as she held open the door for me. "We'll take it slow."

A line of people, fifteen or so deep, stood behind an array of body scanners, presenting passes to a nearby attendant and walking through the scanners one by one. Eager smiles and excited chatter passed between couples and small groups as they waited. We moved forward with the flow until it was our turn. Rose flashed identification to the attendant, and he waved us through.

"In the early days, some people smuggled out some of the most valuable works of art," Rose said once we were fully inside. "We didn't get to all of it, of course, but there are some who believe that it is hidden somewhere in America, and that some of it still may be safe."

"This was painted by an American artist?" I asked as I approached the first piece of artwork I saw.

"It was painted in the late 1800s. A painter by the name of Vincent van Gogh. He wasn't an American artist, he was Dutch, but the painting was housed in an American museum. It was damaged slightly, there in the lower left corner, when it was recovered."

The painting featured black, gray, and blue swirls, a crescent moon, and the silhouette of a building, or maybe black flames. A small town was nestled in the background. It filled me with a sense of melancholy and peace, and I wondered what this Vincent person had been thinking when he painted it.

I looked at the sign underneath.

THE STARRY NIGHT BY VINCENT VAN GOGH
1889
RECOVERED FROM MUSEUM OF MODERN ART IN NEW YORK, NY

I moved to the next painting as other visitors funneled into the alcove behind us.

"Now, this one, here," Rose said with a big smile. "This was an American artist."

A man and a slightly shorter woman stood in front of a house. The woman in the painting wore a disgruntled look on her face, and the man, bald and wearing glasses, was holding a tool of some kind in front of him.

It was the house that my eyes were drawn to. It was the kind of old farmhouse Rexx and I had seen in abandoned America. The type of house where the land itself was more important, and the house was just the period punctuating a well-written sentence. Plenty of room for gardening and exploring the outdoors with no omnipresent cameras in sight.

The sign revealed it was painted exactly one hundred years before the Seclusion.

AMERICAN GOTHIC BY GRANT WOOD

1930

RECOVERED FROM THE ART INSTITUTE OF CHICAGO

I stepped over to the next one, and the image presented before me sent me back to America. An uncomfortable prickle began to lick its way up my back. I felt as if I were standing in my old apartment, removing my clothes next to my bathtub as it filled, while desperately trying to ignore the cameras pointed at my body.

A woman in a red dress and a blue coat stood in the middle of a crowd, in one of many passageways. The infrastructure cast ominous shadows on the ground. She looked scared, or sad maybe. Men in dark coats moved around her, looking angry and determined, but no one looked at one another. A few others looked scared as they ducked into doorways, and I tightened my own coat around my body as I read the sign.

THE SUBWAY BY GEORGE TOOKER

1950

RECOVERED FROM THE WHITNEY MUSEUM OF AMERICAN ART

"Can we move on?" I asked Rose.

"Of course," she said as she led me away from the entrance alcove and into the main museum.

"How many times have you been here?" I asked.

"Oh, I don't know. At least twenty," she said. "It is separated both by category and time period," Rose said. "Shall we start at the beginning?"

"I guess so."

We walked the whole museum in almost near silence, just the two of us, absorbing everything in view. I tried to hide the growing guilt I felt toward how I had spoken to her the night before.

I sought to wrap my head around the displays I was seeing, but it was all so much. Soon, hundreds of years of history started to blur together like shadows in a forest. The displays in each section were alive, featuring holograms and voice tracks when necessary.

We walked past the origins of america exhibit, which, no matter how many times I read the displays or listened to the narration, I could not make into anything more than stolen land and a bloodbath of epic proportions. What followed was not much better.

The atrocities changed as time went on, but they continued as our country developed. Some were recognizable as a shadowy cousin of activities still occurring in America, while others were their own horrors.

People had been kidnapped from other countries and brought against their will. They had been forced into slave labor, hung, traded, and sold like furniture. They'd been stoned, crucified, scalped, burned, raped.

As I walked the displays, trying to understand the timeline, trying to wrap my head around the references I didn't understand and the explanations that felt hollow, the images of the bodies in the library kept popping into my head. The lengths that the Board had to go to hide all of this history from us . . . Well, it was mind-boggling.

Familiar knots formed in my stomach and throat, growing with each step.

There was something inside me, even after everything I'd seen and learned, that still didn't want to acknowledge the truth. I was a little girl who still wanted to cling to the belief that what she had been taught all her life was real.

I peered around at the people who walked through the museum—children excitedly tugging their parents along to the various exhibits; adults holding bags and wearing caps with the words AMERICAN HISTORY MUSEUM printed in crisp letters; teenagers deciding they were bored and wanted to go home.

A familiar defensiveness roared, the same feeling I'd felt the prior evening, even though I knew it didn't belong and was misdirected. An anger at the people making a spectacle of our history, and of our lives. We'd been merely an entertaining cautionary tale.

We wound our way through more of the museum, and the tone shifted. It was happier and more celebratory, with bright colors and bold lighting.

We approached an exhibit titled AMERICAN INNOVATION, which discussed scientific discoveries and the curing and prevention of various diseases. It discussed technology I had never heard of before. There was a vehicle—the Ford Model T—that was apparently one of the first. There was an entire display showing holographic footage of a man landing on the surface of the moon.

Emotions swirled inside me, and I didn't know how to pluck them far enough apart to make sense of them. It all felt so wrong and inconsistent with my reality.

I was shown displays of people celebrating after significant events I'd never heard of. One showed the signing of a document called the Constitution, which I think I remembered the elders mentioning, but I could not remember exactly what it was. There were images of people in the streets cheering after the passing of something called the Civil Rights Act. There was a display with fast-moving images showing businesses turning on their OPEN signs after a new vaccine slowed the spread of a mass pandemic.

We approached the final time period, and I was shown the mass protests precluding the Seclusion. I was shown the final stages of a country falling apart. I was shown the Board dismantling the aforementioned Constitution. I was shown the signing of new laws. I was shown the same video I'd been shown in the Zone 36 community center—the one in which the Board announced the Seclusion and the scrubbing of information and the enactment of what I now knew to be a firewall. Someone must have snuck a copy out early on.

I was shown the Walls being built, and the new immigration policies being horrifically enforced. I thought of Rexx and the letter from his grandfather. I was shown the initial mass exodus, voluntary and otherwise. I was shown testimonials of early defectors.

The weight of everything I'd just seen and heard stacked on top of my shoulders. How could a country have a history simultaneously filled with so much ugliness, so much hope, so much innovation, so much horror? I felt like I was being sealed away brick by brick.

For a split second I found myself empathizing with the Board. I understood wanting to hide this from people. I understood the appeal of a fresh start and erasing all of this from memory with a new generation.

For a moment I understood, and I hated myself for it.

The last exhibit before the museum exit was a small display titled AMERICA TODAY. It showed us current satellite images, explained the basics of a closed economy, and displayed old pictures of America's nuclear arsenal. It explained the negotiations offered to the Board in the past, but that in the fight between giving up its nuclear arsenal for a place at the table and regime survival, the Board had chosen the latter.

I stood staring at that final display for a long time. When I finally turned away, I found my way to a bench and sat down and dropped my head into my hands.

"I just need a minute."

"Of course," Rose said as she took a seat next to me. "You know. That all happened over hundreds of years. Taking it all in at once is a lot for anyone. All of that was covered over several semesters even during my education."

"Yeah, I know what the Board is doing is wrong," I finally said, trying to find the right words to come next. "I know it with everything that I am. The fear, the control, the deception. It has to stop, but would knowing all of this really make people's lives better?" I looked to Rose, and she stayed silent, so I kept going. "Were they right about this one thing? Maybe history is toxic. And maybe we really aren't strong enough to handle it."

"In my opinion," she said as she leaned back and propped an elbow up on the top of the bench behind us, "truth is always the best option."

"What do they do in Canada?" I asked.

"History is taught here. Our history has its atrocities as well. It's not always pretty, but we only learn from our mistakes by acknowledging them and trying to correct and make amends for them if we can."

"Maybe," I said, still absorbing her words.

"It's not always about making people's lives better, Patch. People didn't look up to America because it was perfect. They looked up to it because most of the time, it had ideals it was striving toward. It's like when a parent is disappointed in you. They aren't disappointed because they think you can't be better; they are disappointed because they know you can, and you aren't living up to it. Those times in history when America acknowledged it could be better, that it would be better, well, those were the times when it was strongest."

The day had been long. The museum would be closing soon, but still we just sat, and I absorbed her words and let the remnants of our conversation from the night before hang over us as well. Then I asked the question I had been afraid to ask out loud since I'd arrived.

"They aren't going to help us, are they?"

"They will. They will help you. But I have a feeling that's not what you mean. No, they aren't going to help them. Not unless something changes."

Not unless something changes. The words hung in the air between us. I let them fall over me. The words rang true to everything that had happened so far and their simplicity was comforting, in an odd way.

I thought about leaving. About getting in a car and being driven back to the border. Presenting myself to the Board for whatever punishment they saw fit. Maybe the Board member would stick to his word. Maybe there would be a way for Rexx and me to redeem ourselves. Or maybe I could see him one more time before I died. Maybe they would kill us together.

I remembered Oliver telling me in the garden that the rage inside him felt like a grenade that was going to be detonated at any moment. Ever since I woke up in the hospital, it had felt like he'd passed the grenade to me.

I looked around at the crowds gathered here and there. What would Oliver, what would the elders, what would Rexx want me to do? Suddenly the plan I had been trying to grasp that morning, the fish beneath the murky waters, started to not just swim higher, but to jump.

Maybe it wasn't the leaders I had to convince. Maybe it was the people.

CHAPTER 19

Patch Collins

"LET'S GO," I finally said to Rose, standing up from the bench in the American History Museum. I knew exactly what I had to do, and I had to do it soon.

Once outside, I was relieved when Rose announced she needed to check her messages. She opened a scroll and started pressing buttons, and I saw my window, however small.

"If they don't need us back for anything, then maybe we can grab some lunch," she said. "There is a place on the corner I would love to show you."

"Okay, yeah, sounds great," I said as I searched around, the urge to do what I needed to do becoming increasingly insatiable, like an itch between your shoulder blades that you knew you could reach if you bent just the right way.

We weren't far from the satellite office, and if I'd learned anything regarding how the outside world was different from America, it was that around government buildings, one was likely to find journalists. These were no Aelia Ramey–style news anchors who worked directly for the government. Journalists out here were given more freedom to not just tell the story, but to find the story. The concept was so foreign to me that I still didn't understand it completely, but I had a strong feeling that if anyone could help me, it would be them, and I was about to give them one hell of a story.

After about thirty seconds of scanning, I spotted the group I'd been looking for across a median of snowcapped grass. I cast a quick glance to Rose to confirm she was still engaged with her scroll, then I took a deep breath and made a beeline for the sidewalk.

There were three of them. As I neared, they ceased talking to one another and turned all eyes toward me, perhaps searching for recognition or a reason this strange woman was approaching them with such intensity. My heart was suddenly in my throat and I wiped my palms off on my pants—somehow I was sweating profusely as a light flurry of snow fell around me.

I thought about turning around, but I couldn't. I was being pulled toward the journalists as if I were suddenly gliding across the snow beneath my feet. Underneath the nervousness there was exhilaration and excitement. This was it.

I knew in that moment that I was doing exactly what I had to do, even if it landed in my deportation. This was what Noah and the others would want me to do. I was taking matters into my own hands. I was going to get the truth out to the public.

Suddenly the walk that had seemed long a moment ago was over, and I was standing in front of three people with recording equipment slung over their shoulders and a pop-up lighting gadget of some kind on a tripod on the ground next to them.

"Patch!" I heard Rose yell behind me. "Is everything all right?"

I was right in front of them, and I glanced back quickly to see that Rose was beginning to walk over. I had to hurry.

A woman in the group looked at me quizzically, and before the group had a chance to say anything or pull out their cameras, I held up my hand and began speaking.

"Hello. Please don't react. My name is Patch Collins. Two months ago I escaped from America. I'm being housed in the United Nations satellite office. I've asked leaders to intervene, but they have refused. Things in America are not what they seem. They need your help."

The group looked stunned, and I inhaled what felt like the first full breath I had taken in months.

"Wait!" the woman yelled as she started digging for her equipment, and the other two did as well.

"Miss Collins, please wait. Can you say that again?"

I turned and walked away, exhaling deeply and ignoring the nervous dizziness that tried to take over my body just as Rose and I met in the middle.

Her energy shifted abruptly, and her arm made its way above my shoulder so it was shielding my head. She picked up the pace, pulling me along with her. There was no going back now. I had done it. I'd set a series of events in motion that could not be undone. Excitement ran through my entire body like electricity through a lightning rod.

"You'll want to stay away from them," she said in a stern, concerned tone. I turned my head once more underneath Rose's arm, just in time to see bright flashes from the cameras. "What did they say to you?" I could still hear them chattering behind me.

"Nothing," I lied, but I knew she didn't believe me, that she'd heard them try to ask follow-up questions. Deep down I could feel that she knew exactly what I had just done, and I wondered what she was about to do with that information. I chanced a look up at her face and noticed that it was not angry. Then I wondered something else. Had she stopped there to check her messages on purpose?

When we arrived at the satellite building, Rose escorted me back to my room in a hurry, and told me she would return soon. I tried to hide my rush to step inside, close the door, and be left alone.

I opened my scroll, found one of the top news programs, and projected it onto the wall. I waited for a sign that something, anything, was happening. There was nothing, and an hour or so passed by slowly.

By the time something delectable with cilantro and peanut sauce was delivered to my room for lunch, along with Rose, who insisted on eating with me, nothing had happened. She didn't say anything as she dished up a serving and handed it to me.

I started to wonder where exactly Rose had just gone. What if I had imagined her silent endorsement of my actions? What if she had reported everything that had just happened and my time here was running out? What if I had just set things in motion, but not in the way that I'd intended? What if I had just secured my trip back to America and to whatever punishment Elias Stevens had in store for me?

More questions bounced around my head in quick succession. Should I ask her directly if she knew what I had done? Had she just been sent here to keep an eye on me as travel arrangements back to America were made? What if the group I talked to didn't share what I had said? What if I didn't give them enough to go on, or they wrote me off as crazy? "Well, I tell you one thing I could get used to out here," I said as we ate, in an attempt to distract myself and appear relatively normal. "All of this fresh food and vegetables."

"You didn't have fresh produce in America?"

"We did, but it was hard to come by and expensive. Also, you list the ingredients on everything out here! In there, not so much." I thought about the crates of insect protein Rexx and I had traveled next to on the cargo flats.

"I had a small garden at my apartment, but because of the heat waves, it was only harvestable for a couple months of the year."

"You'd be surprised what they can do with a small gardening space these days, utilizing every inch of height available. I think you'll have a—" Rose abruptly stopped talking. Her eyes shot to the screen on the wall and she used her scroll to turn up the volume.

A photo of me walking away from the camera filled the screen. My heart felt like it was going to leap out of my chest. The words displayed on the screen were also being spoken by the anchor.

Breaking news: story still developing, but we have reason to believe a defector from America is being housed by the Canadian government.

"Oh shit. I have to go. You stay here. Stay here."

She jumped up and ran out of the room, closing the door behind her.

I pulled out my scroll and began searching, ignoring the fear that I'd just secured my own disastrous fate, and instead trying to focus on the hope I felt as the eyes of the world turned toward my country.

Hope continued its ascent as the story broke in more outlets by the minute, each one accompanied by pictures of my face. After several hours, the story was still developing, each outlet trying to make the recycled information seem new. Then the stories refreshing the public's knowledge of the current state of America began circulating.

I had nowhere to place the adrenaline that pumped through my veins, so I decided to peek out of my room. The door opened, but directly outside was a security guard who made it clear I was to wait in my room. I wasn't surprised, but expecting and confirming were two entirely different things.

Then I just waited. Waited to be punished. Waited to be yelled at. Waited to be sent back. Waited for something. I cleaned up what was left of our lunch, then sat in the chair by my desk, imagining everything that might be happening among members of the Security Council at that moment.

Between the waiting, there was a feeling that maybe, just maybe, the page was about to turn and the ground was about to shift.

Rose didn't return that night, and eventually my missed sleep from the night before caught up to me and I fell asleep fully dressed on top of the covers.

When I awoke the next morning, I checked the news feeds and was shocked at what I saw. Demonstrators had lined up on Sussex Avenue, the address of the prime minister, all morning in reaction to the news of the defector from America and the current conditions of their neighbor to the south. They were projecting images into the air. Images with phrases, including *We help our neighbors* and *We demand answers* and *Restore America*. I stared at them, squinting to see their faces. They looked energized and determined.

Security stood in front of the prime minister's mansion, letting the people chant and speak and project their messages into the air, and they did not hurt them or even try to stop them.

An overwhelming warmth and gratitude filled my body. People would be pacified on sight in America for this kind of behavior, yet there they were. I wanted to grab every single one of them and say thank you. I wanted to hug them, and to let them know how much their caring meant to me.

By late afternoon, crowds were spilling onto the lawns, rounding the curve, and overflowing onto the adjoining roads. The cameras toggled between the Sussex Avenue crowd and several other smaller crowds that had apparently been popping up at other locations. Phrases such as *The people demand accountability*, *Free Americans*, *Our voices will be heard*, and *Protection for the defector* crawled across the screen and were also projected into the air or on the sides of large buildings from handheld projectors in the crowd. I spotted my name mentioned on a few of the messages, and some even had digital images of my face. I vacillated between feeling like I was imagining all of it and feeling like it was the most real thing that I'd ever seen.

The entire next day passed without a word, and other than the occasional food being dropped off to my room, I was alone. The silence sent my anxious brain from one extreme possibility to the next, buzzing around like an insect trapped inside a jar. I made tea, and I researched every question that popped into my brain on my scroll. I even played games for a couple of hours to distract myself. Eventually I fell asleep again.

I was awakened the following morning by a knock on the door, and crawled out of bed to answer it. It was Rose.

"The prime minister wants to meet with you," she said with an expression on her face I couldn't read. She looked past me, and into the messy bedroom.

"Look. I'm sorry for the way I handled things," I said. "I didn't mean for your picture to get dragged into this also. I'm also sorry I lied."

"I understand why you did it," she replied as she rolled her head from side to side, stretching out her neck. I felt my body relax. I wasn't exactly swimming in new friends, and I wasn't ready to lose one of the only real ones I felt I'd made so far.

"Why are you being so nice to me, Rose? I'm sure I got you into trouble."

"You're just trying to help your home," she said as she leaned up against the doorframe and finally met my eyes. "It's easy to ignore problems if they aren't right in front of you. Maybe it's your job to keep putting the problem right back in front of them, again and again, until they can't ignore it anymore. I'm not saying it's the right thing; I'm just saying I understand why you did it, and though others might rake you over the coals for it, I'm not going to be one of them."

I stifled a laugh under my breath and was suddenly self-conscious about how disheveled I must look. I reached up and tried to smooth down my hair, then straightened my clothes.

"Despite what anyone tells you, Patch," Rose continued, "you have good instincts. Keep listening to them."

I wondered if there was more to her words than she was letting on, but if she knew what I was about to walk into, she didn't say. I got changed and quickly cleaned myself up, and a few minutes later we were headed back down to the lab where Felix, Rose, and I had been working just a few days before.

When we walked in, four people were already sitting in there—Prime Minister Austin; her chief of staff, James; Felix; and a security guard I didn't recognize. I steeled myself for whatever was to come next, feeling the hope I'd felt upon watching the people in the streets start to disappear as all four pairs of eyes bore down on me.

"Good morning, Patch," the prime minister said coldly as she motioned to the edge of the room where an image hovered in the air. "We have a problem."

I walked toward the image, unsure at first what I was seeing.

"News of the protests and your statement have reached the Board, and they don't seem too happy about it," James chimed in.

The photo on the screen soon became clear—a weapon of some kind. Below the photo was a message.

You have twenty-four hours to return the girl, to stop this, and to renew the trade agreements that have been suspended. Return her, or we will launch our weapons.
—the Board

My stomach dropped through the floor, and even though I knew that what was happening had been a possibility, the fear started to rise around me like mist from water poured on a hot Arizona sidewalk. I looked to the prime minister, who seemed to be doing her best to avoid saying *I told you so.*

Return the girl. Return the girl. I repeated the words in my head, under my breath, possibly even out loud. *Return the girl.*

I stared at the image on the screen as my brain ran through the various scenarios. I ignored the people around me, enclosing myself inside my own impenetrable bubble.

I thought about Rexx and Oliver. I thought about what would happen if I could show the world a close-up view of America now that I had their attention. I thought about the beetles that Felix had shown me in the technology lab a couple of days before.

Return the girl. The fish continued to swim through the murky waters. The edges of a plan. *Return the girl.*

The beetles. The people. The Board. Me.

I knew what had to be done, and it was going to be terrible.

CHAPTER 20

Patch Collins

"I WANT TO talk to him again, and then I will do whatever you want me to do," I said to the prime minister, and I could almost hear Elias Stevens's laughter and satisfaction in my ear.

Shortly after, I was once again standing in the conference room facing a holographic Elias Stevens. My palms started to moisten. He looked so smug.

"I'll admit I underestimated you," Elias began. "Mass protests in the streets. I'd be lying if I said I wasn't a little impressed."

At this he looked down and straightened the hem of his suit jacket before continuing. "I'm surprised you requested this," Elias Stevens said. "We find ourselves in quite a situation here." His vitriol for me was palpable and I understood exactly how he felt.

"Yes. We do," I replied.

"We've had a cordial trade agreement with the United Nations for decades now, and then you came along, getting everyone out there riled up."

"I think you are overestimating the outside world's opinion of you," I said. "The other leaders may have let this slide for so long because it didn't affect them, but now the people know. I have a feeling they won't forget as easily."

I turned to face the window, hoping the prime minister was hearing my message as well, and I turned back to the Board member. "There are no dark corners of the world to hide in anymore."

"You think I give the outside world too little credit. Well, I think you give it too much. As soon as you are eliminated, people out there will forget. They will move on. They will think they had the best of intentions, and that's all that matters. They will pat themselves on the back, and they will move on with their lives."

I was afraid he was right. That people would think they'd tried, that it was enough, but intentions weren't everything. Impact rippled through the world, with the capacity to hurt and to scar. Intentions couldn't be all we clung to.

"Maybe. But I refuse to believe it. I think when people are shown the truth, they will make the right decisions."

"And if you do not come home, then I meant what I said. I am not afraid of a war, and if you are the one responsible for bringing a war into the homes of Americans, into their living rooms, then what do you think they will do?" Elias asked.

I took a deep breath, knowing that part of what he was saying was true, but not all of it. I knew that my word wouldn't be enough, so I had to show them exactly what was taking place in America as they went on with their lives.

"I'll do what you ask."

Elias's eyes grew large and the smirk on his face stretched like a rubber band.

"I'll come home."

"What do you think you are doing?" the prime minister asked as the door slid open behind me. James and Rose rushed in behind her as the form of Elias Stevens disappeared from across the table.

"I'm keeping everyone safe," I replied. "Like you said. The risks are just too big. I can't be responsible for a war. You can label satellite photos yourselves based on what I've already told you, and then shut the file on America. It is of no use for me to be out here, so I'm going home."

"But," the prime minister said, grabbing my shoulder and pulling me aside, and I could feel her steely demeanor, which she'd been projecting my way since the protests had started, begin to soften slightly. "You know you will be in danger," she nearly hissed into my ear. "You've seen what they do in there. They will probably kill you."

"Yes. Yes, I will be in danger," I said, shaking my arm free, "and so is everyone else who is in there right now. That's the point."

She took a step back and pursed her lips and nodded in a way that indicated she was thinking. If she had more questions, she didn't ask them. James stared at me from behind her, waiting for an explanation.

"I'll have to alert the Security Council," the prime minister finally said matter-of-factly. I wondered if underneath all the faux concern, the overwhelming feeling was relief. Relief that I would be out of her hair, that she could go on without someone reminding her both of her past and of what was still taking place next door. Little did she know that that wasn't what was about to happen.

"Can I say goodbye to the team before I go?" I asked.

"James, please lead her back to say her goodbyes, then to a waiting room while we consult with the Board and figure out travel arrangements."

"Why are you doing this?" Rose asked with urgency as soon as I was back in the lab and had explained what had happened.

"This isn't right. There has to be something else we can do." Felix's voice caught on the last words. Moisture was traveling down the bridge of his nose and catching underneath his glasses. His fingers were interlocked loosely in front of him, trembling slightly in an anxious way as his thumbs toyed with each other.

"It's fine. I don't belong here anyway," I said, trying to convince myself as much as him. It was true. Ever since I'd arrived, I'd felt like a desert animal in a cold climate—uncomfortable, unsustainable, and out of place.

"Are you going to be okay? I mean, what are they going to do to you?" Felix asked in a somber voice.

My chest tightened. "Oh, I don't know. They don't really need the real me for most of it. They will probably kill me. Tell people they saved me. Throw up avatars that look like me and put me on the longest episode of *Portrait of a Redeemed Patriot* yet. They'll present me as deranged or misguided and tell everyone they saved me from myself. Use me as an excuse for whatever changes have taken place in the country these past months. But keeping me or Rexx alive any longer will probably be too big of a risk. "

I turned toward James.

"Can we have just a minute, alone?"

He nodded and then walked out of the room, and as soon as he did I pulled Rose and Felix toward me, one in each arm, for a hug.

"I can't just sit around and wait anymore. I'm just being placated. I'm going back, and I need your help. I need one of the beetles. I need to get footage from inside America, and I need it to be broadcast out here. Can you do that for me?"

I felt their bodies stiffen in response, and I waited a moment before pulling away. When I did, I could see Felix was trying to hide a look of shock on his face, while Rose was trying to hide a smile.

CHAPTER 21

Rexx Moreno

IN HIS UNDERGROUND holding location, Rexx remained oblivious to the changes happening outside. He'd tried to exercise as much as possible to build up his strength, but it was difficult. He was still attached to the bed by a feeding tube and the cuffs on his wrists. His back was starting to ache, and he was pretty sure he had sores on his hips, though there was no way for him to check properly.

Depression was settling over him, tightening its consuming grip. The screens on the wall screamed and flashed. He could barely hear them or see them. He was trapped in the depths of the ocean. He tried to find things to hold on to—to conjure up memories of her face, to remember her laughter, or to think of the two of them swimming in the lake under the Arizona sun. Some days it helped, but not today.

Today he was sinking, faster and faster. His mind wandered, remembering the footage of Amara dead on the ground and the scream that had exploded out of Oliver's body when he was pacified, and the letter from his grandfather and the hopelessness it elicited. Everything around him ceased to matter. He ceased to matter.

"Why am I still alive?" Rexx shouted at the camera suspended in the middle of the room. At least he thought he shouted. The words may have barely left his lips. "Why don't you just kill me already?"

Regina Tellman shifted in her chair in the corner, ignoring him.

Rexx knew the answer. He was alive to be used as a pawn. He would remain alive so long as he were still useful to them. He didn't know much, but he knew however he was being used was compromising things. He pictured Patch, and he felt like nothing but a weight around her neck.

He had to remove himself from the equation, and he had to do it soon. He turned his head to look at the Compo in the corner, and as he did so, the moisture from the tears on his pillow pressed into his cheek. He knew he was only making this matter worse. He wanted to die before every ounce of humanity was taken from him, while he was still himself, still someone he recognized. Still Rexx Moreno.

Rexx closed his eyes and waited until Regina took one of her periodic walks outside the room. The cameras were still there. He doubted they would leave him completely unmonitored, so he would have to act fast. He could feel his spirit attempting to claw its way out of the abyss, begging him to hold on, whispering that there might be another way, but he ignored it.

There was a tray of medical supplies just out of reach. He slung his left leg over the edge of the bed to see if it could reach the ground. He could, but just barely. He tried to move the bed, to scoot it, and it took every ounce of strength he had, but it started to wheel closer to the tray. He inched his body as close to the edge of the bed as he could until his shackled right wrist dug painfully into the cold metal.

He used his leg to maneuver the tray of supplies up toward the top of his body. He used to be so coordinated. His physical ease, both in everyday life and in the wilderness, was something others had admired about him. Now he felt a bit like an upside-down turtle. Rexx used his left hand to reach for a scalpel he saw on the tray, almost pulling his right arm out of the socket as he did so, but it was a success. The scalpel was now in his hand.

He wrapped his grip around the cold handle and started to move it toward his throat. He held it right next to his carotid artery and closed his eyes as tight as he could manage. He thought of her face, of her wavy auburn hair, and of her smile and her laugh. He took a deep breath.

"I love you, Patch," he said under his breath. Or maybe he shouted it. It would all be over soon.

A moment's pause was all it took for the plan to fall apart.

The door slammed open, and someone was suddenly on top of him—Regina. She ripped the tool out of his hand, slicing his palm in the process. She wrapped her other hand around his throat and pushed him down onto the bed.

"I was wondering when you were going to snap. You're not getting out of this that easily." She was straddling him, her hand still around his neck, as she threw the scalpel back onto the tray and reached for her pacifier, pushing it against his temple.

"Pull the trigger," Rexx said through moist, glassy eyes, and he meant it; at least, he thought he meant it. The Compo looked at him and cocked her head sideways.

"You would like that, wouldn't you? After everything the Board has done to save you. How dare you. You fucking ungrateful traitors are as low as they come. Don't you have any dignity?"

She kept the pacifier trained on his head as she climbed off him. She fastened another restraint around his left hand, and then also around his ankles. A needle was jabbed into his neck.

Why couldn't I have been quicker? I'm sorry. They were the last thoughts that ran through his mind before everything went dark.

CHAPTER 22

Patch Collins

I SAT ALONE in the same waiting room I'd been brought to the first day I entered this building. I made myself another cup of tea, and once again inhaled the scent of jasmine. The mixed feelings about what I'd just done swirled around my brain, an echo of the tea bag in the cup. I set down the spoon and held the warmth with rickety hands as I thought about what I had just done.

I had a plan, and if it worked, it would be my final contribution to this world. With my last hours, I would show the people out here—not the government, not the special operations teams, but the people—exactly what happened in America and exactly what the Board was capable of. I knew, deep down, that if the Board was ever going to reveal the worst version of themselves, it would be to punish me. Would it be enough? I still didn't know, but it felt like I had to try.

I looked outside the window as I sipped my tea. Snowflakes swirled and landed on the nearby rooftops. There were protestors still gathered down below. I wrapped the sweater I was wearing more tightly around my body as I watched a toddler on the shoulders of their parent wave a sign back and forth.

If Felix and Rose didn't come through, then I would have given myself up for absolutely nothing. I would disappear, the crowds outside would calm, people would forget over time, and the world would move on without me, exactly as Elias Stevens said it would.

I tried to dissociate myself from the fear I was feeling as I pondered what the next few hours or days could bring. Would they be taking me back immediately, or would I have a few hours to get ready? Where would I be taken once I was back in America? Would Elias Stevens chance being out in public and meeting me at the border, or would Compliance Officers simply escort me back to the compound? The hair on my arms stood, and a chill ran up my body, despite the sweater's warmth.

I pulled my scroll out of my pocket, hoping to see a message from Felix or Rose. There were no messages, but there were several news alerts. I didn't check them. I condensed the scroll and put it back in my pocket.

I'd kept the reality of the things I was about to face locked tightly in a compartment in the back of my mind, a compartment that was quickly starting to unhinge to reveal the words inside.

These could be your last hours alive.

I closed my eyes, listening hard for the sound of footsteps. There were none. Not yet.

Just as I was about to make myself another cup of tea, a buzzing in my pocket alerted me to a message on my scroll. I pulled it out, and my fingers shook as I opened it. I remembered something that my father used to tell me when I was a child: *The mind lies much better than the body.*

With still-jittery hands I opened it, hoping with everything I had that the friendships I had formed out here weren't in vain.

Get to the A corridor restroom ASAP—F & R

A few minutes later I entered the bathroom. At first glance it was empty. I took a quick lap around the perimeter. Every single stall was marked with a green oval to indicate they were vacant, but I opened each one individually just to make sure. When I was positive I was alone, I made my way back toward the door and waited.

Several minutes passed and nothing happened. I started to worry that someone who worked for the prime minister would discover I was no longer in the waiting room and come looking for me.

I turned around and faced one of the hand sanitizers mounted on the wall. Because I had nothing better to do, I stuck my hands under it, and they were blasted with steam quickly followed by cool air with a lavender scent. I inhaled the aroma, reminded of the lavender growing in Oliver's garden. I did it again, inhaling deeply, picturing Rexx's face as he worked next to me harvesting vegetables for dinner.

The ache in my chest had changed since that first day on the roof. It was still there, but it was different. Instead of pure guilt and longing, there was hope, just a tiny sliver, that I might see his face again or maybe even get a chance to say goodbye. I thought back to the first day we had met.

I was sixteen, and so was he. I'd just graduated, taken my aptitude tests, and it was my first day of training with the Natural Resource Department. I was nervous, but I was also luckier than most, having been given my top choice. I was lucky for other reasons as well.

My post was in my home city, so I would be near my parents. Not only that, but my best friend, Amara, and I had been assigned to the same training location. If I ignored the Compos, if I followed the rules, if I served the Board, then things would be good.

Amara and I walked in together that morning after spending the first night since we were five not sleeping next to each other—each of us now allocated to our own entry-level apartments. There were times during that first night that I considered breaking curfew and walking to Amara's apartment to sleep on her floor. The feeling of sleeping alone was so foreign.

When we walked into our training center, the room was full of faces we didn't recognize. They were the faces of other sixteen-year-olds brought in from other classrooms across our territory, ready to do their part to serve their country.

Because the specifics of what was performed at one's job was only disclosed on a need-to-know basis, that day we would be finding out exactly what every day for the rest of our lives would look like.

The room was already full, and only two chairs remained empty—two empty chairs next to a sixteen-year-old boy who flashed an inviting smile our way. It was a clear message that the seats were ours if we wanted them. The boy nudged the chairs out from under the table with his feet as we approached.

So, we took them—the two empty chairs next to the boy with the dimples and the jet-black curls.

As we sat down, he turned to me and whispered, "I hear we get to go outside." Then he leaned back and crossed his arms with a satisfied grin.

At the time, I'd thought he'd simply meant that the job allowed us time outdoors. Now, however, I wondered, did he mean outside the city limits? Should that have been my first clue that Rexx saw something the rest of us didn't?

Felix and Rose entered abruptly, startling me out of my memory and back into the present. They forced the sliding door shut and locked it behind them, turning the dial on the inside to a setting marked CLEANING IN PROGRESS.

"We have to be quick," Rose said. "Here, take this."

She handed me a pouch small enough to fit in my pocket. She also handed me a bundle of clothing. I opened the pouch. Inside were several of the small gadgets from the technology lab—the beetles. I counted them quickly. There were ten. Felix had come through, but I didn't know how the rest of the process would work.

"Thank you," I said. "There's one more thing I need you to do, and it might put you in danger."

"I don't understand why you have to leave," Felix said. "There has to be something else we can do from out here."

Rose walked over and grabbed Felix's arm. Her eyes were sharp, and she led him a few feet away and the two of them talked too quietly for me to hear.

After a moment, they turned back to me.

"We'll do anything," Felix said, a look of resignation and sadness in his eyes, and in that moment it became clear that the resignation and sadness weren't about his job or the risks he was about to incur, but rather, about the danger of losing a friend.

"What do you need us to do?" he asked.

"How do I . . ." I began, unsure how to phrase it without sounding like a complete idiot. I pulled out one of the beetles. "How do I make it so people out here can see the footage?"

"There are two settings on each beetle," Felix said. "Live and record. You can control them locally, but that will be difficult in your situation. Or we can control them for you." My eyes widened. "I will get a secure link to a journalist so the feed bypasses the Board's firewall. I'll be able to see the footage being picked up by each beetle and can then control which are set to live and which ones are recording footage to be sent out later. It, well, it would be best to control that part strategically so as to not give away too much at once."

"We'll attach one to you," Rose said, "and the rest you can just drop on the ground as soon as you cross the border."

That sounded easy enough.

"And what will happen to the nine that I drop?" I asked.

"I'll attach one to everyone else that shows," Felix said.

"And what if someone catches you?"

"Then they all go live, and the press takes it from there," he said. "It will be out regardless of what happens to me."

"Thank you," I said somberly. "Honestly, thank you both so much."

"Of course. Now, go put these on under your clothes," Rose said, gesturing to the bundle I was still holding in my hands.

I inspected the clothes. There was a long-sleeved fitted shirt and matching pants. They were made of a stretchy fabric with little specks of a golden copper color sprinkled throughout that caught the light.

"What are these for?" I asked, holding the shirt up.

"They are lined with carbon fiber tape. You wear them under your clothes. They might buy you some time anyway."

"How? What do they do?" I asked as I ran my fingers along the fabric.

"They should take the sting out of any shots from a pacifier, or any other directed energy weapon," Rose said.

"But they won't work if you get shot in the face. So, you know, try not to get shot in the face," Felix chimed in, and I could see the attempt to break the tension with some humor written over his worried face.

"Wait. This is a thing?" I asked. "There is something you can wear to stop the pacifiers from hurting you?"

"Yeah, it's actually pretty basic. The carbon fiber dissipates the charge and protects the target. I couldn't find any gloves or hats in time, though. We were in a hurry. Also, the clothes might be a little big."

I went into a stall and put them on under my other clothes. The carbon fiber fabric was a bit stiff, but the new shirt and pants fit well enough.

I came out, showing off my slightly lumpy outfit.

"It will work, but only until they confiscate your clothes," Felix said. "Still, try to capture as much footage as you can before then."

"By this time tomorrow, the whole world will see what the Board is capable of," I said, knowing full well I would be the catalyst for demonstrating such capabilities, and it wasn't going to be pleasant.

"Now, come here," Rose said, "and give us a proper hug, all right?"

Rose hugged me tightly, and so did Felix, and I wondered if they were the last hugs I would ever receive. We left the bathroom and headed to meet with the prime minister as I carried the weight of the beetles, and the future of my country, in my pocket.

"The Board is still unwilling to have anyone other than a citizen step foot on American soil," Laurel Austin said as we approached, as if we had already been in the middle of a conversation. "But they have given permission for you to be returned using one of our border patrol vehicles. The same kind that picked you up upon your arrival. I see no reason to wait. If you leave now, you can arrive before sunset. And once you arrive, they have promised to take the nuclear threat off the table. I wish you the best, Patch."

At that, she left. I wondered if she'd meant those last words.

I was soon led to a border patrol car, possibly the same one I'd arrived in, and Rose walked with me.

"Well, I guess this is it," Rose said as I climbed in.

"Wait, here—take this. They will if you don't," I said as I dug the scroll out of my pocket, careful not to accidentally remove any of the beetles, and then handed it to her. She clutched it in her hand and nodded.

"Thank you, Rose. Thank you for everything."

"Thank you," she replied. "I hope to see you again, Patch Collins. One way or another."

Within minutes the patrol car had detached from its charging pad, and I waved goodbye to Rose as I lifted up and out of view.

I watched as the city that had been my home for the last two and a half months disappeared in the distance.

The vehicle flew over the Walls so easily, I almost did not believe it. One second the border patrol vehicle was in Canada, and the next, it was in America and descending quickly toward the ground. The Walls didn't stand in its way at all. Of all the reactions I could have had at that moment—I laughed.

The laugh quickly disappeared as the vehicle approached the ground, and a team of people awaiting my arrival stood at attention. There were several Compos, and two men in suits. I could not recognize any of them yet, but one thing was certain—they wouldn't let me get far enough on my own to drop anything out of my pocket.

I thought fast and pulled the beetles out and sprinkled them on the floor of the car, pushing them as far against the door as they would go.

I landed and the door to the border patrol vehicle slid open. One of the men in suits approached, and as he got closer, I realized it was Elias.

"Nice to have you home," he said with that telltale smirk. He reached in and pulled me out of the vehicle himself, digging his fingers and thumbs into my forearms so tight, the bones hurt. I dragged my feet on the ground, determined to kick most of the beetles out of the vehicle, having no idea whether I'd succeeded.

Please, I thought as some kind of band was slipped over my head and secured around my eyes. It fused to the contours of my face, tightening at the same time as Elias' grip tightened around my arm.

"You aren't getting away this time," he said, his words laced with hatred and satisfaction drilling deep into my brain.

The fear was everywhere again, encapsulating me like a cocoon. I saw nothing, except for shapes periodically moving between me and the soft glow that was the sun. I was thrown down, and the cold ground approached with ferocity, stinging my skin, scratching my face, and causing me to gasp to catch my breath.

"Where are you taking me?" I spit out when the wind returned to my lungs. "Where's Rexx?"

"Don't worry. You will see each other again. We just have a little stop to make first." Someone picked up my feet and I was carried clumsily away from the vehicle. Someone kicked me in the side as we passed, and my ribs screamed with pain in response.

A cluster of hands shoved me into a small space, pushing and rearranging, their fingers harsh and unforgiving. Something was fastened around my wrists, and a jab and a sting burned my neck.

Then nothing.

I regained consciousness on a solid, cool surface. My eyes were still covered, and the chatter of people in the distance was vaguely recognizable. I moved my hands and was surprised to discover that they were free. My entire body ached as I made my way to all fours, my ribs protesting as I brought my hand up and pawed at the blindfold. Wedging a finger underneath the taut material, I pulled it down. Where was I? The scene around me didn't make sense, but yet it felt familiar.

I brought my hand down and supported my rib cage. I took a deep breath, feeling the air fill my lungs, trying to quickly decide if my ribs were bruised or broken. *Just bruised,* I thought.

I was on a gigantic oval platform that shined like glass. Bright lights bore down from the ceiling, bathing me in red, blue, and white. The lights were interspersed with thick hanging wires slung in a crisscross pattern. There was a row of seats out in the distance. In the other direction, the national emblem in a vivid and glowing red, covered the wall. It shimmered brightly and accosting, and I squinted. There were curtains in the distance, off to the right, thick and black, letting no light through from whatever was on the other side.

The voices kept chattering in the distance. They were behind the curtains—I was almost sure of it—but no one came into view. Then all at once the lights increased in intensity and I instinctively leaned back on my heels and brought my free forearm up to shield my eyes. The wall behind me lit up with five words. Five words that told me exactly where I was—*Portrait of a Redeemed Patriot.*

I leaned over and threw up all over the stage of the *America One* studio.

CHAPTER 23

Patch Collins

"LADIES AND GENTLEMEN," an amplified voice I knew well boomed behind me. She emerged from the back of the stage—a woman whose face was as recognizable to me as my own. A woman I somehow still had a fondness for because she was etched into my life story like initials carved into wood. Aelia Ramey.

Did she know the truth? Did she know what happened to her redeemed patriots or the lies that were told about what was outside of our walls, or did she truly believe that the role she was serving was righteous, as I once had? I looked up at her, searching her for answers, but found none.

Her chin was held high, and her eyes fixed on one of the cameras suspended from the ceiling and pointed in her direction. Compos emerged from the shadows until they were ringing the edge of the studio floor. Aelia came closer to me, and the ring of Compos raised their weapons. The lambent blue eyes of the pacifier stared me down with a warning to stay where I was. The stage lights intensified overhead, resulting in a blistering brightness that caused me to shield my eyes once again.

"You see before you a wounded animal," Aelia declared, her voice bounding out of her and filling the studio with a resonance she had performed a thousand times before. "An animal who was frightened of something they didn't understand and who ran away. As animals do. An animal who was backed nto a corner, biting and scratching and causing others great harm. What do you do with an animal who can't keep itself and others safe? Why, most would put it down, now, wouldn't they?"

Aelia approached until she was standing directly over me, her foot right in front of my knee. I stayed there, frozen. There was nowhere to go.

"But the Board isn't like most people. The Board is merciful. The Board knows what this animal needs is to be separated from the pack so that her questionable behavior, her toxic behavior, doesn't rub off on other docile creatures."

Aelia walked in circles around me as she spoke. The fog started to lift, my eyes adjusting to the light, and the urge to get out of there began to build. So did the rage. I wanted to run, to spit, to scream.

Aelia continued walking with smooth, confident steps. I wanted to grab her leg and bite. I wanted to watch the blood ooze out of her calf, to hear her scream, to prove to myself that she was as real as I was. Maybe she was right. Maybe I was an animal.

Focus. My eyes searched my perimeter.

I began to work through what I knew in my mind. *This probably isn't live*, I told myself. If I'd learned anything, it was that the Board would want to edit out anything that didn't fit their narrative before delivering their message to the people. I had a feeling this was simply the before shot. They would need a before shot if they were to present me as redeemed in the future.

I searched around me for something I'd almost forgotten. I looked down at my chest, ignoring the searing pain in my ribs as I bent my head, and there it was. Still nestled in the seam on my shoulder where Felix had attached it was one of the beetles.

"The Board knows no one is beyond redemption. This one may prove to be our greatest challenge, but America is a land full of challenges and there is no challenge too large for the Board. So we will prevail with a renewed commitment to safety and security. We will prevail. Say it with me. We will prevail!"

Then, out of the corner of my eye, I spotted something small crawling across the floor and up the hem of Aelia's pants, nearly disappearing as it morphed to match the color of the fabric behind it. It was another beetle. I lowered my head toward the ground to hide my expression.

If Felix had come through, he was controlling the actions of these tiny pieces of technology and it was possible the entire world was watching. What had he said? He told me that they could either be set to live or record. I wondered what they were set to now. If they killed me on this stage, at least I'd accomplished this one thing.

I sank farther back on my heels and leaned on one of my hands. My sudden movement caused Aelia to recoil from me like I was a snake that had just rattled.

Elias Stevens strolled out onto the stage. "That's enough. Time to go," he said, casting Aelia an approving nod. She tossed him a plastered smile and walked offstage, the beetle still clinging to her clothing.

Elias approached until he was standing over me, and his smug smile stretched as he cocked his head to the side and bent down on one knee. He leaned in and whispered, "We put an end to this now, Patricia Collins. Now that the world has gotten a glimpse of you, you are no longer needed. You'll make for a nice little warning. A nice reminder."

I tried to push down the fear, the skin-crawling sensation that his nearness elicited. I remembered his words when I'd spoken to him in Canada. I remembered his promise to reunite me with Rexx. I knew not to trust it, but even so, I'd had the audacity to hope ever so slightly that that was where they were taking me. I hoped they were taking me to him.

Every instinct in me wanted to plead with him to let me see Rexx one more time, as he had promised. *That's not why you came back*, I told myself. *You came back to show them.*

"A reminder of what you are capable of?" I asked through gritted teeth.

A blinding pain obscured my vision after he slapped me hard with the back of his hand. I fell backward as my body contorted sideways and hit the hard floor of the stage, cheekbone first. The pain radiating out from my ribs as I fell was so intense that it quickly eclipsed the pain in my face. I hissed air through my teeth as I opened my eyes once again, determined to not let him win this easily.

I pulled myself back up to my knees and wiped the blood away from under my eye where his ring had lacerated my cheek.

"Why are you smiling, Patricia?" Elias said. He watched with a manic curiosity as I put my hand over my ribs, supported my side, and sat back up.

"I see you're having trouble," he said, the smirk gone and replaced with pursed lips and narrowed eyes. "Here, let me help you." He grabbed a fistful of my hair and dragged me toward him, pulling me upright until I was kneeling eye to eye with him. I tried to put my hand on the ground to steady myself, but I couldn't reach. Panic started to rise in me. I opened my eyes wide, trying to find something to ground me, something to focus on. A vein in his forehead beat beneath his taut, medically enhanced skin.

I held in the pain, letting the rage coat me in armor as my scalp and my ribs silently screamed. I kept my eyes open, unwilling to give him the satisfaction of looking away.

"You know, we have all of these fancier weapons now, but sometimes the old standbys are the best," he said, and with one hand still clutched in my short hair, he removed something from his pocket with his other hand and started twirling it around his fingers. I couldn't see what it was.

"What the Board has built here, Patricia," he said, lowering his voice to a hissing whisper, "is stronger than you. And I want you to feel in your final moments how true that really is. You left. You made it out, and yet you still ended up back here with your life in my hands. That is how powerful I am. That is how powerful the Board is." At that he raised what was in his pocket. It was a multi-tool, and it was currently flipped open to reveal a knife similar to the one Rexx and I had used to cut the chips out of our hands.

"Those words on the National Emblem," he continued, "'security,' 'unity,' 'pride,' 'strength.' They are more than just words. They are a way of life, and when you jeopardize them, you deserve to suffer."

He took the knife and held it up to my throat, tracing the blade gently up and down my carotid artery. Then he whispered, even more softly, "Don't worry, dear. We'll give you a good story. Now, are you ready?"

I tried to imagine all the people who could be watching this very moment. Then I did something I didn't expect. I tried to think of five things, not about one person, as my father had taught me, but five details about those who defined me. Five details about those who made me who I was, and whose strength I needed in that moment.

I thought of Rexx and inhaled beneath the blade of the knife, imagining the smell of his cologne, the scent of cinnamon that filled my senses when I was in his arms. I thought of Oliver, and of his fingers creating beauty and sound that filled the halls of the old church. I thought of my father, and his bravery and conviction. I thought of Noah, and his continuous quest for knowledge and truth. Finally I thought of my mother, and in that moment, I let the forgiveness I felt for her wash over me and hoped that in my final moments, the feeling would travel to her.

Then I swallowed hard, felt the blade press against my throat with just a tiny bit more pressure, locked eyes with Elias Stevens, and whispered back, "Yes."

"That's a good girl," he replied, and pulled the blade away as he wrapped his hand around the knife handle to get a firmer grip, and I finally let my eyes close.

"Sir. Sir, we have a problem!" a voice yelled, accompanied by hurried footsteps.

"Can it wait?" Elias snapped back, his grip on my hair tightening and jerking my head to the side as he turned. I inhaled swift breaths of air through my nose as a tear trickled down my face.

The knife sliced the surface of my skin in Elias's distraction, and I held my breath and stifled a scream.

"No, sir. It can't."

Elias let out an angry groan as he released his clutch on my hair and I fell to the floor. Elias stood and stepped away, making a subtle gesture to a nearby Compo, who stepped toward me and lifted his pacifier, pointing it right at my chest, warning me not to move an inch.

My entire body began to tremble and I grasped the floor for something to hold on to as my surroundings started to blur. I reached my hand up to my neck and it came away covered in blood. I could feel my blood pressure sinking and myself along with it. I wiped the blood on the floor and tried to think.

Stop it, I told myself. *It's just a scratch. You have to keep it together. You're still alive.* I opened my eyes to see a man in a suit talking with Elias. Was it another Board member?

"There has been a security breach. There is leaked footage coming from the studio. We're trying to pinpoint the source."

Elias turned to look at me, and I looked toward the floor, trying to hide my expression.

"It's not her," the other man said. "It's coming from someone else."

"Show me," Elias replied. Then I spotted another beetle crawling up the back of Elias's suit.

"What about her?" the other man asked, gesturing back at me.

"Pacify her and move her out of the way. I'll deal with her later."

The other man nodded toward one of the Compos who had his pacifier pointed at me. Fear began to rise again as I stared at the blue eye of the weapon and remembered what it felt like. Then, without a second's hesitation, he fired, and I collapsed once again to the ground.

The Compo clutched my foot and dragged me across the stage, leaving a trail of blood behind. As he did, my clothing shifted, revealing the dark fabric with the thin carbon fiber flecks. I lay on the floor, forcing myself to be still though my body demanded I move to accommodate the pulsing in my cheek, the aching in my ribs, the searing pain in my neck.

I waited until I could no longer hear footsteps or voices, then I looked around. A large black curtain hung behind me. There were cameras suspended from the ceiling. The weight of everything that had just happened, of how close I had just come to certain death, felt suffocating, but I couldn't let it overwhelm me at the moment. If I was going to make a move, it would have to be fast.

There was a door slightly behind me and to my right, but I had no idea if it would be locked or not. I didn't even know where I was or what was outside of this building. Perhaps I was in the middle of a bustling urban center, or underground, below a compound.

I rationalized that I should at least try. That even if I didn't make it far, that the footage captured of whatever was on the other side of that door could help, and being shot down with a lethal weapon might be less painful than having my throat carved apart slowly.

I gazed at the door. *I think I can make it*, I told myself. *I have no idea what is on the other side, but I think I can make it.*

Just as I was summoning the mental energy to ignore my pain and quickly push off the ground, my leg was grabbed once again, and I was being yanked backward.

I'd lost my chance. A solitary tear fell across my nose.

CHAPTER 24

Patch Collins

I STAYED AS lifeless as possible while unknown pairs of hands hauled me out of the building. When I chanced opening my eyes, I was confused. I was horizontal in the back seat of a flying vehicle that was instantly familiar. Two people were sitting in front of me. There were odd shapes on their faces—dark triangles, squares, and ovals.

I sat up quickly and defensively as one of them slid red glasses down the bridge of his nose and said with a smile, "Temporary tattoos. Fools the facial-recognition software."

It all started to register as the other turned and reached her hand out to me. "You're okay, Patch," Rose said. "Did you think we were really just going to let you do this alone?"

Tears of relief filled my eyes as my head fell back against the seat and I let out a deep sound, somewhere between a laugh and a sigh.

"Yes," I said as my eyes closed, and the relative safety settled over me and I was filled with gratitude and love for the two people in front of me. "For a minute there I thought you were."

I couldn't believe they had come for me. I had never even considered it a possibility. I released a sliver of the tension from pretending to be unconscious, from narrowly escaping death, from trying to ignore pain, from holding back the rage I wanted to unchain on everyone around me for the past day, the past week, the past two months, the past year.

"Hold tight," Felix said. "Even if those bastards didn't see us coming, we can sure count on them seeing us leaving."

Felix pulled up sharply as soon as we were out of the path of the building. He rose high in the air until a sensor alerted us we had reached the highest altitude possible. The sun had long since set, and the lights of the studio faded into the background. He flew for a few minutes, then dipped dramatically, and the ground approached at an alarming speed.

My stomach knotted as my head swiveled from side to side, looking for any sign we were being followed. Even the stars shining brightly in the sky were suspect, as their lights mimicked that of drones.

Felix leveled us out at about ten feet above the ground and all three of us inhaled so loudly that the sound filled the interior of the vehicle.

Felix kept the car low in the dark as we navigated over abandoned desert land that jutted and dipped repeatedly. I realized that now Felix was barely interacting with the control panel. The car was staying a set distance above obstacles—up and down, around and over.

"Surveillance is really spotty anywhere other than urban areas," Felix said. "The Board has really painted itself into a corner there. The drones will be out searching for us soon, though, if they aren't already. They'll expect us to go to the closest abandoned zone, so we'll have to go a bit farther."

"Where are we?" I asked. I'd been unconscious for the trip to the studio and had no idea how long it had taken me to get there. Come to think of it, I didn't even know if it was the same day. "How long has it been since I arrived at the border?"

"You were unconscious for a little over twenty-four hours as far as we could tell," Rose said. "They took you to some kind of holding facility and then loaded you into a plane. They kept giving you injections in your neck."

I reached up and touched my neck. The blood was drying, and it was tender and puffy. A wave of nausea rushed through me when I applied pressure. After needles and knives, I would be perfectly happy for nothing to ever touch my neck again.

"And we're in Nevada."

Nevada, I thought. *So close to home.*

Rose opened up a computer system and set it on her lap. I recognized it as the same system Felix had been updating occasionally in the lab. His words—*I want to make sure we have this information saved somewhere portable*—came back to me.

"I can't believe you guys came for me. I mean, how did you do it?" I said through a fat lip that was getting harder to talk through.

Felix and Rose exchanged a glance I couldn't read.

"Getting in has never been the problem, Patch," Felix said. "Do you really think it's the Walls that have kept people out? They can be climbed with an extension ladder, or a rope. It can be flown over with one of our cars."

Of course I'd realized this, hadn't I? I knew this even before I escaped myself, but there was part of me that still resisted it. The Walls were a symbol, only as powerful as the fear they evoked.

"So you just flew right in? I mean, there has to be more to it than that."

"Essentially, yes, but carefully and in an area that isn't closely monitored. We did it at the exact moment you were meeting the Board at the Walls. We figured most of their attention would be elsewhere. Then we found somewhere to park for the night while we waited to see where they would take you."

"So you've had this planned?" I said, looking around the car and seeing supplies taking up almost every single free inch of space. "When I asked you for the beetles, you brought them to me, no questions asked. How did you know what I wanted to do?"

"We saw it as an opportunity," Felix said. "An opportunity to honor an old friend, and a new one."

"And we didn't get this far for you to just get sent back to be killed," Rose said. "That's not why we joined the team. Now we have a chance to expose the truth, and we're going to make it count."

Rose looked back at me and smiled, the kind of smile you give someone when you are in on a secret together, and then the expression on her face quickly changed.

"Oh," she said. "It's worse than I realized. You're hurt. Why did you let us keep blabbing on like this? Hang on. Let me climb back there."

"What? Oh, no. It's nothing. I'm fine, really," I said as I tried to sit up straighter in my seat to show her I was all right—an unconvincing performance as I hissed air through my teeth and gave up halfway.

"Well, maybe a little," I admitted as Rose turned on an extra interior light, casting a soft blue glow around the vehicle. "It's my ribs and my cheekbone, mostly. I was kicked hard when they brought me in, and Elias hit me. Did you get that on camera? Are people seeing that? Oh my Board, are they seeing us right now?" I looked down to see the beetle was indeed still attached to my shoulder. I cupped my hand over it.

"No, no, don't worry. They can't see us right now," Felix said. "That would put us in some danger, wouldn't it? I'm controlling which ones are set to release footage, and which are just capturing footage for later."

I nodded, and removed my hand as relief washed over me.

"We really lucked out that they took you to the studios," Felix said as he flew. "Was one of the few major locations we hadn't been able to pinpoint yet. Now that we know where the *America One* Studios are, and they happen to be in the same state as the site of the 2029 bombing, I have a good feeling we're going to find the headquarters somewhere around here too. Hopefully, Elias Stevens will lead us right to them. Tonight, if we're lucky."

I remembered seeing the beetle crawling up his back, and the man in the suit telling Elias that footage had been leaked. What footage was it? Felix must have been controlling what had been released if they hadn't found the beetle on Elias yet.

"Right now there is only one currently set to live, and footage is being released as it is captured," Felix continued, as if reading my mind.

"Released where?" I asked.

"To an anonymous drop box James set up that can be accessed by the public."

"James? You mean the prime minister's chief of staff?"

"Yup," said Felix with a smile. "Which means we should have a captive audience of reporters and citizen journalists hungrily waiting for more. For the first time in sixty years, those outside of the government are getting an up-close-and-personal look into America."

His words sank in, and I couldn't help but smile too. We had done something. Even if everything else went wrong, I had done what I'd set out to do. I'd provided a window to the truth.

"Which beetle is still set to live?"

"Oh. Well, we couldn't set the one on you or on Mr. Stevens live just yet, because we didn't want to give ourselves away. So it's the one on that blond woman at the studio. Amelia."

"Aelia," I said, correcting him. I turned my head away for a moment, unable to shake the feeling that I'd just ended the woman's life. When the Board traced something back to her, they wouldn't be kind, even if they knew it wasn't her fault. Making examples of those who didn't deserve it was one of the things the Board did best.

"Yeah, right," Felix said. "Once we get someplace safe, we'll review the rest of the footage captured and release what makes sense. That reminds me—here."

He handed me a small rectangular piece of silver about an inch wide and three inches in length. A slightly indented oval pad sat in the center.

"What is this?" I asked, feeling the smooth rounded outside edge.

"We each have one," he said. "Hold your thumb firmly on top of the face for ten seconds. If you do that, everything that has been recorded so far, by any of the beetles, will be released. But don't use it unless absolutely necessary, as it will give up our location and information that may be best kept to ourselves for now."

"Thank you," I said as I slid it into my pocket.

"That is only to be used if it doesn't look like we are going to make it." Felix turned around in his seat and locked eyes with me as he said the words.

"I understand." I felt the contours of the rectangular device through my pocket, its presence reassuring and anxiety-inducing all at once.

"So James is in on this too?" I asked, still trying to piece everything together.

"Well, we left soon after you did, and we needed someone we could trust," he said. "James doesn't always agree with all of Austin's choices. He wasn't too happy about the council's reluctance to intervene and we picked up on it. Especially considering the prime minister's history."

"Do you mean that he knows—well, do you all know—about her time in America?"

"Well, we had a hunch, and you just confirmed it for us," Rose chimed in.

It was a lot to process, and I didn't know what to ask next. Though I didn't know him well, I was suddenly afraid for James. Plus, as soon as the Security Council realized Rose and Felix were gone, and with them, government-owned supplies, they wouldn't be too happy. Then we would have multiple governments after us.

"Don't worry," Felix continued, as if reading my mind once again. "James's part should be, or will be, over soon. It's probably over already and likely only took him an hour. Luckily, Canada has shield laws in place to protect journalism sources. He should be okay, provided he doesn't do anything too obvious. I told him he could blame it all on me if . . . Well, anyway, they'll realize we're gone soon, if they haven't already."

Rose had climbed into the back seat with me and was digging around behind us for something. She grabbed a bag, hoisted it onto her lap, and started pulling supplies out of it.

"Here, these should help." She cleaned and then put a bandage on my right cheekbone, below my eye. The bandage was cool and instantly soothing. Then she handed me a larger one, helping me to put it over my ribs and readjust my clothing. I unconsciously let out a relieved sigh as the pain in my ribs subsided to a dull ache.

"Is this the same kind of bandage Felix gave me when I hurt my wrist?" I said, realizing as I said it that my wrist had indeed felt better by the next day and had healed remarkably quickly. Rose nodded as she packed away the supplies.

"What are they made of?" I asked.

"They are coated with a mixture of hydrogel, topical pain medication, and sensors that provide a low-grade electrical current to the skin to speed up recovery. Just leave it on through the morning and it should feel worlds better."

"Thank you," I said as I finished readjusting my clothes. "Oh, and thanks again for these. These clothes are remarkable. When I was shot, it just felt like static. Like touching a doorknob after shuffling around on a carpet."

"Glad to hear it," Rose said, and my eyes kept darting to the shapes on her face.

"So tell me again what is all over your faces?" I asked as the blue light lit up the shapes on Rose's dark skin.

"Temporary tattoos," Rose said. "We've found that applying them to someone's face in a variety of specifically designed bold shapes and symbols can fool facial-recognition software. At least, the old kind still used in America. The software is trained to detect the familiar shape of a face, looking for the standard two eyes, nose, and a mouth, but these extra symbols confuse them, so the subject does not resemble a traditional face, and the software often moves on. If the tattoos work correctly, then if we are spotted by a surveillance camera or an overhead drone, it might not even register us as people and hopefully won't send any kind of warning."

"Wow," I said. "You guys really seem to have thought of everything."

"They might buy us some time," Rose said. "But we shouldn't underestimate the Board. They may have handicapped themselves by refusing to evolve and by keeping the surveillance efforts primarily in urban areas, but they aren't stupid."

Rose pulled out a small kit, and before long I had a large indigo upside-down triangle in the middle of my forehead that extended from right above either eyebrow and down the bridge of my nose. I was also given a symbol that looked like an elongated sideways *S* underneath my unbandaged cheekbone.

"Oh. Yikes," I said, catching a glimpse of myself in the reflection in the window, and I started to laugh. "I don't know if I recognize *myself* as human." Felix and Rose laughed too, and before long, despite the pain in my ribs, we were all laughing so hard that it was difficult to stop.

"She can still laugh," Felix said once we all finally stopped. "That's good. We're going to need a bit of resiliency to get through this."

I smiled.

"What else is this? What's in these bags?" I asked, looking around the car. I unzipped one of the bags—a small one. It was filled with beetles. I suddenly had a feeling there was more to the plan than just sharing the footage from the few I'd already snuck in.

"There we have everything we could grab after Austin told us the news we were being shut down, before you even decided to come back," Rose said. I raised an eyebrow, and she smiled. "Everything we thought would be useful and won't be affected by the firewalls. We have some defense equipment, solar panels, food, several beetles, and every personal projector we could find." She unzipped a neighboring bag, much larger than the one that had held the beetles, then patted two others.

There were three giant bags filled with projectors—all the size of a large button. Turns out personal projectors were something almost every single person in the world owned. They were as commonplace outside as the array of video game accessories were in America, and available in bins in almost any place you could buy electronics—and this year's model could hover.

"What are the projectors for?" I asked.

"We just thought they might come in handy if we have to deliver a message," Felix said. "Now that you've been patched up, we can figure out our next move. I'd feel better if we covered at least one hundred miles, so we are headed toward Zone one hundred eight in central Nevada."

We drove through several abandoned towns, and though we could only see glimmers of scenery through the headlights, it was enough to remind me of Wildcliff—the town with the library that Rexx and I had passed through.

As we passed boarded-up houses, gas stations, shops, and warehouses, I wondered how many of these buildings had served as pop-up incinerators for political dissidents. I imagined the towns full, lived-in, a country vastly different from the one I had grown up in.

"You know," Rose said as she settled in next to me, "I've been reading about America for my whole life. When I was eight, I did a history report on it in school."

I smiled at this, imagining her as a child in a classroom where she was permitted to learn about worlds different from her own. Maybe there were other eight-year-olds around the world who thought about us.

Rose started repacking and organizing the supplies in her vicinity. "I gotta tell you, I didn't expect it to have changed this much. I mean, the Board has kept everything going but, Patch, this barely resembles the America of the past. The Board is scared; otherwise, they would never have reacted this strongly. Everything outside of the urban areas is rotting. Seeing it up close and traveling across it only confirms it. They don't have a hold on anything except the urban areas, and they don't have the resources they did when they first started out and the restructuring took place. They are crumbling. Without the Compos, they are nothing."

"Maybe," I said, hoping she was right.

We passed a beautiful farmhouse. It resembled the one in the painting at the American History Museum, and I imagined living in it—planting lavender out front that would encircle a larger gardening bed where I would harvest vegetables for dinner. When I imagined it, Rexx was there with me. We took walks in the yard and worked on fixing up the house with our own hands, as Oliver had with his home in Zone 36.

I let my head fall to the back of the seat as we drove. I let myself feel him, remember what it felt like to see him smile at me from across the conference table at work. What it was like to swim with him in the lake. How much I wanted to be once again in his arms on the floor of the church after dancing to Oliver's music and stepping all over each other's feet. I let the dream linger for just a moment, but then it faded.

This was not that world. This was a world where multiple governments were ready to see me eliminated, and Rexx wasn't with me. He felt so close, yet so far away. *Where are you?*

We continued for nearly two hours in a darkness illuminated only by our headlights, until we approached our destination—Zone 108. A large tower rose up from the ground in the distance.

"The old radar tower," Rose said as she pointed.

A gigantic triangular metal sign, with a diamond in the middle that read NORTH SPRINGS AIR FORCE BASE, was lying on the ground. We navigated around it and toward several large buildings.

"Are you sure this is abandoned?" I asked nervously as the adrenaline started to creep back in. I expected Compos to emerge from the shadows and surround us, but they didn't.

"We went through the satellite footage. There has been no human activity anywhere near this site for years," Rose said.

"Did you bring masks?" I asked. It was the first time I'd thought of it, and I felt foolish. "High levels of air and soil pollution are the top reason for zone designation," I added. "I don't know the specifics on this zone, but we should probably play it safe."

"In that bag there," Felix said, pointing to a case in the back. Rose opened it and grabbed something and handed it to me. I watched Rose put the thing on, and I followed her lead.

"Breathe through your nose as much as you can," said Rose. "The filters are strong, but they don't cover your mouth. These were all we could find in a pinch."

It looked like one of those nasal clips people who snored wore when they were sleeping. It was nowhere near the size of the regulation masks from the Natural Resource Department.

"Do you have the satellite images up, Rose?" Felix asked as we navigated around old shells of airplanes with U.S. AIR FORCE written on the side.

"I've got them here. Go around this building to the left, to the old hangar," she said, pointing to two wide-arched buildings up ahead.

We pulled in front of the shorter of the two buildings. "You both stay here and keep a lookout," Felix said. He jumped out of the vehicle and walked up to the closest door. We watched as he tried it. It was locked.

He took something out of his pocket and placed it on the door. Nothing appeared to happen, but soon Felix easily swung the door inward, disappeared inside, and a moment later the large hangar door was sliding open.

Rose jumped in front of the control panel and navigated our vehicle into the hangar, parking it between two rusted teal airplanes. I wondered if they still worked. We climbed out, and Felix closed the hangar door. We took off our masks and the smell of rotting wood filled my nostrils. Though the beams were metal, the rest of the ceiling looked as if it could cave in on us at any moment. Shadows danced around the perimeter of the hangar, exposing piles of abandoned military equipment that was likely broken or shown to have no value. Dust floated in front of my field of vision as my eyes adjusted, the lights on our vehicle having gone dark.

Felix passed out headlamps, then swung a backpack over his shoulder and grabbed two more with his free hands. Rose carried a few pieces of solar equipment, and I followed suit and picked up two of the large bags.

We skirted the edge of the hangar, carefully stepping over dried puddles of oil and scattered, partially decomposed garbage. My eyes caught a small beverage can lying on its side, similar to the one I'd seen in the van, but this one read LA CROIX. Next to it was a large plastic tub, empty, with the words CHEESE BALLS barely readable on a warped, faded orange label. I kicked some of the garbage out of the way, and walked until we found a small room that looked like it used to be an office.

"This will be easier to heat," Felix said as he led us into it. There was a desk and two chairs knocked sideways in the corner, their fabric looking like it had been chewed through by rodents. Everything was covered in several layers of dust and I reached out my finger and swiped at it.

"I think I saw a broom out there," Rose said as we dropped our stuff on the floor.

Felix illuminated the room with a light, set up a heater, and started unpacking and sorting our supplies. I found myself inching toward the heater as I watched him unpack.

"First things first, we get our solar panels set up," Felix said, "because the battery life on some of this stuff isn't going to get us very far, and then we get one of these little guys on its way to Oliver." He held up one of the beetles. "Chances are, they will notice one soon, so we need as much information as quickly as possible. We are far from the compound, so best for it to start the journey now so it will be ready and waiting in the morning."

Felix left to take the beetle outside and set up the solar equipment.

Rose grabbed an old, decaying wooden trash can from underneath the desk and began sweeping up some of the trash and dust on the floor, which filled it easily. The rest she pushed to the edge of the room, resulting in a pile the size of a large load of laundry.

"Door or desk side?" she asked as she then opened three inflatable sleeping mats she'd unpacked from a curiously small bag.

"Hmm. I guess I'll take desk side."

"I'll take the middle, and give Felix the door," she said as she started rolling out the mats. "Knowing him, I bet he'll be up to check on his gadgets a few times anyway."

When Felix returned, he ignored the dust-covered desk completely and began setting up a workstation in the corner that included the same monitor Rose had been holding in the vehicle, a small light, and a couple of the unpacked bags. Questions were on the tip of my tongue, but my eyes were heavy, my body ached, and the sleeping mat was calling to me.

"I'm going to stay up a bit longer," he said as he dimmed the lights, "so I can check on our released beetles one more time, but you two try to get some rest. Things will move fast tomorrow, and I have a feeling we are going to wake up to multiple government leaders angry with us."

Rose tossed me an inflatable pillow and a thin blanket, and I settled down on the mat next to the desk. It was surprisingly comfortable and molded to my spine, and I stretched my body nearly the full length of the mat and pulled the blanket up underneath my chin.

I looked across the space between me and Rose as she took the band out of her braid and lay down. Her full purple hair swirled around her into a crown as she ran her fingers through its curls. I closed my eyes as a flash of Amara and me in our dorm room as children raced through my head.

The building creaked around us, and the air was suddenly too thin and, despite the space heaters, slightly too cold. I didn't know how sleep would be possible, with all the information running through my brain about a plan I still didn't fully grasp and the aftermath of everything that had happened today.

I opened my eyes and looked once again to the mat next to me.

"Rose?" I said.

"Yeah, Patch?" she replied in a sleepy voice as she yawned and covered herself with the blanket.

"Thank you," I said as I reached my hand out through the space between us.

"No. Thank you," she said as she smiled. She wrapped her hand around mine. Suddenly I was eight years old again, in my dorm room bed, holding the hand of a friend, and I let exhaustion overtake me.

CHAPTER 25

Robbie Webb

AFTER THE END of another extended shift, Webb walked straight home from work and fell face-first with exhaustion onto the couch, throwing his helmet onto the floor but not bothering to remove his bulky boots or uniform. He was still thinking of the old man from the other day, and of the mark on his arm.

Webb hadn't seen Constance in over a week. Ideology classes were extended, and things had ratcheted up at the Compliance Department as well, though there was still no specific reason given to the public for the changes. As Webb lay there on the couch, he thought about that morning, when Commander Lewis had walked in and made an announcement.

"I have bad news, Officers," he'd said. "Footage was leaked from the *America One* Studios. The Board is still trying to determine if this is the fault of a traitorous operation, or of foreign terrorists. As we work to pinpoint the source, this doesn't leave the Compliance Department. We are operating on extended shifts today. The Board is confident the threat will be addressed quickly."

"Thank the Board," every single Compliance Officer said in unison, including Webb, though the pit in his stomach that had been present for months suddenly seemed to double in size.

The commander spoke up to the line of officers. "With the threat level climbing over the recent days, we are also going to have to work harder than ever to weed out potential traitors within our borders. Good thing is, we've been preparing for this our whole careers." As Lewis said the words, a look of hunger and yearning spread over his face.

"Anyone with subversive thoughts needs to be eliminated from the public population." He paced back and forth in front of the officers. "Immediately."

Lewis walked past each individual Compo, stopping for a spell to make full eye contact. Each returned the gesture with a straightened spine and a nod of confirmation, like players on a football team being given their play.

"This is a new challenge before us," Lewis continued, "but we are not the strongest and safest nation on Earth for nothing, and I expect all of you will rise to the challenge. Your country needs you."

Webb's arm hung to the floor off the edge of the couch and his wrist started to buzz, pulling him out of his recollection. There was a message on his ID.

Ever since he had visited Zone 36, a feeling washed over him whenever his ID beeped. That feeling was dread. Dread of what that message contained. Dread that the moment would finally come when he would be taken out of his daughter's life forever. Dread that he wouldn't get to see who she grew into, and whether it would be someone who questioned or followed blindly, and which one he even hoped for at this point.

He lifted his arm and pressed to bring the message into view.

Mandatory live viewing. Swipe your chip on the nearest viewing device, or press here.

Webb sighed loudly. It was after ten p.m. There was almost never a mandatory viewing in the evening, especially this late. The camera in the corner would have caught his exasperated sigh, but he was starting not to care. Webb pressed the triangle on his ideation device, not even having enough energy to flip over and watch whatever it was on the full-wall screen.

Webb's ID projected a viewing square into the area above his wrist. The words *America One: Helping Our Nation Succeed* scrolled across the screen, followed by the words *Emergency Edition.*

Webb sat up abruptly. *Shit, what now?* he wondered, but part of him knew. He knew the Board would have to craft a narrative for the public to explain the recent changes. A narrative that would both reinforce the knowledge of the Board, and fill citizens with a sense of duty to step up for their country. His exhaustion vanished and was replaced by adrenaline.

Aelia Ramey walked on-screen, and it was evident immediately that something was wrong. She was limping. Her white hair, normally smooth and perfectly styled, was in ruins. As she walked closer to the camera, it became obvious she'd been crying, and trails of makeup stained her cheeks. The camera zoomed out, showing more of the stage she was standing on. Webb's stomach dropped. On all sides were Compliance Officers, their pacifiers pointed directly at Aelia.

Canned gasps escaped the screen. Aelia kept her eyes straight ahead, as if she were looking—no, pleading—with everyone watching. Webb stared right back at her, and he soon projected the image on the large screen across the room.

A voice interrupted the display. It was loud and deep and unrecognizable by Webb. A man stepped into view. Like his voice, his face was not one Webb was familiar with and he squinted instinctively to look closer, despite the largeness of the screen.

The man was wearing an outfit that matched the look of those Aelia usually wore on-screen—designed specifically to coordinate with the set of *America One*. His suit featured glistening stripes of vertical red ribbing down the sides.

"Allow me to introduce myself: I am the new host of *America One*. Before we get to our regular programming, I have a special message for you today from the Board. Do as they say, and everything will work out just fine. You will be safe. You will be secure. You will be united."

A chill started to inch its way up Webb's spine. The man held out something between his thumb and forefinger—a tiny piece of technology the size of an insect.

"Some of you may have heard that there have been rumors of rogue Americans acting in a way that does not have our best interests at heart and puts all of us in danger."

A camera zoomed in on the piece of technology as he let it settle into the palm of his hand. It seemed to disappear until the camera zoomed even closer, and Webb found himself forgetting that Aelia was on the same stage as he strained to get a good look at the object. It melted into its background, shifting color to the same hue as the man's chalky skin.

"If you find one of these, you are to report it immediately. You might be wondering what it is, but do not worry. The Board will worry about those details so that you don't have to. All you need to know is that these are dangerous and they do not belong. Check your clothes and your surroundings when you return home from work, and if you see one of these on the floor, on yourself, or on someone else, it is to be immediately reported to the Compliance Department."

The man walked in a small semicircle behind Aelia, and he handed the piece of technology to a Compliance Officer standing nearby.

"Let's see what will happen if you do not."

"No, no, no." The words came out before Webb had time to stop them.

The Compos surrounding Aelia walked closer to her until they were each only about two feet away, and then they raised their weapons. An invisible force struck Aelia and then she was convulsing on the stage. Her head hit the floor with a sound so terrible, it made Webb jump. The Compos didn't let up there, the way a Compliance Officer was trained to stop once the suspect was incapacitated. They each took a step closer, and the electricity kept its hold on Aelia's petite body, bending and thrashing it in unnatural ways as the camera zoomed in closer.

"No! What the hell do you think you're doing?" Webb was no longer looking at the scene unfolding; he was now staring directly at the overhead camera in his own living room. "For Board's sake, stop! This isn't protocol!"

His eyes landed back on the screen. The Compos kept at it, and a red-hot anger grew inside Webb to a level he had never felt before. Anger at being one of them. Anger at convincing himself for years that he was there to protect anyone other than those in power.

His door swung open behind him. Webb heard it, and in that moment he knew with absolute certainty that his actions had finally caught up to him.

He didn't turn around. Not yet.

"It's time to go, traitor," Evan said.

Webb let Evan's words circle him as he stared straight ahead, his eyes still on Aelia's white hair spread across the floor and her usually meticulous clothes now skewed and untucked. She was the image of the perfect American patriot, the one who kept every single American company each night, and she was now nothing but a vulnerable shape sprawled out before him.

Robbie's cheeks grew warm, his muscles grew tight, his body suddenly a vector for the rage pulsing through him. He watched as the limp body of Aelia Ramey was dragged off the stage as an example and warning to every single person watching that not even the most loved and admired among them were to be trusted.

When she was gone, Webb slowly turned to face his coworkers. Evan and Jason stood in the doorway. They didn't run at him, didn't pull out their weapons. They just looked at the camera, and then looked at him.

Webb took several resolute steps forward and held his arms, still pulsing with rage, out in front of him. His problem wasn't with them, and this was the only way he would be allowed back in the station.

Thirty minutes later an alert showed up on Celeste Webb's ID.

Robbie Webb is being held in federal custody on charges of treason. An investigation into the charges has begun. You will be informed of the results.

CHAPTER 26

Rexx Moreno

ELIAS STEVENS WALKED into Rexx's room in the middle of the night with footsteps that were heavy and loaded. The lights flashed on, and Rexx squinted to see him. His face was beet red and his brow was misted with sweat that glistened in the overhead light.

"How are they doing this?" he screamed in a voice so laced with contempt that Rexx's body tensed as he tried to make sense of his surroundings. Rexx didn't know who "they" were and what they were doing. He didn't have any answers, so he didn't offer any. He had a feeling the Board member knew this, but just needed somewhere to direct his frustration.

"How is she doing this? I had her!" he yelled, the change from *they* to *her* not lost on Rexx as he watched the man pace in front of his bed. The Board member looked manic, his pupils dilated. "We had her. We had her. There must have been a weapon malfunction." Elias threw something at Rexx, and it landed on his chest. It was a small piece of technology. It looked kind of like a beetle and was very obviously broken.

"Do you know what this is?" he roared at Rexx but gave him no time to answer. "All of our work. All of it. She doesn't know what she is doing. This is insanity."

The man continued to talk, but his words were no longer aimed at Rexx and they were largely intangible, rapid mumbles, as if he were attempting to talk himself through a math problem. Was Patch back in America? Rexx didn't know for sure, but he knew something she had done had rattled the man in front of him. It was almost as if the Board member had forgotten that Rexx was there as he paced, now looking paler and sallower than the red shade he sported when he'd first walked in.

Rexx didn't know what to say, so he opted for some thoughts that had been swirling through his mind since he'd emerged from his coma. "You know you can't condition human nature out of people," Rexx finally said, causing the Board member to turn to him with a startled expression. "But I suspect you already know that, or why would the compounds exist in the first place?"

Rexx expected rage to follow, but the Board member just stared at him, his manic eyes imploring him to continue.

"I mean, seventy years ago, sure," Rexx kept on. "You tried. But to still need them today. To still need the facilities to hold that many people. That many political prisoners. Well, your plans must not be as successful as you thought they would be. Not working as well as you would like to think."

"What do you know about our work?" the Board member spit back, the red returning to his cheeks. "How dare you pretend to know anything about what we have built and why."

"Fine," Rexx said. "Then tell me why. Why not just let the rest of the world in? Why keep this up after all this time? If Patch really made it out and elicited this response, then there is more out there for us. More than what we've been taught."

The Board member leaned over the bed, putting his hands on either side of Rexx's feet.

"Listen, boy," he said. "We are the greatest nation on Earth, and we will not have the legacy of our fathers and grandfathers ruined. We will *not* have a twenty-two-year-old girl make us look like fools."

"She's always been smarter than most." As Rexx said the words, his lips cracked into a smile. "She would never have stayed in the mold people kept trying to make for her. Even without the van. Even without Zone 36. Hell, even without . . . me." Rexx paused after this last part. "It would have happened, eventually. She would have started questioning, eventually."

The Board member's eyes narrowed on Rexx, but in addition to the mounting anger evident by the pulsing vein on his forehead, there was something else. He was restraining himself, imploring Rexx to continue, so he did even though he was frightened. "You guys like to drill it home that we all know just what we need to do our jobs. Nothing more. Well, a scientist's job is to find answers where there don't seem to be any. To follow a thread and see where it might lead. So that's what she did. She did exactly what you trained her to do."

Rexx could feel the Board member's fingers grip the thin blanket on either side of his feet. He knew he wanted to take his anger out on someone and Rexx was an easy target, so why wasn't he? Was it possible this wasn't the right moment? Maybe the Board member didn't know where Patch was, or didn't know how to reach her. Rexx knew saying much more was dangerous, but he said it anyway.

"It seems to me that if letting Americans and the rest of the world know the truth makes you look like fools, you have already lost."

The Board member's face got even redder. He pulled his hands up and then stepped to the side of the bed. The taut skin of his face looked like it might snap, and it continued to tighten as he leaned down closer to Rexx. He wrapped one hand around Rexx's throat, as a reminder of who was in control.

"Don't test me, Mr. Moreno," he hissed as his thumb and index finger tightened their grip. "Yes, I'd rather your death work more in my favor, but believe me, it is going to come either way. If I thought your little friend would believe an avatar, you would be dead already."

Rexx tried to inhale but couldn't. His windpipe was closing. He started thrashing, but his arms were still restrained. He kicked, but his legs did not hit their target. He had nothing. He could feel the color draining from his face, the oxygen not reaching his brain, his final seconds ticking away.

Then the Board member let go. Rexx gasped for air, choking as the man kicked the lower corner of the bed, causing indescribable pain to shoot up Rexx's spine.

The Board member emitted a rage-filled holler. He turned away from Rexx and punched the nearby cart of medical supplies. A loud crash echoed throughout the small room as the supplies scattered. The Board member raised his hand, and Rexx saw crimson droplets dripping onto the floor.

"Sir, is everything okay in here?" Regina Tellman was standing in the doorway.

"Clean this mess up," the Board member spit before storming out of the room, leaving Rexx in a state of agony until the pain began to dull.

CHAPTER 27

Patch Collins

I AWOKE TO Felix digging for something in one of the bags and Rose stretching in the corner, bending her body in a way that I would never even dream of attempting. A small amount of light was making its way through the dust-caked horizontal row of windows at the top of the hangar door.

"What time is it?" I asked as I sat up on the mat and leaned forward, stretching my back and taking in my surroundings in the daylight for the first time. I felt the injuries on my body, including my ribs and my cheekbone, and was pleasantly surprised to find that they were less tender to the touch.

"A little after seven," Felix said.

"Did you get any sleep?" I asked, noting the dark circles surrounding Felix's eyes, magnified slightly by his glasses. His normally shaggy hair was extra shaggy this morning and pointed haphazardly in multiple directions.

"About two hours. Don't worry about me, though. We can take turns sleeping today."

"Why don't you use the desk?" I asked as I watched Felix sitting cross-legged on the hard floor, just inches away from the pile of garbage.

"I'm honestly afraid one of those chairs will break underneath me," he said with a slight laugh. I looked at the chairs once more in the small light of day, and realized he was probably right.

"Here," I said, jumping back up and dragging one of the mats over so that we could both sit on it.

"Right," he said. "The obvious solution. I suppose I should have thought of that."

"Well, you've barely slept, and it looks like you've accomplished plenty, so we'll let it slide this time."

My eyes wandered longingly at the stack of food piled into a pyramid in the corner, realizing I hadn't eaten anything in an exceptionally long time. Felix noticed and reached over and grabbed a bag of mixed nuts and dried fruit and tossed them to me.

"Sorry, I didn't have time to make anything from scratch before we left."

"Thank you."

"Eat up," he said, tossing me another as I was mid-bag. "We all need to have energy for whatever comes next."

"Show me what you've found," I said as the hunger started to subside.

"Good news! Elias Stevens led us right to the headquarters, as I suspected he would, and it sounds like Rexx might be in there too."

I wasn't sure if I had heard him correctly, he said it so casually. "Rexx is in the headquarters?"

"Yeah, it looks like it," Felix said as he ran his hand through his hair. "But they may have seen the beetle attached to Elias. The feed cut out shortly after an interesting exchange. Watch."

"What exactly are we watching?" I asked as my heart started to race at the thought of learning something about Rexx's whereabouts.

"We're watching beetle number three at ten-times speed," he said, clicking on one of the many camera feeds and enlarging the footage. There was someone riding in a vehicle, and then walking, and then going through gates. There was sound too, but it was sped up so that it was impossible to follow and sounded like a couple of screech owls quarreling.

Then, having apparently caught up to the spot he wanted to show me, Felix slowed the footage down. "Here, listen closely," he said.

Elias Stevens was talking to someone out of view.

"Aelia Ramey. Has she been taken care of?"

The view was obstructed partially by what looked like part of Elias's suit. The beetle must have been perched on his chest, or maybe his belt buckle. His hands moved in front of the camera sporadically so that you could only catch glimpses of the surrounding view.

"Yes, sir. About an hour ago on *America One*."

I swallowed forcefully as I thought about the woman who I had been watching on television since I was a child, and the realization came over me that I was responsible for another death. After what I was put through yesterday, why did I still care? I guess I cared because I had a feeling she was being used just as much as the rest of us.

I knew the Board was certainly capable of worse and liked to make examples out of people, but I had a strong feeling they might have been underestimating how Americans would react to this. It was easy enough to write a neighbor or a classmate or an unknown face on a screen off as a traitor, but people are attached to their celebrities. I had a feeling it wouldn't sit well with the public.

"Good. Good," Elias was saying, pulling my attention back to the footage. "That will help make sure that everyone sees what not reporting one of those gadgets we found will result in. Who knows how many of them are already out there? We have to rein this in quickly. I want to offer five credits for all reports at the see-something-say-something booths this week. Have the new host announce it on tomorrow's episode."

"Very good, sir."

"The boy," Elias Stevens said, and I was suddenly holding my breath. "Is he up? I want to pay him a visit before I retire for the evening."

"We can certainly wake him, sir. He has been conscious all day and appears to be stable now."

"Yes. Let's do that. I'll walk there now. Alert Officer Tellman, will you?"

"Sir." The voice opposite Elias was now suddenly full of alarm and speaking at a higher volume as if he were chasing after Elias, who, based on the movements of the camera, was beginning to walk away. "Stop where you are and hold very still," it said.

There was some rustling, some loud crunching noises, and then the camera went dark.

"Maybe they spotted the beetle, but just brushed it off as if it were a bug?" I said hopefully, knowing this was not the case. They knew what the beetles looked like now.

"Maybe," Felix said, humoring me. "But they are built to withstand a simple brushing. For the feed to cut out completely, it would have to sustain some damage."

"And I assume that's not great."

"Well, I was hoping we had a bit more time for footage of the headquarters."

"That footage we just watched. Are you going to release it?" I asked.

"Already have," Felix said to my surprise. "Now that we suspect the Board may have found a beetle or two, we need to get as much information out as quickly as possible. Overnight

I released all the footage from beetles that attached themselves to a host, except for yours. So, Elias's, Aelia's, and four of the Compos' whom you met at the border, though Aelia's and Elias's are now dark."

If they were attached to the Compos, then that meant the outside world would soon start to see what the inside of Compliance Departments looked like. I'd been taken into custody more than once now, and still never passed through a Compliance Department that I knew of. I made a mental note to ask Felix to show me some of that footage when he didn't seem occupied with something else, if that ever happened.

I was suddenly feeling very hesitant about the beetle currently making its way to the compound near the Northern Barrier, and the thought of it being anywhere near Oliver.

"On the bright side," said Rose, who had stealthily come and sat next to us without me noticing, "now that Elias has led us to the headquarters and we know exactly where it is"—she pointed to a map on the screen that showed the trajectory of each beetle—"we should be able to get a good view via satellite. Can I see that, Felix?"

"Of course," he said, moving out of the way so Rose could sit in front of the monitor.

When I was a young girl, maybe eight or nine, I would lie awake in my dorm bed and conjure images of what the Board headquarters looked like. We were never told where it was located, for our own safety, but I knew it had to be impressive. I knew how the Tier 1s and 2s lived, each in their own individual row houses with their own yards, and I knew the Board must have even more luxury.

When I asked my parents about the headquarters one day, I was quickly hushed and told we didn't discuss such things, but that didn't stop me from imagining. I never once envisioned the location would be southern Nevada, so close to home.

I pictured, at the center of everything in this fabricated city, a table like the one we saw on the towering billboards in the urban centers. There were hands folded atop it as important things were discussed and "details" were sorted out. I often wondered if they were handed across the table something concrete to hold and destroy, or if these details were more abstract. Were they, like a wildfire, simply deprived of the oxygen they needed to spread?

I imagined that room, that table, in the middle of a fortresslike city. Did the entire Board live there, all together in their own neighborhood? Were there thirty houses, thirty large yards, and thirty cars? They were allowed their own vehicles, of this I felt certain as a child.

I imagined the houses connected to the Boardroom through bridges and tunnels and grand walkways. There would be plenty of real wooden trees, not the plastic ones scattered throughout the urban centers. Even as a child, I loved the thought of real trees. My version of the headquarters was an oasis.

Suddenly I felt myself cascading back into my childhood as Rose zoomed in on an ominous complex that took up the entire screen. There were no flowers, no trees, and no yards with happy children of Board members playing.

It did resemble a fortress, but not like the one I'd imagined. My throat grew tight as I took in the image of what resembled a rigid clay-toned castle set inside a vast ravine. I unintentionally held my breath as I stared at the scene that was at once captivating and spine-chilling.

I felt like I might topple face-first into the screen and suddenly be staring up at the meticulously arranged stone walls. They were framed by the edges of a canyon ascending and descending around it, so you didn't quite know where the complex began and ended. It felt as unknowable and unrelenting as the Board members themselves had been to me in my childhood.

I felt Rose's hand on my shoulder, and I reached up and held her hand in my own.

"Where is this?" I asked, surprised at how shaky my voice was when it emerged.

"It's . . ." Rose said, not finishing her sentence, like she didn't fully believe the words that were about to follow.

"What? What's wrong?" Felix and I asked simultaneously.

"It's the Hoover Dam."

"What's the Hoover Dam?" I asked.

Both sets of eyes jerked to me with astonishment.

"You worked in the Natural Resource Department and you don't know what the Hoover Dam is?" Felix said, his voice laced with shock. "The Colorado River supplies a large portion of Arizona's water."

"I know what the Colorado River is," I shot back, suddenly feeling defensive, "and we were told our expected annual water supply, and made request adjustments when necessary, but no, I was not told about the Hoover Dam. It looks like it was outside of my territory."

"Sorry," Felix said. "I was just surprised."

I nodded and we all turned back to the image.

Compliance Officers ringed the edges of the complex like ants on the rim of a fruit bowl, just like they had the crater that Rexx and I had discovered in Nevada.

Rose zoomed out so we could see both the bombing site and the headquarters in the same image. I couldn't believe Rexx and I had traveled so close.

"Of course," Rose said, laughing under her breath. "Limitless electricity, natural cover, and the chances anyone would go searching there after the bombing and risk radiation poisoning would be slim."

"Fear wins again," I added, feeling as if I were emerging from water. I tried to shake off the feeling that had taken over me moments before when looking at the headquarters. That hidden, awful part of me that, when years of indoctrination took over, was still left in awe of the Board.

"Exactly," Felix said, chiming in. "They probably moved there from D.C. as soon as they knew the waters wouldn't recede on the East Coast, and that Nevada would be relatively safe. They likely continued to let the public think it was dangerous. I wonder how long radiation stays in the air after an explosion like that."

"One to five years," I said matter-of-factly, happy to have an answer for once, "but it will remain in the soil longer, which may explain all the concrete."

Felix looked at me, impressed.

"Studying and reporting on the radiation levels found in the air and soil was a large part of my job," I said.

He nodded. "Guess we'll just ask you, then!"

"Any signs of the nuclear arsenal nearby? It would make sense to keep it close. Maybe even in the canyon," I said.

"No sign yet," Rose said. "Though it would also make sense to keep it underground."

"Looks like our little bug is about thirty minutes away from Oliver," Felix said, switching his attention to something else. "We'll park him somewhere close to wait until outside time for the prisoners."

"So what do we do while we wait?"

"Well, now that we know where it is, we start by deploying more of these little guys to try to get some more footage of the headquarters. Based on that footage of Elias Stevens and his reaction, they have probably already issued a warning to their Compliance Departments, and possibly even to citizens, to destroy these on sight, so we need to move on to the next part of our plan."

"What's the next part of our plan?" I asked.

"I need you and Rose to analyze the footage we brought from Canada and select what you want to add to a message to show Americans. Can you do that? Can you record a message to American citizens?"

My eyes widened as I started to understand that there was indeed more to Rose and Felix's plan.

"Sure," I said hesitantly. "But what are we going to do with the message?"

"Well, though so much is wrong with America and they haven't evolved too much technologically after the Seclusion, the firewall is still surprisingly strong."

Felix stood and started walking toward the pile of supplies.

"At first this seemed to take away any hope of getting a message to people, but then I realized something else. We don't have to rely on breaking their firewall. Why not take one of their biggest methods of control and use it against them? What have they done to try to keep the people subdued? They moved you all to compact urban centers so you could be under constant surveillance."

He dug around in the pile until he found what he was looking for. "We have some pretty rudimentary technology in Canada that will do the trick."

Then he pulled out one of the three large bags, and it all became clear. The answer was so much simpler than I had ever imagined.

"Oh," I said as I watched him open the bags containing hundreds of hovering projectors. Then louder: "OH!"

"You think everyone will watch?" he asked.

"Yes," I said without hesitation.

It all started to come together—use the beetles to show America to the people of the outside world, and flood the urban centers with these simple hovering projectors to show the outside world to the American people. In the end, all we could do was offer them the truth. They would have to take it from there.

"Everyone will watch," I said confidently. "When there is an alert, video or otherwise, we read it, we watch, we listen. It's what we were trained to do. They will put down what they are doing, and they will watch. It will be everyone, all of the Tiers, the Compliance Officers, everyone."

CHAPTER 28

Patch Collins

"BEFORE YOU AND Rose record your message, I want you to know how to operate most of this stuff in case we get separated," Felix said. "Do you still have the kill switch in your pocket?"

"Yes." I pulled out the silver rectangular button and gently ran my thumb along the outside edge, careful not to press any part of it too firmly, remembering what Felix had told me. Once the button was pressed, all footage that had been recorded up to that point, as well as a signal that sent out our location, would be released. I carefully slid it back into my pocket.

"Great. Always keep that on you," Felix said before beginning to list an inventory of all the items he and Rose had brought. There was a mix of things swiped from the lab, and items readily available to anyone in Canada. There were the beetles, the projectors, and kits for disabling a variety of locks, which I realized, as he pointed, must have been how he'd broken into the hangar. There was a stash of food, as well as supplies for harnessing solar energy to work the equipment.

Felix grabbed an interesting miniature drone-like apparatus from a bag containing six or seven identical devices. It reminded me of the drone Rexx and I had encountered while riding on the cargo flats, but smaller and sleeker.

Felix's face lit up as he held it in front of me and turned it from side to side, showing it off. "This," he said, "can fly away and then explode on command. It's not great for combat, but it's an excellent diversion should we need one."

After going through everything, we carefully divided the supplies into those we might need in an emergency, and everything else, then put the bags near the vehicle in case of a quick departure.

Next, Rose showed me the footage they had brought, and we picked favorite segments that illustrated life outside of the Walls and then planned how to piece it together with a recorded message. It was exciting.

Once we were fairly certain of the messaging, Rose and I got to work recording multiple takes of me speaking to a camera. We set up in the large open space of the hangar, next to one of the airplanes. We laughed after the first round, when the two of us realized too late that, in our excitement to hit record, we had not removed my face tattoos. We paused and spent a few minutes getting me cleaned up so that I didn't look like parts of my face had been removed like puzzle pieces. Rose had a bit of makeup with her, but the bulk of it was suited to her black skin, not my pale and freckled complexion. We did the best we could to clean me up—a touch of lip gloss and eye shadow helped tremendously.

Felix interrupted periodically, filling us in on what was happening with various beetle footage, and providing other updates. A fleet of drones had passed by at one point but moved on quickly, he told us.

"Should we be concerned?" I asked, the urge to run surfacing.

"It's hard to tell," Felix said. "If they didn't see our vehicle inside the hangar, we are probably fine, but we'll want to move somewhere else before long. Rose, be sure to get those tattoos back on her face as soon as you're done recording."

"I think this is as good as we're going to get," Rose said later that afternoon when we had finished patching together my recording with the outside footage. When we had finalized the message, we went to find Felix.

"I think the prisoners will be let out soon," he said when we walked into the office. The beetle he had released the night before had apparently arrived at the compound. On his monitor, Felix had the camera footage from the beetle up alongside the satellite footage. The beetle was perched and waiting atop one of the lightning rods that circled the compound.

We could see the yards of the compound clearly, and there were three Compos stationed within each pie wedge, but there were no prisoners in the yard. I knew from personal experience that prisoners were allocated only fifteen minutes of outside time per day, and that privilege could be taken away for disciplinary measures.

It was surreal to see the scene laid out in front of me with an up-close view through the beetle's lens. There were two layers of fencing outside the yard, with one at the end of the pie wedge, then another about two hundred yards from the first, forming a loop around the entire complex. A vivid memory surfaced of Webb helping me in the pouring-down rain through the gates of both fences.

"I don't know which wedge I was in, and Rexx and Oliver were held separately, but when I got out, Webb led me through one of these gates," I said as I pointed. "Someone caught us in the middle section here, but Webb pacified him, and then helped me out through the last gate. Then he gave me back my map and told me which way to run. Rexx was waiting for me at the tree line here."

I'd likely already told them this, but they humored me anyway. I felt my chest tighten as the first prisoners filed out into the yard. They were not filling the section with the infinity symbol, but rather, the one next to it.

"If they let out in the same order every day," Felix said, "then Oliver's section should be next, meaning we have approximately fifteen minutes to wait."

Fifteen minutes ticked by, then one section emptied and another one filled. One prisoner walked immediately into the yard with his head down and began walking on the path where the grass was worn as if nothing else in the world mattered to him.

"That's him," I said loudly, my voice jumping out of my throat with urgency.

His thick hair was gone, and it looked like he had a few patches of completely bald skin on his scalp, but I recognized him as Oliver right away and I didn't think my heart could beat so quickly. I swallowed through a tight throat. He wasn't well and I was filled with the overwhelming urge to reach into the screen and grab him.

"What do we do now?" I asked.

"We get the beetle on him," Rose said.

"Already on it," Felix said.

"Wait," I said, grabbing Felix's shoulder as a sour feeling circulated in my gut. "Does it have to be him?"

"Who would you rather it be?" Felix asked gently, and I lowered my hand and nodded.

Felix navigated the beetle out into the yard. It hovered close to Oliver, then moved down until it crashed onto the leg of his pants. It was a bit disorienting, as the camera was filled with nothing but the gray fabric of a compound uniform.

"Is that what was supposed to happen?" I asked.

"Not as precise as I would have wanted," Felix declared. "I think it will be best to have it on his shoe or waistband. They tend to be a little less noticeable there, and we know the Compliance Officers are already looking for them. We can wait until he is back in his cell and move it when we see the opportunity. Switching angles now."

I imagined Oliver spotting the unfamiliar piece of technology crawling across the floor of his cell. Would he worry, thinking that it was something from the Board, or had he already seen the warnings that were issued? Was it possible he would see this unfamiliar piece of technology and realize that we were trying to help him?

"I don't feel good about this," I said. The gray fabric disappeared as Felix switched the camera angle on the beetle. My palms started to sweat, my body started to tremble mildly, and Rose noticed and set a hand on my arm. I closed my eyes as the feelings of being there came crashing back.

I took a deep breath and returned my attention to the camera, watching the footage move in unison with Oliver's steady, intentional steps. I pretended I was someone outside America, seeing what was happening inside these compounds for the first time.

CHAPTER 29

Oliver Shelling

OLIVER WAS SITTING in his cell when he noticed something sticking to the hem of his pants. He looked at it carefully. It appeared to be a small device of some kind and it blended in almost perfectly with his gray compound-issued jumper. It glistened ever so slightly as he rocked his leg back and forth. There was a tiny dome protruding from the center, like an eye, or, he realized, a miniscule camera lens.

"What the hell?" he murmured.

He tried to pull it off, but it clung. Its tiny pronged legs looped tightly through the threads of the fabric. He looked away, turning his attention back to his work assignment, before someone might notice him staring too long.

He looked to the two trays sitting in front of him. With his raw fingers, he took a standard pacifier from tray number one, popped off the protective cover, and removed the battery from inside. He placed the old battery on tray one and grabbed a new one from tray two. He inserted the fresh battery into the pacifier, closed the protective cover, and put the fixed equipment on tray two.

He repeated this process for over three hours, until tray one was filled with old batteries, and tray two held only repaired pacifiers. The whole time, his mind was on the bug-like thing sticking to his leg. Was this something from the Board? That didn't make any sense. There were plenty of cameras in his cell already and all around the compound.

In Zone 36, the elders had gone over all of the various types of security equipment with Patch and Rexx, but he had never seen anything like this. If this was the Board, it was a huge leap from where he knew they were technologically.

He placed both trays into the slot on the wall. After it registered the weight to be exactly the same weight as when the two trays arrived, the slot closed, and the trays were taken away.

Oliver had a brief break until the next round arrived. He leaned back against the wall and took a deep breath. *What can this thing be?* he thought as he tried to inspect it without drawing any more attention to himself.

He suspected it had attached to him for a reason. Could it be that someone out there had not forgotten about him? A lone tear escaped from his eye and rolled down the bridge of his nose. Had his message worked?

CHAPTER 30

Patch Collins

"THIS IS UNBELIEVABLE," Rose said. Her hand was over her mouth as she leaned in and watched the footage the beetle was capturing from Oliver's cell. Currently, the screen was playing a scene of a mother and child, both skinny as a rail, obviously malnourished, seeking help and shelter in the middle of a deserted landscape.

This is what happens outside our walls was scrawled across the bottom of the screen. *Inside, you are safe, you are secure, you are united.*

"I've never seen anything like this," Rose said. "This kind of stuff played all day in there?"

"Not just in there," I said. "It played pretty regularly everywhere. Interspersed with our lessons as children and in our television programs. I've seen this exact message before. Multiple times."

"Let's publish it," Felix said without hesitation as he started the process of connecting with the drop box. The same feeling I'd had when the beetle had landed on Oliver's uniform returned, and Felix seemed to read the worry on my face.

"You said this cell looks identical to the one you were in," he said gently, "so hopefully they are all identical. We'll just hope figuring out the source takes them awhile."

I thought back to the words Oliver had spoken in the garden in Zone 36, and held on to them like a lifeline. *And then it just hits you. . . . None of your plans will work. Or even if they might, you are too scared to try. . . . It just makes you feel so small. . . . It makes you feel so damn small.*

I wished we knew how the outside world was reacting to the footage they had already seen. I would feel better if I had confirmation that something was happening.

"Well, we might as well release those too," Felix said as he looked at a pile of supplies stacked by the door. "Are you ready for this, Patch? As soon as we release them, we leave."

By "them," Felix was referring to thirty high-altitude mini-cargo drones carrying a total of over five hundred personal projectors. They were programmed to be sent to the largest urban centers in America, and each would carry the recorded message Rose and I had been working on. It wouldn't be enough to reach every set of eyes in the country, but the message would reach thousands.

An hour later the drones had been released, and we finished packing up the vehicle as the sun started to set. We would head to another abandoned zone while we waited for the aftermath, just to be safe. Rose walked over to open the hangar door for our final departure, but before opening it, she peeked out the windows to check that the way was clear.

"Uh-oh," she said with a tone that demanded an immediate reaction. Felix and I rushed over to where she stood, and look outside. Search drones hovered in front of the hangar.

"Those are the same ones that passed by earlier," Felix said. They were also the same kind Rexx and I had encountered, as far as I could tell. There were at least five of them, but they moved so quickly that I had trouble counting.

"What do we do?" I asked as I watched the drones swarm around like bees outside the window. Felix opened his mouth to say something, but before he could get a word out, an explosion sent us all to the ground.

I opened one eye. The hangar wobbled and smoke swirled around us. The garage door lay on its side, half in and half out of the hangar. A siren filled my head, and I couldn't tell if it was real or an echo of the aftermath of the explosion. Was I hurt? I brought my hand up and touched the back of my skull, then lowered it. It came away awash with crimson, thick and jolting.

I ignored it for now, turning my hand over and pressing it into the ground as I lifted myself onto all fours. Memories began to flash into my head, faster than usual—waking in the *America One* Studios, being interrogated by Elias Stevens, being pacified in a field. I squeezed my eyes shut as hard as I could. *Stay in the present*, I reminded myself. *You have to deal with this.*

Debris is falling from the community-center roof. Rexx just lit it on fire. No, debris was falling on the far end of the hangar.

"Find Rose and Felix," I said out loud, as if I were standing beside myself issuing orders. I looked around slowly, carefully. If I moved my head too quickly, I would surely pass out. Rose was a few yards away. She was standing half on the fallen garage door and was yelling something at me, but I couldn't hear her.

The siren morphs into the sound of footsteps—mine, Rexx's, and Oliver's—running through the sewer. No, it was the sound of wobbling sheet metal.

I spotted Felix. He was on the ground, unconscious, crumpled at the base of the hangar door. I'd been right next to him and Rose when the explosion had happened. How had I landed this far away?

Rexx's leg, it's been crushed by a boulder. No, one of Felix's legs was wedged underneath the hangar door.

Rose was trying to lift the door off of Felix and yelling words that were inaudible to me.

My eyes instinctively moved away from the intense scene, focusing on something on the ground beside them—a pair of red glasses, lying on the floor, scratched but not broken.

With the glasses as my focus, I crawled over as quickly as I could, pausing twice when my vision started to blur. I picked the glasses up and put them in my pocket. Then, and only then, did I look at Rose again.

"Pull!" she was yelling over and over, barely audible against the sound of wobbling metal.

"We have to move him," Rexx is saying as an unconscious Robbie Webb lies beside the riverbed. No, it was Rose. Rose was the one talking.

Snap out of it, I reprimanded myself, but the memories were too strong, and I felt as if I were trapped inside a digital picture frame while it shifted from photo to photo.

You have to focus. You're in an old military hangar. You're with Rose and Felix. The Board has Rexx. Oliver is in the prison compound. Your father is dead. You will be soon too if you don't focus.

I moved over to Felix and checked his pulse. It was there. I grabbed him underneath his shoulders and pulled him until his leg was clear of the wide door.

Rose fell to her knees and started turning back and forth in a semicircle. She was searching for something. The physical exertion caught up to me, and my surroundings started to blur once again as I fell backward, still clutching Felix under the arms. I could feel my blood pressure dropping, and I was worried I would pass out.

The side of the building had been blown out, and the drones still hovered, scanning for signs of us. Did they recognize us as human, or were the tattoos working? Even if we weren't recognized, they would capture footage of the vehicle.

I stood, ignoring the stabbing pain in the back of my head, and pulled Felix as hard as I could, dragging him across the ground toward the vehicle.

There was another explosion—this one felt closer, but I managed to keep my footing. Suddenly Rose was beside me, helping me pull Felix.

"Where are our bags? Our individual bags?" she was yelling.

"Underneath the front console!" I yelled back as I put Felix down next to the side door. Rose climbed in and leaned over the seat and yanked one of the bags out and quickly dug. She pulled something out and programmed it. It flew out of her hand and away, and a moment later there was an explosion in the distance.

She grabbed another one and did the same. There was another explosion, this time farther away. I glanced out the window. The drones were retreating.

"We have to go now. They will be back," she said as she jumped out and helped me hoist Felix into the vehicle. She then put the bag she had been holding on my back. "Do not take this off," she said. "Under any circumstances." She put another one on herself and clipped it across her chest.

Then, before long, we were out of the hangar and making a beeline for anywhere but where we had been.

CHAPTER 31

Robbie Webb

WHEN WEBB CAME to, he was sitting in a dark room. He recognized the room he was in as one of the two holding rooms at the Compliance Department, where those taken into custody would wait for transport to one of the compounds.

A bit of light shined through from the rectangular windows that faced the street outside the department. His wrists and hands were fused to a panel behind him with magnetic cuffs, the same kind he carried with him for arresting civilians.

At the moment he was alone in the room, but he'd seen as many as twenty people crammed into the space before. There were magnetic panels lined up against three of the walls, so that when people were sitting on the built-in benches, they could align next to one another like cans of soup on a shelf.

All he could think as he sat there was how different everything looked from his current angle. A metallic taste filled his mouth, and the left side of his chest, where the pacifier had hit him, had pins and needles running up and down it. How could he have been so damn stupid?

He looked through the metal grate covering the top half of the door to the holding room, and watched for movement or any other sign that someone was there. Nothing. As night fell, the room was plunged into total darkness. What felt like hours passed until he heard a commotion that rattled him awake in the early morning.

His neck had been hanging in front of his chest as he slept, and pain shot through his upper back as he stiffened at the alarm bells beginning to blare.

"What's going on?" he shouted as he saw Evan run past.

"We don't know. Incoming threats in our airspace. Level Red." Evan's panic was palpable.

"Well, let me out! I can help!"

"No chance, traitor," Evan shot back as he ran in the direction he had come from, but the nervousness in the officer's voice took the sting out of the words.

Webb turned as much as he could to look out the window. His body tensed as he realized something was headed toward the building—actually, multiple somethings. They looked like lightning bugs from far away, but as they got closer, they moved apart until only one was near the station, hovering in the middle of the street.

Was it a weapon? Was it about to explode and take the entire Compliance Department with it? He wondered why someone wasn't knocking it down. He craned his neck to see more of the surrounding area, and then he saw why.

There were too many of them, and they hovered just out of reach. Little dots lit up the sky on every block, almost like lumicomms. Was this the Board, trying to subdue its citizens, or was this something from the outside?

He felt completely helpless. Though if he were out, he didn't know exactly what he would be doing. Ignoring the pain in his neck, and in his wrists as the cuffs dug into his skin, he strained to get a better look.

An image filled the sky, projected from the floating orbs. It was similar to how IDs projected, but on a larger scale. Each image was the size of a movie screen.

Then there she was. Webb squinted to make sure he was seeing correctly. She didn't quite resemble the young woman he'd met in the woods—the woman who had knocked him out with a rock and altered the course of his entire life. She didn't resemble the woman he had last spoken to outside the fence of the prison yard, emaciated and beaten down, but it was definitely her.

On the screen was Patricia Collins. Her hair had grown out a few inches, and she had put on a healthy weight. She looked strong. Her blue eyes pierced through the screen with determination. Tears trickled down Webb's cheeks before he could stop them. They had done it. They had reached the outside. He now knew for sure. Was the boy the one who had held the camera as she recorded this message?

He looked out at the early-morning streets. People were emerging from their houses to see what was going on. Compos on the streets yelled, but their primary attention seemed focused on the orbs in the sky and the hovering image of the young woman.

"Say something," Webb whispered under his breath. Then, as if she were answering him, the sound broke through.

"Good morning, everyone. My name is Patch Collins." Her voice was clear and crisp. Her head was held high, her jaw set in a state of defiance. Those piercing blue eyes were looking straight at Webb. Compliance Officers outside the window were rushing around, and Webb could tell from their demeanor that they didn't quite know what to do.

"Nearly three months ago, I escaped America through the northern border and into the outside world." The cameras showed the Northern Barrier, then pivoted to show a towering city that looked like it was plucked out of a video game, full of architecture and other scenery Webb did not recognize.

"If you don't believe me, please notice how this message is reaching you. Does this look like technology from the Board? It's not. I have visited a city in Canada, our neighbor on the other side of the Northern Barrier, and I have met with the leaders of other nations. I have not been beheaded, tortured, or encountered anyone who resembles the monsters in the photos we have been shown our entire lives."

The screen cut to more footage of families and people interacting in foreign places. Emotions flowed through Webb, some recognizable to him, and others not. There was one that stood out above the rest. It was the same emotion he was told time and again he should feel for his job, for his leaders, and for his home. He was realizing he had never really felt it properly until now. Pride.

"Not everything out here is perfect, but I don't think anything, anywhere, is perfect. I'm here to tell you that everything you have been taught about the outside world is a lie. Outside, people are free to come and go as they please. They are free to follow the education of their choosing. Innovation is encouraged and even rewarded. The world is thriving without us. There are global alliances working together to solve some of the largest problems facing life here on Earth, like air pollution and water shortages. America has fallen behind because of the Board.

"Though I have seen no sign of the nightmares we in America are shown on the screens day in and day out, here are a few of the things I *have* seen."

Patch disappeared from the screen and instead there were several small snippets of video showing life taking place. A few of the snippets stood out to Webb. There was a panorama of the ocean and a beach where people were swimming and sunbathing and reading in chairs. There was footage of the inside of a building, the walls filled from floor to ceiling with books, and people reading those books. Webb swallowed hard as he thought about the book from the bottom of Patch's backpack and the day he had found it.

Patch was then back on the screen. "I know it's hard to reconcile these images with what you have been led to believe, and honestly, I don't completely understand the motives of the Board or why they have done this to us. What I do know is that our walls are not there to keep us safe. They are there to keep us subdued, keep us scared, keep us weak, and keep us fearful. Whether it is pride or whether this has gone on too long for them to admit they were wrong, I don't really know. I'm sure the answer lies in the details they have always told us are so dangerous."

Now there was footage of prisoners, scenes that looked like they were recorded at the camp where Webb had been stationed.

"The military redemption centers do not exist. I should know, for I spent two months in a compound like this one. All of your loved ones who have been taken over the years did not join the military. They were held captive, forced into labor, provided with the minimum amount of exercise and sustenance to keep them alive, but barely."

Webb found himself nodding along with her words. Any Compliance Officer who had been assigned to a compound knew this truth. They knew it, but they did not say anything. Other Compliance Officers were not trained in what they did not need to know. They did not know the fate to which they were sending those they had captured. But Webb knew.

"It's all a lie," Patch continued. "The videos they show us of the outside world are a lie. The *Portrait of a Redeemed Patriot* videos we are forced to watch are more lies produced in a studio. There are people in our country who have tried to show us. People who remember what happened or who have passed on that information. Who knew the truth about what was outside these walls. They are not traitors. They were trying to warn us. Those people have ended up as victims of the Board. This has to stop.

"I know it's hard to understand. I didn't understand at first either. It is really scary to have your whole world dismantled, to admit that what you believe might not be right. But when you do it, when you open yourself up to realizing there might be another way, then the world is suddenly full of possibilities. I think deep down you know, the same way I knew, that something isn't right. Something doesn't fit. People shouldn't be treated like this. We should be able to ask questions, to talk openly, to contribute more than we are allowed to. That there is a reason they are silencing us. Together we can do this. We can demand it be another way. There are only thirty of them, and there are millions of us. We should not have to live in fear of being ripped apart from our families if we ask the wrong question. We should not be taught that to learn, to be educated, to question, is wrong. Look."

The cameras turned to reveal a crowd of people—well, more than a crowd. An entire street overfilled with people gathering and projecting signs into the air and smiling. Webb couldn't really read the signs from his current angle.

"This is what is really out here. People who want to see you free and happy. People who want to help you see what our country used to be, and what it can be. You might ask, how can everything you believe be wrong? I understand, trust me, but please just ask yourself one question—what if the information out here isn't toxic to us, but what if it's toxic to them? What if it shows all of us who the Board really is?"

Then there was a picture of a group of people lined up in three rows, shoulder to suit-lined shoulder. Webb had never seen their faces before, yet they were somehow instantly familiar. Webb's stomach hardened as his eyes scanned the faces. Was this who he thought it was?

"This is the Board. Thirty men. They have faces, and they have names. They are not the deities we make them out to be. They are simply men who have let their pride lead an entire nation into ruin."

It can't be, Webb thought. *They're so small, so insignificant, so, well, human.*

"And to the Compliance Officers, I say, help us. I have met compliance officers who know deep down that what they are doing is not right. Without you, compliance officers, the Board members have nothing, they have no power. So find out for yourselves. Find out if what you are 'working for' is what you have been told.

"I have so much to show you, there is so much that we can be, but first we have to show them that we aren't afraid of them, and that is going to take tremendous courage. The whole world is watching. For the first time in sixty years, we are all seeing the truth—us about them, and them about us. So now is the time. If you've been waiting, now is the time."

When the feed was over, the screen was imprinted with a symbol resembling a sideways eight. It was the same symbol Webb had seen on the map Patricia had in her backpack and that Webb had seen on the prisoner's arm the day before, but what did it mean?

After Patch's message, Webb could hear commotion outside, but he could not get a good look. Prisoners soon started to be shuffled past his door, some protesting, and some unconscious, on the way to the other holding cell. Webb saw Commander Lewis walk past.

"Let me out, Chief," he said loudly. "You know you need all the help you can get." Webb didn't know how the commander would respond, but to his delight, Lewis walked forward so that Robbie could see his face through the silver grating on the top half of the door.

"Now, why on earth would I do that, Webb?" he said with the flat tone of a father disappointed in his son. "You disobeyed orders. You drove to an unsanctioned area, Board knows why. You have been unstable and acting odd for months. Now, I don't exactly know what is going on right now, but I've no reason to trust you. Trust and loyalty are everything around here. You know that."

Lewis brought one hand up and gripped the grating in the door and leaned his forehead against it. He looked overwhelmed. Webb cast a brief look out the window to see that the unrest outside was intensifying.

"I understand I've let you down, Chief," Webb said, meeting Lewis's eyes. "I've been unpredictable. My stint at the redemption camp, well, it just shook me up, is all. I saw some things that I've been processing. Was too weak, that's all, but I'm starting to feel like myself again, and I want you to trust me. I want to earn your trust back. I want to, above all, serve the Board."

Lewis sighed and scratched behind his ear. He grabbed the grating with a second hand. He was considering it. If he wasn't, he would have been gone by now.

"Can you at least loosen these a bit, Chief?" Webb asked. "Haven't I earned that much after my years of service?" Webb gestured his head toward the cuffs suspending his arms up and against the magnetic wall behind him.

Lewis didn't say anything for a moment. Then Webb heard the telltale sound of the door lock opening after Lewis had scanned his biometrics. Webb readied himself to act fast.

"You been drinking, Robbie?" Lewis said as he crossed the holding cell.

"Not for days, sir, but it got out of hand for a while there. I guess I didn't hide it as well as I thought I did."

Lewis chuckled under his breath. "No, no, you didn't." He surveyed Webb from a few paces away, studying his face. "I'll see what I can do for you, Webb. I'll try to put in a stay of transport, but there's only so much I have control over, so no promises."

"That would be good of you, sir."

Lewis walked over and set his thumb on a biometric pad on the cuffs. They opened.

"You still have to wear them, but I'll switch 'em to the front for you."

There was no time to switch them to the front. Webb hit him hard with his elbow, between the eyes like he'd been taught if a perpetrator was acting up or if a weapon wasn't easily accessible.

He kicked Lewis in the midsection so that he doubled over. The man swiped in Webb's direction, but his aim was off. Webb grabbed the cuffs out of Lewis's hand and brought them down hard on the commander's head. Then, gripping the commander firmly from under the armpits, he started dragging him out of the holding cell, across the next room, and into the commander's office. He clicked the office door shut just as Stokes, with an unconscious woman's head pinned in his elbow, spotted him.

"Officer, what do you think you are doing?" he said, dropping the woman on the floor without a second thought. "Open this door immediately!" Stokes looked from the holding cell to the office, then moved forward and looked through the office window, seeing Commander Lewis unconscious on the floor.

"Open this door! Webb!" Stokes was screaming now. "This isn't funny. We have a real emergency out here. What the hell has gotten into you, man? Are you possessed or something?"

Graham walked in, saw Stokes banging on the commander's door, and joined him.

"Stand back," Graham said as he tried fruitlessly to break open the door. Webb did his best to ignore the activity just a few feet from where he stood. He approached the commander's interface system. His heart rate had never been so fast in his entire life. He wiped the sweat off his brow with one hand.

Robbie grabbed the commander and hoisted him up so that he was supporting Lewis's body on his knee. Then he quickly used the commander's biometrics to access the messaging device, having to first swipe his fingerprints and chip, and then hold his eyelids open for an iris scan. As soon as he was in the system, he dropped the commander with a thud. Webb felt like his stomach fell along with the commander and was now residing on the floor.

He worked as quickly as he could with sweaty fingers, typing out a message, then hitting send before he had time to have second thoughts. It might not reach the whole force, but at least it would help. At least he'd done something.

There was a booming noise behind him, and soon Graham was grabbing him around the neck and pulling him backward, but it was too late. A message had been sent to every single Compo and commanding officer in the Portland Territory.

Lay down your weapons—directive from the Board. Alert neighboring precincts.

CHAPTER 32

Patch Collins

ROSE FOUND A covered bridge about fifty miles away and set down underneath it with a rough landing. We both peered around nervously, since the dim headlights served as the only illumination.

The bridge was about thirty yards in length and looked so unmaintained that it wouldn't have surprised me if it collapsed at any moment. The road in front of us was cracked and brittle, as if cars had not driven on its surface for decades.

"Be right back," Rose said. She jumped out and slung something that looked like a tarp over the vehicle, covering the windows and plunging the interior into near total darkness. Rose climbed back in and turned on a couple of interior lights.

"What was that you put over the car?"

"Camouflage sheet," Rose replied. "It takes on the texture and pattern of its surroundings and makes it difficult for any drones to spot the vehicle underneath. It also serves as a thermal disruptor for any heat-tracking devices."

"Wow. That's incredible," I said, imagining how much easier my and Rexx's journey could have been with something like that.

I looked at my bloodstained hands and pulled my top shirt off so I was wearing only the carbon fiber top. After wiping my hands off as best I could, I held the bundled-up shirt to the back of my head, inhaling sharply through my teeth as the piercing pain radiated outward with the pressure.

"Hey, Felix," I said as I spun in the seat on my knees and leaned over. "Can you hear me?"

He didn't answer, but his eyelids were fluttering ever so slightly.

Rose helped me rearrange him so he would be more comfortable, then together we tended to his injuries, which seemed mostly confined to a large scratch on his leg from the hangar door and whatever blow to his head had rendered him in this state.

Rose used her thumb to open his eyelids, checked his pupils, immobilized his neck, then broke open an ice pack and instructed me to put it underneath his head.

"Will that do it? Do you think he will be okay?"

"Time will tell," Rose said in a wobbly voice, and I noticed moisture in her eyes as she avoided eye contact. "There isn't much else we have on board to deal with anything affecting his brain. Let's just hope he wakes up. Now, come back up here next to me and let me take a look at your head," she said. I climbed into the front seat and then she gently separated my hair to inspect the damage.

"Well, your hair is an absolute mess," she said, laughing as she peeled away the blood-soaked clumps of strands to unearth the injury. "The cut doesn't look too deep, but it's about three inches long, and I'm sure it hurts like hell."

She took more supplies out of the medical bag.

"Is everyone in Canada trained in first aid?" I asked, impressed by her prowess.

"No, not everyone, but basically everyone who accepts a job with the government," she said.

She cleaned up the area and then applied a glue-like substance to the cut. "This is going to have to do for now. It will hold it together, at least." After the glue dried, she applied a cooling gel. The pain dulled, though my brain still felt slightly like an egg that had been scrambled inside its shell. Rose leaned back and let out a deep sigh, then dimmed a few of the interior lights and reclined her seat. She reached over and squeezed my hand.

"Let's try to get some sleep. I know it won't come easy, but a few hours are better than nothing." I nodded and rearranged myself to be as comfortable as possible. I didn't know how long had passed before I awoke to Felix rustling behind me.

"It's okay," I said as I pawed around, fruitlessly trying to remember where Rose had pressed to turn the lights on. "We're inside the vehicle. You hit your head." I finally located the lights and smiled at Felix. He looked very pale, but he was upright.

"What happened?" he asked groggily. Rose woke and was soon scrambling over the seat to hug him.

"There was an explosion at the hangar," I said as Rose practically kicked me in the side trying to get to Felix. "You were knocked out."

I fished for a bag of almonds in one of our supply bags. "Here, try to eat a couple of these."

"Was the message released?"

"You don't remember?" I asked.

"Not clearly, anyway," he said as he popped a couple of almonds into his mouth.

"Yes, it was," Rose said, a big smile plastered on her face, revealing just how much she had been downplaying her worry about Felix. After spending some time getting him up to speed on what he had missed, he asked Rose to hand him his computer monitor.

"Let's check on how our little message is being received," he said. As he reached for the monitor, he let out a moan then fell back against the seat.

"Can you do it?" he asked Rose as he put his hand up over his eyes and turned a little green.

Several satellite locations were bookmarked on Felix's system for easy access—the headquarters, the site of the 2029 bombing, a couple of urban centers, and the compound. Rose scrolled through them, quickly reviewing the satellite footage of each over the last several hours.

"Looks like there was a bit of unrest," she said as she fast-forwarded through some of the urban-center footage of Houston, Texas, showing crowds of people outside, watching the projectors. Some citizens went back inside their homes immediately, while others wandered around in confusion, trying to get answers from their neighbors. Some congregated into groups, and the Compos broke them up. The footage also showed the streets cleared within an hour.

"That's it?" I said, my voice sharper than I had intended. "That's the reaction? A bit of confusion and then, what, they just go back inside? After everything we've done? How can that be it? No. I don't believe it. Look at another."

Rose switched to the footage of a different urban center, this time Nashville, Tennessee. It was the same. There was some mass confusion followed by everyone dispersing at the sight of a line of Compliance Officers approaching.

"Show me another one," I said sharply. "Show me Portland," I said, picturing Noah, Sophia, Mason, and Ethan.

"Oh," Rose said as we watched the Portland footage. "This one is a little different."

The unrest went on longer than in the other urban areas. There were Compos out, but their weapons were down, and more people had piled out into the streets. I watched with my eyes glued to the screen, my heart lifting and falling over and over as pain and hope fought and clawed for top billing. Then, at about three in the morning, arrests began again, and the streets were clear by daylight.

"It's not going to be enough," I said, and my chest felt tight. Our vehicle suddenly felt too small. "This isn't going to be enough."

"We don't know. People need time to process, Patch," Rose said. "You can't expect them to upend everything they believe right away. You know that better than most. It's not our main goal, remember? Our main goal is to show others outside what is happening in America."

Her words felt empty, like a cup of water poured on a fire that was already consuming an entire room. My rage had nowhere to go. Had this vehicle always been this small?

"But why would they help if the people in America don't seem to care!" I was yelling now. "How can that be the only reaction? We showed them. We showed them what it is like out there. We showed them what has happened to their loved ones. To their friends, to their partners, to their family. To children, for Board's sake. We showed them the truth." My eyes grew hot as the fire crossed the threshold into the next room.

"They don't know what to believe," Rose said, putting her hand on my shoulder. "Give it more time."

"We don't have any more time!" I yelled, knowing my anger was misdirected, but I couldn't contain it. "Oliver, Rexx. You know as I do, they are nothing but examples waiting to be made. You know that Elias Stevens is just waiting for the right moment to use them against me. That their lives are expendable and our window to help them is small. This was our plan.

This was it. There is no more time." My voice continued to rise. "There has to be more. It can't end like this!"

I started to fumble with the buttons on the door, trying to open it, but where would I go? I just knew I couldn't stay in that vehicle any longer. It was practically shrinking. If I'd learned anything, it was that I was nothing but a danger to the people near me. Maybe Felix and Rose could return home and plead for a lighter sentence. Maybe they could pretend that I manipulated them somehow, or maybe they wouldn't be pretending at all.

Felix began to shift behind me, leaning forward in a way that I could only assume was causing him great pain. He reached his arm out to me and I paused.

"Stay, Patch. Let's look at a few more. We don't know it's the same everywhere."

Rose switched to the view of the compound where Oliver was held. Nothing notable happened throughout the night, and then, as the footage caught up to the present moment, people started to gather outside the gates. We exchanged worried glances. There were several Compos lining up right outside the fence.

"What is that? What are they doing?"

Rose zoomed in. A group of people were gathered, and not just Compliance Officers. There was a vehicle, with large bold letters written on the side in blue and red—*AMERICA ONE* STUDIOS. People stood in an arc shape, facing something—a large clearing in the field outside the compound. The clearing was a perfect circle.

Rose zoomed in more, and my heart jumped into my throat as I spotted Elias Stevens standing in front of the group, his hands clasped in front of his crisp suit. His chin was raised, and a familiar smirk decorated his face.

"What is that?" I asked. "What's happening?"

Rose turned to me. Her eyes were wide and filled with alarm, and I searched them as I waited for an answer.

"I think he knows we're watching."

CHAPTER 33

Oliver Shelling

OLIVER HAD BEEN sleeping when the door to his cell slammed open.

"What's going on?" Oliver croaked to the Compo staring openmouthed at the smattering of blood on the wall. It was the first time someone had set foot in his room in days, and certainly since the solitary orders had been lifted.

"Uh. I've been ordered to search your cell," the Compo said, her eyes still on the mural, looking it up and down. She brought her hand behind her head, pacifier still in it, and scratched.

"Is this your blood?" she asked, sounding more perplexed than angry. Oliver didn't really see the point in lying.

"Yeah. I thought it would be fruitless to ask for paint," he said dryly, sitting himself up against the concrete. "But search away."

"I'm gonna have to report this," she said, waving to the image, which was now dried a rust brown. Oliver's eyes darted around, trying to pinpoint where the tiny piece of technology was perched. "Now, move to that corner, Mr. Shelling," she said as she followed him with a pair of magnetic cuffs that she activated once they reached the panel.

Once he was contained, she turned and started searching the room, though there wasn't much to search. She looked in and behind the toilet in one corner, and flipped the thin mattress on the floor in the other.

She turned and walked toward Oliver, her eyes searching his body as she approached. She started at the top, running her fingers over his scalp, down his neck, and under the collar of his shirt. He bit down on his lip, and the taste of blood coated his tongue as his lip burst back open.

"What is this?" she asked as she yanked something off the waistband of his pants. She held the tiny bug-like piece of technology out in front of him.

"Uh, I don't know. I don't know. I've never seen—seen it before," Oliver said unconvincingly as a chill ran from the cold floor underneath him to the crown of his head. "I can't see it well. It's awfully small. What is it?"

"You tell me, Mr. Shelling. It's in your cell, and someone has been leaking footage from inside these walls." The Compo's tone was now hard as a rock.

"It looks like a toy," Oliver said. "Like a little robotic toy. Maybe—maybe a prisoner with a child had it in their pocket when they were brought in. I'm sure it's nothing."

What Oliver didn't know was that the world was watching this very interaction, perhaps breaking records for the amount of people watching a live event at the same time in history. He also didn't know that the UN Security Council was convening at that very moment for a vote on the authorization of intervention.

The Compo demagnetized the cuffs, but left them on, before taking the small piece of technology with her out of the room. "I'll be back," she said. The door slid shut behind her and Oliver sank down against the wall until he reached the floor.

Someone has been leaking footage. Her words played in his head. If footage from his cell had been leaked, then it was being used. Tears came to his eyes as he realized that somehow, in some small way, he might have been useful. That this might not all have been for nothing.

A short while later, when Oliver was led out of the compound, he knew what was about to come, and of all the emotions that he felt, there was one that was stronger than the others—relief. Relief that this nightmare might all be over soon.

Four Compos guarded him from all sides. The footage from the now smashed and destroyed beetle was no longer live, but the world still watched via satellite.

They watched as Oliver Shelling was marched past *America One* cameras, which were thrust close as a buzzing of excited and eager voices and footsteps followed him like a swarm of provoked bees. Had Oliver provoked this swarm? Did he deserve what was about to happen to him?

The world then watched as Oliver was led to an empty, haunting field, and then to a large ring-shaped area, lined with metal bricks at least twenty feet across. In the middle, there was a circular metal pad covered with a thin layer of ash, with mounds along the circumference. The procession stopped and Oliver stood at the edge.

Underneath the mounds of ash pushed to the sides, Oliver saw something. A bone. Possibly a femur, he thought with a strange detachment.

Oliver was handed a brush and instructed by a Compliance Officer to clear the area. He dropped down to his knees and, with smooth strokes, swept the ash off the round pad. His fingers were cold in the brisk late-fall air. He looked outside the circle, where the earth was barren.

When he was done clearing the area, he admired his fingernails. He thought of his garden, and he thought of his home. He thought of Patch and Rexx, and of Yasmine. He didn't weep. He didn't attempt to run. He leaned back on his heels, ignored the Compos and the cameras, and looked up at the sky. It was still early. Swirls of pinks and purples danced above the mountains.

He inhaled deeply through an air tinged with ash, and he hoped. He hoped that it would be fast, and that it would be painless, but more than anything he hoped that this one final contribution would make a difference.

Then the whole world watched as Oliver Shelling was instructed to lie down in the middle of the circle.

They watched as the straps were fastened around his body.

They watched as a switch was flipped.

They watched as a body burned without flames, until there was nothing left but essence and bones.

They watched as a final layer of ash was picked up by the wind, mixing with those before it.

The world watched, and it was in that moment that the call was made to do more than watch.

CHAPTER 34

Patch Collins

THE SCREAM WAS primal, guttural. It left my body of its own volition, its journey unalterable by my conscious, singeing my throat with its intensity on the way out. Rose's arms were around me, hugging me tightly to her body, but I was not in her arms; I was somewhere else entirely. A place where all I could see was fire and smoke, where my eyes were blurred by an all-consuming grief and rage.

Oliver.

It took minutes, or hours, for the smoke to clear, and then there was the pain. The incapacitating physical pain that comes along with grief. We bury this pain in our memories; otherwise, how would we go on with life? It was like someone twisting a knife into your abdomen, pulling it out, then doing it again, deeper and with more pressure than the first time. You lost someone, and that pain never went away, but you forgot the intensity with which it was delivered, and the agony of every breath. Then you lost someone else you loved, and it happened again, unique and unyielding until you were made of nothing but knife wounds with scraps of your former self in between. *What have I done?*

"Patch. Patch!" Felix was in front of me, out of his prone position in the back seat. I finally met his eyes.

"He left a message for you," he said, turning the screen toward me.

The crowd had dispersed, but the screen still displayed the area outside the compound. On the ground, in the middle of the circle, Oliver's body was no longer there, but a message was.

I expect to be seeing you at the Board headquarters, alone, or you know who will be next.

I turned to Felix and Rose and, without hesitation, said, "Take me there."

The headquarters and the site of the bombing were both visible in the distance. We began lowering down about three miles from our destination. It still resembled a fortress, but the canyon's size took on a whole new meaning when soaring above it.

I could see how if one were looking at the headquarters from the side, or from anywhere other than my current vantage point, really, it would melt seamlessly into the landscape against the edges of the dam. Had Rexx and I passed by it on the cargo rails without knowing?

The Compos were no longer simply visible behind the protection of a screen. They would be there, waiting for me. We landed on the dusty earth, and we were all silent for a moment. Oliver's death and the pending goodbyes hung over us like a cloud.

"No use running now," Felix finally said, and then he pulled something out of his pocket. It was his kill switch. There were tears in his eyes and he pushed his red glasses to the top of his head and wiped the moisture away. Rose began to dig in her pocket, and I did the same, until the three of us were holding the small, rectangular buttons in our hands.

Then, without needing words, we all pressed at the same time, releasing every single second of footage that hadn't been released yet, and giving up our location to the outside world.

Rose climbed over the seat until she was sitting next to me, and she tenderly helped me clean my face, removing the temporary tattoos. When she was done, she pulled out a small digital pad of some kind from one of the nearby bags.

"Before you go," she said, her voice cracking slightly, "can you do something for me?"

"Anything," I said, looking from Rose to Felix, who now had his head in his hands as if he knew what she was about to ask.

"Can I capture your fingerprint, just in case?" It took me a moment to understand what she meant, but then it hit me—the tattoo on her temple, the fingerprint of the friend she had lost.

I obliged, swallowing hard and ignoring the tears streaming down her cheeks, because if I was to let either her or Felix's emotions in, I would lose my resolve. If I stopped to think about these two people in front of me and what they had done for me over the past several weeks, I felt as if I would melt into the floor.

Instead I held on to the fresh pain and rage of Oliver's death, letting everything else continue to be blanketed by it, and I said the only thing I could think to say.

"Thank you both for everything." I reached to open the door, but Felix's hand on my shoulder stopped me.

"No matter what happens," he said as he squeezed his fingers into my shoulder, "we won't forget, Patch, and we won't let the world forget either. We promise you that."

I brought my free hand up to my shoulder and wrapped it around his fingers, and we stayed there for just a moment with his hand in mine. Then we both nodded, and he let go.

I climbed out and let the door slide closed between us. I began to walk, not looking back until at least five minutes had passed, knowing that if I did, I might change my mind. When I finally turned around, Compos circled the area where the vehicle had just been. They were looking up at the sky. A few of them turned in my direction, but they did not pursue me. I had been invited.

The plummeting sides of the canyon walls approached on my left and I walked parallel to them. The thought of stepping right over entered my mind a few times, and I pushed it away, holding on to the rage that propelled me forward.

Oliver. He loved to garden. He was a painter. He had the biggest, brightest smile of anyone I knew. He collected things. When he played the piano, you felt like everything would be all right. Five things. Five details.

I approached a wide, twisting outdoor staircase. The national emblem was engraved in stone above it. A Compo at the top of the staircase nodded. I walked down it. It seemed to go on forever, until it wound to reveal a vast set of double doors that opened as I got to the base.

At first glance the compound was empty of anyone but Compliance Officers. I wandered, continuing to take even, measured steps, wondering if I was the only civilian to have ever walked the steps that I was walking.

A crunch underneath my foot caused me to look down. There, on the ground, was a beetle, crushed. A few yards in front of it was another one. I walked toward it, only to see another. I followed.

There was an explosion in the distance and the ground below me shook slightly. All heads turned, but I continued. Several Compos retreated, moving toward the sound, but enough stayed. When the trail ended, I was at a door, propped open. There was still no sign of anyone other than the Compos, who watched me intently.

Then I was in a hallway with barely any light. I could make out stairs on the far end. Tentatively, I stepped forward in the dark. Another explosion outside crashed me down to my knees, and I hissed air through my teeth as the pain radiated up my leg. The explosion felt close. I suddenly remembered that we were inside a ravine. The right spot, and this entire complex could be buried in rubble.

I pulled myself back to my feet and clutched the wall to my right as I inched toward the stairway. There was an opening immediately before the stairs where small amounts of light escaped a door's edges. I approached it cautiously. I was nearly there.

I pushed open the door, and my eyes adjusted to the light. There, on the left side of the room, was a hospital bed. My heart flipped into my throat, piercing through the numbness and anger that had cloaked me all morning. Suddenly the armor of rage I'd worn into the room felt as thin as if it were made of leaves.

It was Rexx.

He didn't turn his head. Did he assume I was simply a Compo returning? I inched closer to the bed, worried if I startled him, he might scream.

"Rexx," I whispered from where I stood. I wanted to walk toward him, but I felt like I was anchored to the ground below me. I was afraid if I touched him, he would disappear beneath my hands like a hologram. He turned his head. His eyes widened and tears began to coat them.

"Patch," he said through a raspy, warm voice. My own tears dripped to my bare shoulder. His curls had grown back. Not as long as they once were, but he looked more like Rexx than the last time I'd seen him in person.

"No, you can't be here," he said. His eyes were fearful and had hardened slightly, but they were still his, captivating and kind. His lips quivered, as if he didn't know whether to draw me closer or push me away, and the urge to go to him was stronger than gravity.

"I'm here anyway," I said, and soon the anchors lifted and I was crossing the room as quickly as I could, wanting nothing more than to touch him, to hold him, and to promise him everything was going to be okay, even if I knew it was a false promise.

He didn't take his eyes off me as I threw my arms around his thin body. It was as real as mine. It was really him. Not a hologram. Not an avatar. It was Rexx Moreno.

"You have to go. They're going to kill you," he said, his voice weak. His cuffed hand just barely found the back of my head and I hissed in pain as his fingers grazed my injury.

"You're hurt," he said with alarm.

"No. It's okay. I'm okay. Just a scratch," I said as I inhaled. "I know what you're thinking. They used you to get to me. I know, but I'm here anyway." Somehow he still smelled of cinnamon.

"You can't be here. The Board," he said again, but his voice caught and his body trembled and he didn't finish his sentence.

"Rexx, they were right. Noah, and—" Another explosion shook the ground beneath us, and I fell backward. His hand caught mine and held until the shaking ceased. When it stopped, I looked up at Rexx—still cuffed to the bed and completely at the mercy of this situation. I didn't know what was going on outside, and I didn't know how much longer I had left.

I stood back up and climbed into the bed next to him. I reached up and inspected the cuffs keeping him secured. They looked like the ones I'd had on in the compound and during my capture when I reentered the border, impenetrable for all I knew.

The world exploded around us and I let the weight fall out of my head, and out of my body, letting myself melt into him for just a moment. He held me as best he could, and I stared at his face, and he stared at mine—at the lines, at the scars, and the pain. Were they still the faces of the kids playing video games in my parent's living room? Were they the faces of the scientists swimming in the lake, or the criminals on the run who woke up on the floor of the church in Zone 36?

I pressed myself up, brought my lips to his, and kissed him. When we parted, the shaking ceased. The silence was so deafening, and a feeling that we were no longer alone settled over me.

"Where are you going?" Rexx whispered, worry lacing his voice as I climbed out of bed.

"I just want to check on something. Stay here," I said as I started walking back toward the doorframe, only to find that I was right. We were no longer alone.

I didn't move or scream or take a step backward. Instead I just stared at Elias Stevens as he stood in the doorway. It was as if he had compelled me toward the frame like a magnet. Part of me knew that he would be standing there, waiting. Perhaps he'd been standing there the whole time, watching us.

Elias took a few steps into the room. His face was bruised, and he was limping slightly. I looked behind him, expecting to see an array of Compos ready to march in and detain me. There were none. He was alone.

Rexx tried fruitlessly to reach for me, to do something protective. I moved farther away from both the bed and the doorway, willing Elias's attention to follow me.

"How? How could one stupid girl cause so much trouble?" He breathed rapidly. His pupils were huge and his eyes manic. "I told you. Repeatedly. That you didn't know what you were dealing with here, but I have you both now." His smirk widened and he took two more steps toward me.

I was no longer afraid, but the rage and the hatred directed at this man standing before me was as real as it had ever been. He took two more steps. He was now only a few feet away as he pulled a pacifier out from inside his jacket and waved it in the air.

"You know, I've actually never fired one of these myself," he said. "There's always been someone around to do it for me, but I told the others that you two"—he waved the pacifier between Rexx and me—"are all mine."

"You might have us, but this is over, Elias," I spit back at him. "You hear what is going on out there. They must have concluded you are no longer a threat. Your weapons were duds, weren't they? Even I, one of your lowly scientists, know you have to maintain nuclear weapons. You have nothing left to hold over the rest of the world anymore. You have failed. Everyone is seeing you for what you are. It's over."

I knew I should be looking for something to use against him, a weapon of some kind, but I didn't. Instead I asked him a question. "Why did you really do it, Elias? Why? Was the Seclusion really the solution?"

He smirked as he took one final step toward me and pointed the pacifier right in the center of my rib cage, and I looked down to see specks of copper shining in the light.

"Goodbye, Patricia Collins," he said as he pulled the trigger. Static.

I smiled, and he looked at me quizzically.

"I guess you should have pointed it at my neck," I said. Then there was a moment of confusion as he looked at the pacifier. He aimed it at Rexx, about to test its function, and I saw my opening.

I kicked Elias square in the knee, harder than I thought possible. All my anger and resentment somehow found its way into that one kick, angled right at the base of his kneecap. He fell to the floor with a scream, and the pacifier flew across the room as he lost his grip.

Rexx was yelling something to me from the corner, but his words were garbled as I dove for the pacifier, my fingertips just barely grazing the edge as I felt myself being pulled backward. I couldn't reach it, but there was something else, something I could reach. I twisted my body and lunged for the leg to the medical supply cart and pulled.

Metal crashed to the floor. Whether it hit Elias or not, I didn't give myself time to check. His grip on my leg loosened and I hoisted myself up and ran, grabbing the pacifier and turning around swiftly. Elias had his hand on his face as blood ran down his temple. He was struggling to get back to his feet.

"Down, on the ground," I demanded, pointing the weapon at him.

"You stupid, naive girl," he said as he smirked at me. "That only works in my hand, but I think you know that."

I did know it, but I was hoping at the moment he might forget. As I was looking for something I could use to buy time, a loud crash caused us both to turn. The hospital bed was lying completely on its side, Rexx still attached by the wrists. I didn't know how he did it, but he'd managed to topple the bed over onto its side.

I ran as fast as I could and threw myself on top of Elias.

"I guess I'll just have to use your hand, then," I said as I grabbed his arm and twisted. He tried to wrestle his arm away, but I kneed him in the face, hard. Blood from his nose coated my pants as his head dropped toward the floor. I wrapped his fingers around the handle of the pacifier, and with his biometrics touching the weapon, I pulled the trigger.

He collapsed the rest of the way onto the ground, a seizing mess, right before another explosion sent me to the ground along with him.

EPILOGUE

EVERYTHING HAPPENED QUICKLY after that. The swarms soon came from both borders. Laurel Austin publicly disclosed her history as an agent who'd served in America, and she was put in charge of directing the mission. I'd been right about the nuclear weapons. The arsenal, when it was found near the site of the bombing, had not been maintained.

Some Compliance Officers fought on behalf of the Board, but others were too shocked to see the onslaught of outsiders come in to challenge everything they thought they were serving. It became overwhelmingly apparent how far behind American technology had fallen. After over a week of fighting, weapons were eventually laid down. Some Compos even volunteered with aid.

The Board members were ordered to be captured alive and the headquarters was thoroughly searched by soldiers, drones, and volunteers. Four escaped. Where they were, we didn't know. Over the years that followed, there were many theories about what had happened to them—they escaped to another country, they changed their appearance and lived a quiet life, or they were squatting somewhere in a secret bunker, scheming and plotting their return. It didn't really matter. Their power was gone. The people knew the truth and there was no longer anything that could be done about it.

The Board members who were captured, twenty-six of them, including Elias, were held to await charges of crimes against humanity.

The compounds were opened, aid was rushed in via air. Living prisoners were bused back to their urban areas to be reunited with remaining family members or friends. Ethan and Mason, both alive, returned to Portland.

Over the days and weeks that followed, it was revealed just how many released prisoners identified with the Veritas Ring—thousands in the early decades, and it seemed Rexx and I had met some of the last remaining uncaptured members.

The future of America was unclear—where we would go, who would be in charge, how our children would be educated, or how we would rebuild. They weren't easy questions, and we didn't have any easy answers.

Separating fact from fiction continued to be a blight on America, but one thing that most agreed on was that hiding the truth was not the right course of action. The firewalls were dismantled, and the process of rebuilding trust began.

* * *

A year later Rexx and I moved into our new home—an eighty-year-old farmhouse that needed plenty of work—located ten miles from the Tucson Urban Center. A gift of soil, seeds, and other supplies was delivered—courtesy of James, Felix, and Rose—shortly after we'd moved in, with a promise that they would visit soon. We spent long evenings tending to the garden, which contained all of Oliver's favorites—with extra mint and lavender.

Mid-spring, we received a special invitation, and we packed up and headed south. When we arrived, a large crowd had already gathered. Families sat huddled together on blankets, and pop-up chairs were arranged haphazardly around the dry, dusty Arizona ground.

We unloaded our stuff and walked through the crowds until we saw them. Webb and Celeste were sitting behind freshly rolled-out caution tape, on a blanket with a feast of fresh fruit and vegetables arranged in the middle.

"I grew them in my garden," Celeste declared proudly as she ran up to meet us. After a few minutes of catching up, Webb gave us an update.

"I've put in a job application for a few positions here in Arizona," he said. "Keep your fingers crossed for me."

Rexx shot me a look and nudged me with his elbow. "You don't need to keep looking," I said with a smile.

"Someone," Rexx said as he gestured to me, "just became the founder of the Global Research and Innovation Center here in Tucson, and there's a position there for you if you want it. We would have to get you together with Felix to train you in some engineering. Do you think you can handle that?" A large smile spread across Webb's face.

"Well, if you think it would be a good fit. Wow. Wow. I don't know what to say. I would love that," Webb said, and then he reached down and grabbed a package off the blanket.

"Here, I made this for you," he said as he handed it to me. I opened the package to see a small wooden shadow box filled with dried lavender.

"I went back to Zone 36. I was able to salvage some wood from the rubble. This was made from Oliver's front door, and the lavender is from his garden. It's for your new place."

"Thank you," I said as I held the gift to my chest and thought of Oliver.

A short while later, as Celeste was removing lids from containers inside the picnic basket, she gestured with her head toward a woman who was walking, slowly and nervously, up to our group.

"Do you know her?" she asked.

"Mom!" I yelled as I jumped up and ran to her. Her fingers spread through my hair as she pulled me close.

"Mrs. Collins! So happy you could make it!" Rexx said as he wrapped his arms around both of us. Several minutes later we all settled down on the blanket.

We didn't need to talk about everything we had been through. The deafening absence of Oliver and my father said enough. So we just watched.

We watched for hours as piece upon piece of the Walls came down.

At one point, I saw something scurry out from underneath the blanket. It was a lizard, a gecko probably, about six inches in length, tail curled against its back. We locked eyes for the length of a heartbeat, blue and lizard green connecting, and then it turned and scrambled away, into the direction of the world outside that was finally starting to reveal itself.

ACKNOWLEDGMENTS

Like the process of writing this book, the past three and a half years have been full of ups and downs, and I often felt like the only thing holding me afloat was a life raft of friends and family.

First, to my husband, Bart Castle, and my children, Tristan and Willow. Thank you for providing the space and support needed to write this book even when space and mental reserves were both hard to come by. I am so proud to be part of your team.

To my writing family. Thank you for always being willing to bounce ideas around, work through plot holes, or just sit on a coffee shop patio or a Zoom call alongside one another until the words come. A special thank-you to Mary Pembleton, Matt Harry, Alex Morrissey, Jason Stokes, David Voyles, Anna Ray Stokes, Jason Chestnut, Cari Dubiel, Becca Spence Dobias, Micaela Green, Myrth Killingsworth, and Matt Nilsen.

To the team at the Indie Author Project, thank you for believing in me and my writing enough to name me your 2020 Indie Author of the Year. A special thank-you to Alissa Bankowski, Emily Gooding, and Mitchell Davis.

Thank you to Adam Gomolin, Avalon Radys, Noah Broyles, Tim Barber, Sarah Nivala, Kaitlin Severini, and everyone else who worked on the editorial process of *The Chasm* and who I'm sure saved me from many mortifying mistakes.

Finally, to my mother, Sue Regan, who passed away in 2019, for always being my biggest cheerleader and best friend.

GRAND PATRONS

Lawrence David Rogers

Michael Ostrowski

Nicholas S. Ludington

Noelle Molter

Rick Olshak

Skye Mallory

Sue Regan

Susan K. Hamilton

INKSHARES

INKSHARES is a reader-driven publisher and producer based in Oakland, California. Our books are selected not by a group of editors, but by readers worldwide.

While we've published books by established writers like *Big Fish* author Daniel Wallace and *Star Wars: Rogue One* scribe Gary Whitta, our aim remains surfacing and developing the new-author voices of tomorrow.

Previously unknown Inkshares authors have received starred reviews and been featured in *The New York Times*. Their books are on the front tables of Barnes & Noble and hundreds of independents nationwide, and many have been licensed by publishers in other major markets. They are also being adapted by Oscar-winning screenwriters at the biggest studios and networks.

Interested in making your own story a reality? Visit Inkshares.com to start your own project or find other great books.

CPSIA information can be obtained
at www.ICGtesting.com
Printed in the USA
LVHW030445190522
719127LV00003B/236

9 781950 301331